The Sirens of Space

By Jeffrey Caminsky:

The Referee's Survival Guide
All Fathers Are Giants (ed.)
The Sonnets of William Shakespeare (ed.)
The Guardians of Peace series:
    The Sirens of Space
    The Star Dancers
    Clouds of Darkness

Coming soon:
    The Guardians of Peace

The Sirens of Space

A Novel

Jeffrey Caminsky

NEW ALEXANDRIA PRESS
LIVONIA

Published by New Alexandria Press
PO Box 530516
Livonia, Michigan 48153
www.newalexandriapress.com

The quote attributed to Friedrich Nietzsche first appeared in 1885, in the book *Beyond Good and Evil.*

Hardcover Edition:
ISBN-10: 0-9790106-6-7
ISBN-13: 978-0-9790106-6-8

Softcover Edition:
ISBN-10: 0-9790106-3-2
ISBN-13: 978-0-9790106-3-7

Quantity discounts are available on bulk purchases of this book Special books or book excerpts can also be made available to fit specific needs. For information, please contact *sales@newalexandriapress.com* or send written inquiries to New Alexandria Press, PO Box 530516, Livonia, Michigan 48153.

Printed in the United States of America

10 9 8 7 6 5 4 3 2

2008934583

To Mom and Dad,
  with love and gratitude....

Acknowledgments

WHILE TECHNOLOGY ENHANCES our lives in many ways, nothing will ever replace the people close to us, or those who help us confront the challenges we encounter along the way.

Writing can be a lonely endeavor. Producing a book, however, is impossible without the assistance of a great many people—many of whom an author never even gets the chance to meet, let alone to thank. Among the many who have helped bring this book to print are many whose contributions are no less critical merely because they pass largely without notice—including the workers running the printing machines, who literally bring a book to life.

Often taken for granted is the indulgence of an author's family, as they patiently listen to a thousand worries and complaints, as well as enduring the endless debates and controversies within the author's own mind which occasionally are vented audibly—often about minuscule revisions and word choices that would otherwise pass unnoticed, and are often undetectable by the human eye. During the many years of writing this series—spanning the entire Reagan and Bush Administrations, as well as the first two Clinton Years—and the even longer time it took to bring the work to print, it was a great comfort to be able to count on their tolerance and forbearance, no matter how maddening or difficult I might be at any given moment.

Other friends and colleagues, in and out of the legal profession, have proven to be a constant source of strength and help. While they number too many to list, I have to give special thanks to Mark Cavanagh, James Shaw, and Kevin Huntsman for their early encouragement; to my son, Jason, for helping to keep me from giving up hope after the entire work was completed and nobody seemed the slightest bit interested; to Jeff Joyce, Marilyn Eisenbraun, Jaimie Powell, my parents, Wallace and Alice Caminsky, and my wife, Nonie, for providing feedback and suggestions, and for helping me proofread and edit the text in order to get it ready—or, at least readier—for print; and to Nadine Dyer and Christopher Reaske, my favorite English teachers, for correcting as many defects in my writing as they could manage in the short time they had.

Despite everyone's help and best efforts, the shortcomings in what follows are mine.

JEFF CAMINSKY
September, 2008

Author's Note

THOSE INTERESTED IN EXPLORING the historical context of the ensuing chapters can find information about the era from a variety of sources. Unfortunately, most of those sources are not yet in print.

To aid readers curious about the years to come, the Author has convinced the Publisher to share some information about what the Future may hold in store for our relatives, taken directly from the prize-winning work of a renowned historian.

Excerpts from Toomey, *From Earth to Isis: The Rise of Humanity*. (New Alexandria, cc:343-0874; 3191 OE; 1055 Is)(Reprinted by permission of the author):

From the Introduction to Volume VI: THE CONFLAGRATION

On this side of the vast Crutchtan Cloud a mighty empire once stretched westward, reaching into the heart of Greater Isis. Like many nations of pre-cosmic antiquity, its divergent cultures were noted chiefly for their inability to unite long enough to apply the most obvious solutions to the simplest problems of social policy, and for a stubborn unwillingness among their people to let the pressing concerns of the day intrude upon their daily lives.

Like its Old Earth predecessors, and for many of the same reasons, this early empire has now disintegrated into the many feuding and contentious parts that we know today. And while their never-ending squabbles no longer threaten their neighbors, they offer unexpected insights and occasional amusement to the curious.

This, of course, is the Terran League of the Second Cosmic Century....

From Volume IV: THE ASCENSION OF TERRA

In the dying days of the twenty-first century, a previously unknown amateur mathematician named Caldwell Covington published his first and last paper, entitled SUBATOMIC PARTICLES AND SUBSPACE: AN INFERENTIAL ANALYSIS, *in an obscure professional journal. That same year some graduate students at Earth's Massachusetts Institute of Technology, trying to help a professor complete a paper of his own before being denied tenure, thought they saw in its turgid prose the key to unraveling a mystery of physics: "Irregularities in the behavior of some subatomic particles," Covington had written, "are explicable only by positing the existence of a non-universe, or subspace, where charged particles can go for a time and then return, almost at random, and not always in the same place."*

Caldwell Covington was no scientific radical. In fact, he had intended his paper as a sarcastic riposte to the sloppy methods and theoretical involutions of a whole school of subatomic physicists. But however accidentally, he had hit the mark. And though they failed to save their professor's job at MIT, the students soon devised an hypothesis, some rough equations, and a few crude experiments that cracked the bedrock of twenty-first-century science.

They found that all atoms, and hence all objects in the physical universe, produce emissions caused by the constant, random passage of subatomic particles into subspace. With proper equipment these emissions are instantly detected across great distances, since time is not a subspace dimension. Light, too, has a subspace component called, with typical scientific poesy, subphotons, and the speed of light is nothing more than the simultaneous passage of observable phenomena through two separate universes. While nothing in nature travels faster than light, its speed could no longer intimidate human ingenuity.

More importantly, these subspace emissions quickly led scientists to a powerful new energy source, which we now call gravitronics. Like magnetism, we can control it by using simple electricity, and researchers soon found that it let us bend gravity, shred atoms and molecules if focused properly, and carry images and sound waves. It also lifted Man's horizons and truly opened the heavens....

...[M]en and women, machines and molecules exist, like Light, in the physical universe. With limited exceptions, we cannot enjoy the instantaneous travel of "pure" forms of energy, but Science soon realized that, while matter could not outpace energy beams, it could hitch rides with them. Speed through space was now limited only by Man's imagination—or his technology, which is really the same thing....

* * *

Toward the end of the twenty-first century, and in Year 1 of the cosmic calendar,[1] MIT developed the first spacedrive engine prototype.

By the early twenty-second century—or cc:4-4009, to be precise—extensive research in high energy physics had produced the pressure-resistant crystalline metallic alloys needed to withstand the extreme stress of faster-than-light travel. Ten years later, the first interstellar flight returned from a fifteen-month round trip to Alpha Centauri; on its return, the ever-bickering nations of Earth established the Cosmic Guard, to direct and control interstellar travel and exploration.

CosGuard discovered the first known inhabitable planet outside Earth's solar system by the middle of the century. Nineteen light years away, Athena became Earth's earliest self-sustaining colony. In rapid succession, the Guard discovered the planets now known as Gaea, New Babylon, and Zarathustra, and soon had explored and charted all star systems within fifty light years of Earth....

---

[*]The cosmic calendar is a chronometrical system used to standardize astronomical time: 100 seconds = 1 cosmic minute; 100 cosmic minutes = 1 cosmic hour; 10 cosmic hours = 1 cosmic day; 10 cosmic days = 1 cosmic week; 10 cosmic weeks = 1 cosmic month; 10 cosmic months = 1 cosmic year. Cosmic time differs from solar time, which varies from planet to planet and time zone to time zone, and is used by science to compute units of mass, volume, distance, time, and the like. As used in this book, one cosmic day equals about 27.8 solar hours; one cosmic year equals about 3.2 solar years, a cosmic century, about 320 years.

To further complicate matters, one cosmic light year is called a "parsec;" a "light year" refers to the distance light in nature travels in a standard solar year ie, one Earth year. A "meter" remains as defined on twentieth century Earth; however, the standard unit of distance in the twenty-sixth century is the "foot," which is defined as the distance light travels in 0.000000001 seconds (give or take a decimal point), and roughly corresponds to the "foot" used in the old English system of measurement. An "astrometer," by contrast, is defined as the distance light travels in 1 second; and an "astrokilometer" is 1,000 astrometers, or the distance light travels in 1,000 seconds—defined as the average diameter of the orbit of Planet Earth around its sun. A "second," correspondingly, was redefined in 2206 as the time it takes light to travel 1/1,000 of an astrokilometer—or one astrometer, which is approximately 186,000 miles, calculating under the old English system.

Aside from the use of local time by every planet, this system of measurement finds acceptance everywhere in twenty-sixth-century Terra, except for a few provinces on the North American continent of Earth.

Like moths drawn by the beacon of adventure, Earth's brightest, best trained, most curious minds drifted skyward. The end of the twenty-second century saw human colonies on nine planets, including large settlements on New Babylon and Zarathustra; and still the mass exodus continued. Humanity formed the Terran League, to govern itself and help the Cosmic Guard keep the fractious and stubborn member planets from warring among themselves over such cosmically significant causes as tariffs, trade, and immigration....

New Babylon itself enjoyed many advantages, conferred both by nature and by accident. It was among the first inhabitable planets discovered outside the planetary system of Earth; and like the planet Zarathustra, which was discovered at roughly the same time, it was a garden teeming with life lovingly spawned from its warm and salty seas. But the twelve parsecs—about thirty-eight light years—east to New Babylon took a full solar year less to travel in the early days of interstellar flight than the ninety-six parsecs west to Zarathustra, and most of the major inhabitable planets that the early Cosmic Guard discovered were to the cosmic east of Earth—Athena, Gaea; later Ceres and Demeter. And of the fifteen member planets of the Terran League through first half of the twenty-sixth century, the only planet west of Zarathustra was tiny Isis, a small outpost on the way to the then-as-yet unvisited Rigel star system. So, by default as much as by the beauty and bounty of the land itself, New Babylon became the Mecca for the first flood of emigrants from Earth; and the Cosmic East became the focus of Humanity's destiny, while the two planets of the West seemed destined to be Man's forgotten stepchildren....

What historians call the Babylonian Exodus stirred the human soul like no event since the dawn of civilization. The cream of a generation, dazzled by the chance to participate in the greatest adventure they could imagine, and anxious to escape the squalor and misery of Earth, scratched and clawed for the chance to claim the future for their descendants. Soon, they had flooded the virgin world with shining cities and great universities, with roads and factories and great modern farms stretching endlessly into the horizon. Before long the planet blossomed with a modern, cosmopolitan culture, embracing all human accomplishments while leaving most of Humanity's problems behind them on Earth....

* * *

As what was now called Terra expanded eastward, Earth remained its most populous planet. But with each succeeding generation, the skilled and educated fled as far as their money and talent could take them, searching for a new life and a less dismal future. The constant flow of Earth's boldest, most energetic, and most adventuresome offspring to the beckoning new worlds of the East drained her vitality and robbed her of hope. And the very eagerness with which the East welcomed its immigrants, often including relocation subsidies for professionals in fields suffering critical shortages, gave the talented and ambitious few reasons to stay behind. Meanwhile, Earth's ancient problems—hunger, poverty, ignorance, mindless and contentious division—chased away all but the poor and the helpless, and the most hopeless of idealists....

Soon, like the dawn that follows the sunset, Terra's cultural center followed the emigrants, and before the end of the First Cosmic Century, the Terran Senate moved the capital. The debate was emotional and traumatic, but history had already decided the outcome; and in the Earth Year 2334, Terra finally abandoned the Old Earth for New Babylon, and the gleaming and ascendant city of Covington....

...Once its leaders had escaped the filth and squalor of our ancestral home, Terra found it could focus on nobler aspirations. Freed from constant reminders of Humanity's humbler beginnings, art and science soon bloomed in a new Renaissance, a phoenix rising from the ashes of Earth.

And freed from the clamorous misery of Mother Earth, Man was free to conquer the stars.

From Volume V: **THE DEMETRIAN REVOLT**

[A]s lush as any planet in Terra, and jealous of the attention lavished on New Babylon merely because that lucky planet was the focus of the First Migration, Demeter loomed sullenly in the east, like a younger brother resentful of a doting parent's praise of a prodigious sibling....Just south of the galactic plane, and forty parsecs to anticenter of a line drawn between Earth and the new Terran capital, Demeter's hospitable climate and ambitious people produced an industrial colossus that quickly rivaled and soon surpassed the early settlements of the older worlds....

* * *

[By] the Earth Year 2349, barely a century after its discovery, Demeter found itself the center of a social upheaval and ferment unknown since the darkest days of the Bloody Century...[as the] stubbornly independent worlds of the eastern frontier rose in revolt against the very concept of union as defined by the ruling Federalists, preferring to chart their own course in the pursuit of the riches to be found in the giant gas clouds and uncharted systems of eastern Terra, rather than suffering the indignities imposed by the government of Austin Prendergast.

* * *

[But] the rebel faction of the Terran Civil War was doomed from the start....All the factories and farmlands of Demeter, Ceres, and their outlands could not long stand against the rest of Humanity—or, at least, against the troops of the Terran Army, and the ships of the Cosmic Guard. So, inevitably, peace descended on the brooding planet, and its leaders were taken to judgment. And though its populace grudgingly accepted union as a practical necessity, they quickly took to heart the concept of planetary sovereignty advanced by the nascent Tory Party. In the meantime, the devastation of war soon faded into memory with the rebuilding of the ecomonic muscle of a people too proud to allow the lack of victory to spell defeat....

* * *

And in its own way, Demeter finally had its revenge, for by the twenty-sixth century, Demeter would come to dominate the economy of eastern Terra in much the same way as New Babylon dominated the West....

Though inconceivable in the war's immediate aftermath, the same planet that chafed at the visible presence of the Cosmic Guard would later feel wounded by the decision to move Eastern Fleet headquarters "from Mullinberry's Star to Ishtar," and the factories of Demeter would soon outbid and outperform their eastern rivals in building ships and equipment for their old nemesis. And as surely as one day it would lead the agitation against a new menace from the East—which by then would sport a reptile's countenance rather than a lilting Demetrian brogue—the pocketbooks of its citizens continued to fatten with the advance of technology. Two centuries after his forces reduced New Dublin to ruins, the velvet voice of Prendergast would find a Demetrian echo in the crescendo of warnings from another silver-haired prophet of doom determined to profit in the next election by proving his manhood; and another chapter of History—alas, requiring another volume—would loom in the blackness of space.

From Volume VI: THE CONFLAGRATION

By the year 2496, reckoning by the Old Earth calendar, the Terran League had grown to fifteen full members, each with colonies of its own....

In midyear, a CosGuard monitoring station detected the faint but unmistakable subspace blips of alien vessels in the space far beyond the planet Ishtar....

* * *

The discovery of alien civilizations had long been the dream of scientists and visionaries. The literature of five hundred years had glowed with anticipation of the day when the enlightened races of the Universe would deliver the answers to the conundrums of creation to the human race, and lead them from the chaos and disorder that they had built for themselves. But as with many things, the anticipation was far different than the reality, and the sudden confirmation of alien ships built by alien technology proved more traumatic than any event since the Terran Civil War. Disorder ruled the streets of every major city for months as the authorities struggled to control the panic—caused foremost by the knowledge that Terra was not alone, and helped along by the handsome profits to be found in the doomsday trade. In the capital the government fell, unable to persuade the Senate that it could guarantee the safety of the people. A crisis government rose in its place, committed to preserving Terra's security whatever the cost, and Terran science was once again conscripted to military ends, striving to improve the ships and technology that were Humanity's only defense against an unknown and therefore terrible menace....

* * *

To help secure the border and preserve domestic peace, the Cosmic Guard began constructing a monitoring station and starbase ninety light years past the agricultural colony in the Hodges Binary system, and clamped strict, if futile, restrictions on further settlement or private exploration in the area. Within ten years Starbase 102, christened "Looking Glass" by a forgotten media wag, was plotting alien trade routes and tracking the steady progress of alien colonies toward Terra. Slowly the panic subsided, but it remained a shadowy memory lurking beneath the consciousness of every man and woman, like the knowledge of mortality, an unpleasant reality pushed into the seamless future....

* * *

...[I]n 2547, some unlicensed Terran ore miners landed on a fertile planet 50 parsecs beyond Looking Glass, seeking easy riches and a comfortable home base. Instead, they found a small alien settlement. Within hours, Humanity's first contact with an alien civilization had produced the first interstellar massacre, and threatened interstellar war.

* * *

IT IS 2550.

Three years of negotiating with the alien Consortium have not brought peace. The Senate echoes with fifty years of warnings about the alien menace.

And Terra's factories are desperately making starships.

THE PLAYERS

The Cosmic Guard
Yeoman Lars Anderson, *shift supervisor*
Commander Jeremy Ashton, *ship's systems officer*
Denny Barrett, *crewman*
Captain Tom Chandler, *a starship captain*
Admiral Porter Clay, *commander of the Eastern Fleet*
Yeoman Chief Gregory Connors, *supervisor of enlistees*
Roscoe Cook, *a native of Planet Isis*
Ens. Kirkland Dexter, *apprentice systems officer*
Captain Brian Fitzgerald, *a starship captain*
Ens. Tom Gerlach, *apprentice weapons officer*
Commodore Jefferson McKinley Jones, *senior wing commander, Demeter Command*
Andrew Larsen, *crewman*
Lt. Cmdr. François LaRue, *first officer of the Cruiser Constantine*
Jim Martindale, *crewman*
Ens. Mary Mathison, *apprentice radio officer*
Commodore Jason McIntyre, *senior wing commander, Looking Glass*
Ens. Connie McKenzie, *apprentice navigator*
Lt. Janet Mendelson, *ship's helmsman*
Lt. Vera Nkwete, *supervising communications officer, Ishtar Command*
Lt. Karen Palmer, *weapons officer*
Yeoman Rick Sillars, *shift supervisor*
Tom Sullivan, *crewman*
Lt. Ronald Talbert, *ship's navigator*
Captain Art Tanana, *a starship captain*
Lt. Dennis Underwood, *communications officer*
Lt. Cmdr. Bruce Van Horn, *ship's chief engineer*
Admiral Winthrop Weatherlee, *commander of Demeter Command*
Commodore Miriam Wright, *commander of Looking Glass*

Spacers and Assorted Riff-Raff
Cyrus McGee, *spacer and former pirate*
Mason McGee, *brother of Cyrus*
Chadborne Wilkes, *a space pirate*

Terrans

Andrew Cook, *Roscoe's father*
Cornelius Cook, *Roscoe's uncle*
Thomas Cook, *Roscoe's grandfather*
Jonathan Osborne Grant, *Terran Ambassador*
Duncan Heathcoate, *senior senator from Demeter*
E. Emerson Hollenbach, *senior senator from Earth*
Irene McGinnis, *senior senator from Isis*
Nicholas Schiller, *a Demetrian industrialist*
Mikos Sarkisian, *President of the Terran League*
Suzie Yang, *presidential aide and journalist*

Veshnans

Munshi, *a translator*
Zatar, *a diplomat*

Crutchtans

G'Rishela, *the Imperator's ambassador to Terra*
Ja'Rend XCVI, *Imperator of the Crutchtan Empire*

A SELECT GAZETTEER
OF OBSCURE HEAVENLY BODIES

Athena, *a Terran planet*
Balarium, *seat of the Grand Alliance of the Consortium*
Ceres, *a Terran planet*
The Crutchtan Cloud, *a vast natural formation of rocks, gases, and precious elements*
Demeter, *third most populous Terran planet*
Earth, *former capital of the Terran League, most populous Terran planet*
Gaea, *a Terran planet*
The Great Divide, *the Crutchtan name for the Neutral Zone*
g'Khruushte, *ancestral home and capital of the Crutchtan Empire; also, Crutchan Empire*
Gr'Shuna, *a Crutchtan planet and regional capital*
Gutterman's Gap, *a narrow passage to Isis through the Nakahashi Storms*
Hodges Binary, *an agricultural colony east of Ishtar*
Ishtar, *Terra's easternmost planet*
The Ishtari Belt, *a formation of rocks, gases, and precious elements near Ishtar*
Isis, *Terra's westernmost planet*
Khu'ukhana Rift, *a narrow passage through the Crutchtan Cloud*
Looking Glass, *colloquial name of Starbase 102*
Mullinberry's Star, *the star dominating the Demeter system*
The Nakahashi Storms, *a large and intense formation of gases and rocks east of Isis*
New Babylon, *capital of the Terran League, second most populous Terran planet*
New Calais, *a Terran planet*
Pirate's Alley, *a dangerous stretch of space from the Ishtari Belt to Demeter*
Riley's Station, *a private starbase and interstellar port of call along the Terran frontier*
Shun'Galanga, *a Crutchtan scientific outpost*
Valhalla, *a Terran planet*
Zarathustra, *one of two inhabited Terran planets west of Earth*

I SWEAR UPON MY SACRED OATH to renounce all bigotry, racial and religious; to forswear for my term of service all planetary allegiance; and to serve Humanity as a guardian of peace, dedicated to preserving human life wherever it wanders. I swear to uphold the laws of the Terran League and all its member planets, and to conduct myself at all times in a manner consistent with integrity and justice. I pledge to serve my superiors faithfully and obey their lawful orders, and to treat any discretion that befalls me as a sacred trust not be abused, nor perverted for personal gain or aggrandizement. And I pledge full devotion to all of my appointed tasks, no matter what the cost to myself.

To fulfill my duties to Humanity, and to the Cosmic Guard, I pledge my name, my life, and my honor.

COSGUARD OATH OF ALLEGIANCE

The Sirens of Space

He who fights with monsters must take care not to become a monster. For if you stare long enough into the abyss, the abyss will stare back at you.

FRIEDRICH NIETZSCHE
Old Earth Philosopher
1844-1900

Peace comes from self-discipline and self-awareness, from enlightenment, and not from power. In much the same way, Science can give us numbers and books can give us words, but we must each must supply our own thoughts.

P. J. HOLLANDER
Isitian Poet and Sage
2295-2393

Prologue

"WHAT'S THAT, GRANDPA?"

Tom Cook looked at the screen and felt his heart freeze in mid-beat. Instantly, he knew what it was. He'd seen the anomaly once before and it scared the wits out of him that time, too. He didn't like the thought of facing it again, especially not with his grandson on board.

"Grandpa?"

Tom wasn't paying attention. All he could think about was staying out of the way. He trimmed the engines, veered hard to port, and prayed to God that the object would miss the small sloop. All the while, he couldn't keep from watching. Frightened as he was—and as terrifying as it must be for the youngster—his eyes were drawn to the eerie light stream bearing down upon them, dead to starboard. Some pleasure outing, he mused. Even if it didn't kill them both, it might be enough to make the boy's parents forbid him from taking the lad sailing again. And that, the old man thought, might be worse than dying for both of them.

He peered through the observation window. The approaching object was bright blue, streaked with white, trailing a wispy tail like a comet. It streaked toward them like an ion storm, at speeds that would leave a star cruiser foundering in its wake. Passing the sloop off the starboard beam, the object swerved suddenly, passing in front of them—then behind them, in a tight spiral of light, swirling around them like a spiraling eddy, inching closer and closer, until it was so close that it seemed Tom could reach outside and touch it.

Then, suddenly as it came, it sliced past the ship's stern and off into the blackness, leaving the small craft shuddering in the energy waves it left behind. Though never prone to space sickness, Tom felt his stomach weaken under the strain, and he entertained the passing notion of making a dash to the head before it was too late. But first, he wanted to reassure his grandson. He turned, only to find young Roscoe giggling and grinning from ear to ear.

"Grandpa!" The boy ran to the stern porthole and rested his chin on the ledge, gazing out into the space beyond the fragile hull of the ship. Putting the controls on automatic, Tom walked over to the boy and knelt beside him.

"Roscoe," Tom began.

"It was the Ancients!" Roscoe exclaimed, his eyes bright with wonder. "We saw them! It was the Ancients, wasn't it Grandpa?"

Tom smiled and placed an arm on Roscoe's shoulder, wondering how to explain it. People had been seeing these same anomalies since interstellar travel began. Four hundred years had passed since then, and still nobody knew what they were.

"Well, maybe you're right at that," he said at last. Leaving the boy aft, Tom returned to the controls and set course for home. He'd had enough excitement for one outing, he laughed to himself. And he counted himself lucky that a six-year old didn't know enough to realize how frightened he should be.

The old man looked to see his grandson still gazing out into the darkness astern. An hour later, the boy would still be there, curled on the window ledge and fast asleep, dreaming of myths and magical adventures.

* * *

From the UMN Trans-Terran Dispatch, 28January2547:
ALIENS ESCAPE SITE OF MASSACRE
by S.L. Yang
COVINGTON, New Babylon
January 28, 2547

With shock waves resounding across Terra from news that humanity's first encounter with an alien race has led to a bloody massacre, the government of President Mikos Sarkisian is reeling from allegations that the actions of the Cosmic Guard permitted the aliens to escape responsibility for the slaughter.

Initial reports released yesterday by Central Command portrayed efforts by a squadron of frigates near the Hawkins Star system as instrumental in saving a large number of civilian craft from attack by alien warships. Interviews with the spacers themselves, however, suggest that the frigates actually interfered with pursuit of the aliens by those who had witnessed the encounter, allowing the aliens—whom CosGuard now calls "Crutchtans"—to flee the region and escape to the east.

"We are going to get to the bottom of this," promised Admiral Winthrop W. Weatherlee, commanding officer at Demeter Command and a member of the hastily convened board of inquiry that will be investigating the incident. "CosGuard exists to protect people, and heads will roll if we discover that any officer of the Cosmic Guard willingly allowed the perpetrators of the massacre at Hawkins Star to escape justice."

Citing military protocol, Weatherlee declined to release the names of anyone involved in the preliminary inquiry. Senior military sources speaking off the record identified the squadron leader as Lt. Commander Roscoe Cook, who is serving his second tour of duty in the Hodges Sector. Cook, a native of Planet Isis, was unavailable for comment

Meanwhile, in the Senate, leaders of the opposition Tory Party demanded that the President appoint an independent special prosecutor to conduct a thorough inquiry into the circumstances of the Hawkins Massacre....

Chapter 1

THE CROWD WAS BOISTEROUS AND rowdy. Clinking glasses and bawdy laughter mixed with scuffles and shoves, and the air reeked of lager and sweat. At the bar, the patrons jostled to fill their steins with the chilled, intoxicating brew that warmed their nights and made life on the cold, arid planet bearable. Men from a dozen worlds drank and sang, churning the room with their stories and songs. Lights glowed warmly through the frosted windows, and laughter and music floated beyond the walls to be scattered by the wind.

> *For it's Springtime on Ishtar, me darlin*
> *It's payday, come lager an' carolin*
> *An' me dusty, dry glass needs a-fillin*
> *By a lusty young lass who's a-willin.*

A tall, muscular man broke through the cluster at the bar, carrying four steins of lager. Swarthy and bearded, he wore maroon thermoflax coveralls and black leather boots. He ambled tenuously to a round wooden table in the center of the room, with most of his cargo intact. At the table, three others sat by candlelight, two in native attire and a Cosmic Guard yeoman. They were engaged in heated conversation lost in the din of the crowd.

> *Now the girlies o'Ishtar ain't pretty*
> *Nor graceful, nor charmin, nor witty*
> *But it scarce matters me, as I dally*
> *While the icy winds roll through the valley*
>
> *An' it's Springtime on Ishtar, me darlin....*

"Laddy," said a native with a heavy Ishtari accent. Scraggly patches of beard covered his craggy face, and he wore a blue knit cap. "Ain't no slimy lizard can tell me, pack up an'leave. A scant six month gimme bare time to 'coup me costs o'gittin there, an' they have the bloody gall to swoop down from the sky an' farce me off, an' escort me half-back here."

The bearded native distributed his catch from the bar. "Well, Cyrus," he said. "Ye did after all let them carry ye off, wi'out liftin s'much as a hand-laser agin them. Ye know, we seen how they scattered when the laddies came after'em proper at Hawkins. If ye'd just stood your ground—"

"Pssh." The second native made room for the bearded one at the table and cast a side glance at the green-shirted yeoman sitting across the table. "Ain't no blamin Cyrus, now. Ye know bloody well it's these limp-wristed Cozzies what's too bloody sissified to be protectin decent folk agin them stinkin sallymanders. If it showed us anything, Hawkins taught us that, it did."

Cyrus sipped his lager. Bloodshot eyes flashing, he turned to face the yeoman. His mouth twisted into a sly grin, as if welcoming the fight he hoped to provoke. "Spacer," he hissed, "ye say ye're not lackin sympathy. But them lizards is gittin bolder by the day, makin it so's honest merchants like us can't survive. 'Twixt them an' the pirates, we risk our hides ev'ry time we sail, an' all we git from yer kind is preachin and promises. Well, laddie, where's our help?" The others at the table gently pounded the table, indicating their agreement.

Like all servicemen in the region, the yeoman had become quite adept at deflecting questions like this. Locals accosted CosGuarders randomly on every planet and colony along the frontier, demanding answers to the alien threat. It never helped to remind them that if they stayed on Terra's side of the Neutral Zone, the Crutchtans wouldn't bother them.

"Gentlemen, we have our own problems," he began, reaching for his stein. "We can't ignore Crutchtan abuse of our citizens, but it's bad tactics to confront an enemy without knowing his capabilities. Besides, the human race doesn't revolve around Ishtar."

"Bosh an' bahanna!" bellowed Cyrus. "Them lizards has pushed us out o'too many systems already. If we don't draw the line soon, they'll be half-back to Earth herself afore the rest o'ye even blink. An' besides, all we be hearin from ev'ry corner is not to worry, because our ships is so superior.

"Well, the whores can all go lonely for the good it does us, if we still git ourselves pushed around. An' if you Cozzies keep givin ground each time they hiss at ye, there's naught akeepin us from the lizards' stewpot." His companions all agreed.

The yeoman shook his head sadly. Reasoning with spacers was like teaching algebra to a mutluk, he though. And reminding them that the Crutchtans were vegetarians only made matters worse. "I've no love for them either, but they're hardly savages. They're advanced enough for space flight, after all."

"Cozzie," rasped Cyrus, his eyes blazing in the candlelight. "Ye never met them creatures face to face, like I did. Never felt their slimy hands on your skin, nor looked in them slitty eyes to see the devil's own soul." He emptied his stein and wiped his mouth in his sleeve.

"I tell ye, them monsters won't be restin until they've destroyed us."

Fortunately, one of the spacer's friends interceded. "Laddies," said the one lately returned from the bar, "we've enough trouble these days, wi'out goin for each other's throats. To spacers," he said, lifting his stein. "The sorriest lot o'bastards in Terra."

"To spacers," chorused the others.

Around them, the clamor grew like a dust storm on the Ishtari plains. Old friends shouted greetings across the dimly lit room, and the talk became militant on subjects ranging from trade tariffs to the shortage of women on the frontier. Everyone drank as if dying of thirst, and hoarse voices raised hearty choruses about asteroid mining and Demetrian summers, pirate raids and outlaw heroes.

> *For ten long years, they never found him.*
> *Ten long years, they'll ever hound him.*
> *An' the night he left New Dublin town*
> *A star rose in the sky,*
> *An' the light that burns forever*
> *Is the gleam in Danny's eye.*

The yeoman and two of his new friends joined in the singing, which shook the rafters and echoed in their groggy heads. It felt odd, celebrating one of CosGuard's darkest moments; but he was a Demetrian, after all, and Danny O'Donovan was a legend in the folklore of his youth. Cyrus stared ahead, his jawbone twitching. At his table, he alone refused to join the merriment.

> *A hundred howlin' Cozzies couldn't catch him.*
> *No outlaw band could make a stand to match him.*
> *An' one day, for fun he stole a frigate*
> > *From the Cosmic Guard*
> *An' gave it to the settlement*
> > *At Mullinberry's Star.*

"They'll destroy us," muttered Cyrus, oblivious to the cheer resounding through the pub. Amid the chorus of voices, none could tell that his accent had changed. "Or we'll be destroyin them."

OUTSIDE, FIVE small figures, shivering in the cold, emerged from the shadows and walked tentatively toward the pub, looking about nervously with each step. They could feel the warm glow inside, and heard the laughter and singing. The voices sounded guttural, like animals at play. Yet there was something familiar, almost friendly, about the sounds, as if beneath the snarling bluster beat hearts pulsing with kinship and kindness. Huddling together for warmth, they paused in front of the door.

After more than a few moments of hesitation, they entered and walked down the steps to the inner door.

A STUNNED SILENCE fell over the bar. Ninety-five and one-half pairs of eyes followed the small creatures slowly walking from the door to the bar. The wind whipped against the outside wall; inside, hushed voices carried whispers of the carnage to come.

There were five of them. The tallest stood almost five feet tall; the heaviest weighed about a hundred pounds. Even without the strangely colored outer cloaks and their eerie, floating manner of walking, their bald pates and translucent skin were unmistakable. Slowly, whispers crept across the room as lips mouthed the hated word: *aliens.*

They were Veshnans, from the diplomatic mission negotiating on behalf of the reptilian race of Cruthtans who claimed the disputed region of space on the other side of the Neutral Zone. Tiny skin flaps on top of their heads hid their aural membranes, and two small slits squeezed between two large, pale pink eyes, served as nostrils. But a human-sized mouth, in an oddly familiar place at the conflux of cheek and chin bones, gave them an unexpectedly human appearance. Quilted gold tunics beneath their cloaks draped their bodies, and slate gray scarves dangled from their necks.

An ominous murmur pulsed through the crowd. Sullen men withdrew from the bar as the aliens, closely grouped and clinging to each other for safety, approached. Timidly, one of the creatures grasped the railing and stood, tiptoed, peering over the bar into the curious face of the barkeep.

"Five glasses of prune juice, please," it said in a clear and unaccented voice. Jumping with surprise, the startled barkeep knocked over a half-dozen glasses, which shattered loudly on the floor and caused everyone nearby to yelp in alarm. But he had the presence of mind to overcharge his strange customers for their drinks, and watched in wonder as they strolled, prune juice in hand, toward the center of the pub to survey the room, blissfully unaware of the tension growing around them.

Presently, one of the aliens pointed to a table at the far corner of the pub, near the entrance to the sanitary annex the building shared with the one next door. The others nodded and exchanged a singing chorus of voices. After several moments of melodious debate, the aliens started walking toward the table. Before them, the crowd parted; angry stares followed them.

Lost in thought and seated at the table was a CosGuard officer, with the eyes of a poet. Sitting quietly by himself in the farthest corner of the pub, he seemed uncomfortable and out of place, and looked to all the world like someone who'd just lost his best friend. The three gold stripes on his space-black epaulets showed him to be a full commander, and the subordinates aboard his ship knew his sharp voice with its edge of steel and ring of command. But the lager had dulled his senses along with his mind, and his eyes had long since gone glassy with drink. Among the crowd, he was the only one who'd failed to notice the strangers' arrival in the pub, and it was only by chance that he raised his eyes to see them walking slowly toward him. By the time he cleared his windpipe of the drink that his sudden gasp drew into his lungs, the newcomers had arrived at his table and were busy making themselves at home. Under the murderous glowers of the crowd, he realized that he was beginning to perspire.

"Excuse me, Commander," one of them said, "but we recognized your uniform and thought it would be interesting to chat. Do you mind if we join you?"

The commander would come to wonder why he was not surprised by the alien's flawless speech. At the time, all he could do was take a deep breath and emit a soft, involuntary whimper. His eyes quickly darted about, desperately seeking help. When he'd entered, the pub had sparkled with Cozzie colors, mingling with the natives. Now, he searched vainly for a friendly face.

"Please sit down," he said at last, clearing his throat. Despairingly, he caught sight of the last remaining Cozzie discreetly slipping out the door. It meant, he realized to his horror, that he was now trapped, surrounded, and quite alone. As his mind struggled to free itself from the effects of the lager, all he could do was wonder why having a quiet beer by himself was proving to be such a problem.

"Making peace means making contact," the alien linguist said in a tone that seemed to admit no debating the point. "It is more than merely talking across a conference table. We decided to mingle, as you call it, to help us better understand each other."

"Admirable," said the Terran, his voice cracking. He'd heard stories, but always wondered what bar brawls on Ishtar were really like.

"This world seems far too cold," the alien continued, shivering at the memory of walking outside. "Why do so many chose to live here?"

"It's close...to...resources," the commander said absently, gazing about him.

"But a quarter-billion people? Our scientists say that your biology is similar to ours, and that we prefer similar climates. So, when we first arrived...."

Nodding politely, the commander was not paying attention to his guest. He was watching the crowd, and he did not like what he saw.

* * *

Minutes seemed like eons.

The commander felt every eye watching him. Murmurs coursed through the room and darkened with anger, the tone growing more menacing with each passing heartbeat. As his head struggled to clear itself, panic rose to take the place of the beer. Across the table, the alien kept chattering merrily, as if they were all long lost friends exchanging pleasantries and gossip. Either fear was as alien to Veshnans as they were to Ishtar, he thought to himself, or they had no sense of the trouble they were causing.

"We find your music interesting but incomprehensible," said the Veshnan. "There is so much noise, there is so much chaos. But our hearing senses are quite similar, so we are told, and we know that there must be something we are missing. Perhaps it is some structural form or convention?"

"It's the emotional content, I think," the Terran said absently. "Your experience with us is too limited to sense clues we grasp immediately, but barely notice. And our musical instruments are probably different enough to confuse you."

The alien smiled. For an instant, the danger they shared faded from the Terran's mind, and the commander found himself charmed to the point of captivation. In the middle of a room filled with hate, it shined like the gentle sun of an Isitian Spring, warming everything and everyone with the glow of renewal. The alien's smile, to the Terran's amazement, looked like the sweet, innocent smile of a human infant.

"You are very perceptive, Commander."

The officer smiled lamely and shrugged. "I just know a bit about music," he said, looking nervously about.

Turning around, his back was to the lockers as he saw them pushing toward him, cutting off any chance of escape. They were big and mean, and anger flared in their eyes.

"Plebe," snorted one. "You've much to learn about respect."

The young man stood his ground, but said nothing. He watched their advance impassively, his arms filled with books and computer files. Though scared to death, he would not give them the satisfaction of showing fear.

"*Some folk don't think much of Isitian daisy-sniffers pretending to be spacers,*" smirked another. The plebe saw amused scorn flash in their eyes. As if by signal, they dropped their school books to the floor.

"*So I've heard,*" he answered.

Soon they stood pressing him on all sides, nose to nose to ear. He could smell the liquor on their breath, and felt the mindless hatred in their souls. With all the inner strength he could muster, he forced himself to relax. Surrendering to panic would only admit defeat.

"*What's that you're carrying?*" demanded the third.

"*Navigation disks, a biology text, and some music.*"

"*What kind of music?*" Snatching a disk from the plebe's arm, the upperclassman knocked everything else the young man carried onto the floor.

"*VanSlambrook—and Mozart!*" the upperclassman chortled derisively. His companions laughed.

"*Sissy music,*" scoffed the first, taking the tape. "*For Isissies and other losers.*" He threw down the disk contemptuously, then cracked and shattered it under his boot.

The plebe's eyes darted to the ruined music disk, then challenged the upperclassman's haughty stare. "*Midshipman VanderMuelen,*" he said, quietly but firmly. "*That was my personal recording. I expect you to pay for it.*"

VanderMuelen's eyes narrowed.

"*Plebes don't talk that way to upperclassmen.*"

"*This one does,*" said the plebe. He saw rage flash in their faces, felt their fists clench, sensed their arms draw back to strike. You prat-head, he told himself; you never learn.

"So every winter Ghilgh'a'sin's spirit returns to the ground, to sleep until spring.

"Is that not a lovely legend, Commander?"

A tall, sneering spacer rose from a table at the other end of the room and emptied his stein. Pushing away from his friends, who tried to pull him back to his chair, he glowered at the aliens sitting at the officer's table and began staggering toward the aisle.

"Commander?" repeated the Veshnan.

"Yes, it's a beautiful story," answered the Terran, but his attention was elsewhere. The mood of the crowd was now livelier, almost festive. Looking about, he saw everyone's eyes following the spacer's progress, their faces giddy with anticipation.

"You see why Terra has nothing to fear from the Crutchtans?"

As the spacer neared them, the commander heard drunken voices raising in hearty encouragement. His head had cleared enough to know full well the danger they faced, but not enough to let him plan an escape. He felt a surge of resentment toward his companions for placing him in this predicament. It quickly passed, for he realized that they were not responsible for the lowlife of Ishtar, and knew no better than to wander into a spacer's bar.

"Any culture where the strong give their lives for the weak, and an act of love becomes a source of renewal, will be friendly and peaceful," said the Veshnan. "And they will be the best sort of neighbors. All they need is a chance."

The spacer was twenty feet away and closing. The crowd was definitely enjoying itself; the prospect of blood always warmed the Ishtari soul. "Listen to me," said the commander, calmly but intensely. "We have to leave. Tell your friends to put on their cloaks and prepare to follow me."

"Is anything wrong, Commander?" asked the alien. "Have we done something— "

"I'll explain later. Just do as I say—quickly, but with no sudden moves." The Veshnans donned their cloaks and fastened their waistbelts as the commander rose to put on his heavy gray overcoat. The spacer stopped short and chuckled.

"Ye wouldna be leavin us now, Mr. Cozzie," said Cyrus, his voice thick with drink. "I be needin a ward wi'your lizard-lovin friends, there."

The commander had no illusions about what "a word" with somebody blocking the exit meant on Ishtar. Painfully aware that he was out of his element, he knew that the time for fear had passed. Now, he needed the clearest thinking his own muddled brain could muster. That, he thought, and about a year's worth of luck.

A quick glance and the beleaguered officer had sized up his adversary. The haze in the spacer's eyes promised a slow reaction if they tried to slip past him. But he was a big man—bigger than the commander, anyway—and would be far stronger, even in his drunken condition: the lower gravity of the officer's home planet guaranteed that the spacer would beat him senseless if they came to blows, and few Ishtaris would pass the chance to help someone dust off a CosGuard officer. Even in the best of times, Cozzies were not very popular here; someone would surely stop them from escaping if they tried rushing the door.

Even worse, they might just grab the Veshnans. A physical attack on diplomats in a pub—the commander shuddered to think about the complications.

No, he thought. They had to ease past him gradually. A sudden move could provoke a riot. And the honor of the Guard required at least one try for a graceful retreat before dashing for the hatch like a whipped puppy.

"My friend," he said firmly. "Please step aside and let us pass."

Cyrus folded his arms and smirked. Sweat coursed down his face. Hate burned in his eyes like glowing coals.

"My friend," the commander smiled coldly. "We'd love to stay and share a lager-pitcher with you, but I'm afraid we're due somewhere else, and running a bit behind schedule as well. Perhaps another time."

"I'm wantin no drink wi'you, matey," stormed Cyrus, his eyes searching the officer for the smallest reaction, the faintest hint of fear. But the Cozzie held his ground and returned Cyrus' hateful stare without flinching. He even folded his arms and stiffened his back, defying a closer approach by the drunken spacer. Taken aback by the show of resolve, Cyrus spat out his words like acid. "Kindly tell your wan, wee friends to be steppin over here."

A wave of gleeful hate filled the air. Several men moved to block the aisleway, the only route to the door. Hurriedly, the bartender began clearing bottles and glasses and other breakables from the top of the bar. Then, amid cheers from the center of the pub and a quietly sinking heart from the lone Cozzie in the room, a huge man rose and lumbered past the others to stand beside Cyrus.

"Hello, Cozzie," said a giant that the increasingly alarmed officer recognized from a past encounter, though the Cozzie had quite forgotten the Goliath's name. The spacer had once tried to slip past a CosGuard blockade, bent on making a run to one of the illegal colonies past Hodges' Binary. He'd spent the next week in a Cozzie brig, his ship in tow to Looking Glass, and the brooding, sullen man had never forgotten.

At least my luck is consistent, thought the Cozzie. His hopes now ran less to escape than to the prospect of a short convalescence.

Suddenly, the commander noticed an annoying pressure, from a source he took pains to avoid when leading his ship into battle. By reflex, he started to look over his shoulder to the narrow hallway leading to the kitchen and—

To safety, he thought, dismayed at the time it had taken to arrive at the obvious solution. The doors weren't very sturdy, but it didn't matter. Once inside, he could lock the door and signal his ship. The molecular transmitter on board could whisk them out of danger long before the door gave way. Must be the lager, he thought, smiling as he realized that the lager led him to the answer as well.

"Listen carefully," he whispered to the Veshnan linguist. "Take your friends down the hallway behind us and wait for me in the room with the small ceramic pot in the middle of the floor."

The alien had heard the exchange between the Terrans, and understood enough to be frightened beyond measure. Quietly, as their officer friend kept talking, the Veshnans backed toward the hall.

"What the— " the giant puzzled dumbly.

"Beelzebub's ghost!" thundered Cyrus, when he understood what was happening.

"Move!" barked the commander, tipping over chairs and tables to cover their retreat. Quickly, he ushered the Veshnans into the room with the sign marked "Johnnie," then slammed the door, bolting it shut just ahead of Cyrus' lunging body, hoping that it would hold for a few minutes. Outside in the bar, a crush of laughing and sneering spacers followed the two ringleaders to the hallway.

"A fine display o'Cozzie courage," scoffed one.

"I ain't had this much fun since the day Paddy Hassib got tored apart in the Collyseum," cackled another.

"Look, what I found," said a third, stooping by the abandoned table. There, from the floor, he picked up a CosGuard mobile transmitter; in the rush to escape it had fallen from the commander's pocket.

"Stars to smile on a spacer's heart," crowed Cyrus, as someone handed him the radio. "Cozzie," he bellowed with a laugh. "Ye dropped your squawker. There's no way to be gittin out."

The response was silence.

"We'll let ye go, we will," cooed Goliath, a bloodthirsty glint in his eye. "It's your puny friends we want."

The silence from the locked men's room only made the mob angrier.

"Ye can't stay in there forever," Cyrus shouted. In the hallway the crowd cawed and whooped.

"We're a-comin in after ye!" Goliath warned, to the cheers of the others. He started ramming the door with his body. Others joined him, shouting with glee. Furiously they hurled themselves at the flimsy metal, trying to shake it loose from its crumbling concrete frame. Each grunt fanned their blood lust; every bruised shoulder whipped their animal fury.

Finally, the door started moving. With a fierce howl, the frenzied men threw their bodies into one smashing thrust at the buckling frame. The hinges ripped from the wall, the door slammed onto the floor, and the blood-crazed men charged into the head in a blind rage. In an instant, the crush from the rear threw the leaders nose-first against the back wall, and Cyrus cracked his shin against the commode. The pain crackled up his leg to echo in his lager-soaked brain, but except for the mob, the room was empty.

Within seconds, someone noticed a frozen chill to the air. Goliath looked toward the ceiling in the right corner of the room, where the air-chute was ripped open. The opening was barely big enough for a man, surely big enough for the small aliens. As the drain in the commode finished its cycle, the cold night air poured through the hole, driving the attackers back into the hallway.

The giant was furious.

"Ye noodle-noggined mushbrain!" he bellowed at Cyrus. "Ye should o' thought he might sneak out some back way, the tricky bastard. Ye simpleminded twit." He punched the wall as hard as he could, breaking his hand.

"Don't be a-blamin me, ye loud-mouthed fanny-noodler," snarled Cyrus. Too drunk and angry to know better, he stomped on the larger man's foot and aimed an elbow at his solar plexus. He hit the monster's belly instead, and the enraged giant lifted Cyrus off the floor with his good arm, hurling him into the crowd, knocking several would-be brawlers down and forcing the rest into the center of the pub.

"Fight, fight!" chorused the mob, eagerly joining the melee, little caring whose side they took.

AFTER RUNNING for several blocks, the cold air burned their lungs. On the Terran's signal the group stopped to lean against a wall, breathing deeply. Their hearts were pounding like hammers.

"Your pubs—seem friendlier—from the outside," the alien gasped between breaths.

The commander laughed, as much from relief as in response to the alien's jest. He rested his head against the wall and looked up at the shining stars and lightening sky. "I'll walk you to your hotel," he panted. "The rowdies are out in force tonight, and the nights here are short. Dawn will break soon, and it would be better if you were home when the sun comes up."

They started walking, slowly to help them catch their breath. Before long they were trotting as quickly as they could without stumbling over the cracks in the pavement. The wind pierced their clothing like knives, and soon they were shivering again.

"By the way, Commander, I am called *Panche'teMunshi*. And we are renting a house, not a hotel."

"My name is Roscoe Cook," said the commander. He returned the Veshnan's bow as they ran, nearly tripping over some cracked pavement in the process.

"Welcome to Ishtar."

Chapter 2

I HAVE NEVER SEEN ONE close up before."

"How ever do they breathe through those long, pointed snouts?"

"Munshi says this one is quite friendly, though painfully shy. It hardly said more than a few dozen words on the way back from the riot. But it seems intelligent—and look at the way it moves around the room, examining everything in sight. It is curious as a schripan't."

"Is it male or female?"

"Who can tell?"

"Short hair—and Munshi says it has a deep voice. I think, perhaps, it is a male."

"Maybe Zatar will not feel so out of place, now."

"You know, he really need not be so lonely—not if we send Gh'sienna to tell him we have a guest."

"Be not crude, Doshanda. Besides, 'Sienna hardly went into heat on purpose."

"I will go."

"No, I will go; you flirt so shamefully, we shall never get you out of his room if you go. And you have been eating so much you are likely to go into heat yourself."

ZATAR OF IBLEIMAN was a handsome man, tall and powerfully built, with firm, angular cheekbones and a well-rounded chin. Even approaching middle age, his skin retained the whiteness of youth, for the yellowing of age came slowly to his proud and distinguished family. As befitted a scion of the House of Ibleiman, he was not easily given to wearing his thoughts on his countenance, but his eyes had almost lost their color and a look of bewilderment had seized his brow. He was, in a word, incredulous.

"Are you sure?" he asked again, as if repeating the question would alter the facts. His aide stamped her foot in annoyance. He knew that dwelling on the obvious was foolish, but the cold, dry planet sometimes affected his hearing and he wanted to be certain he heard things correctly.

"I saw the Terran with my own eyes, Ambassador," she replied tartly. Men were impossible, she thought; you could repeat things a dozen times and they would still ask if you were sure. Even so, she could not stay angry with Zatar for long. It was the one benefit she could see in working for a man, and mischief soon darted across her cheek muscles.

"They say it is a male. Imagine that—but then, I suppose even Terran males are not without their charms."

Irritation clouded Zatar's face. Even after so many years of service together, his aides still delighted in showing themselves unawed by his credentials or accomplishments. As a senior procurator for the High Council of the Grand Alliance, Zatar had been places and seen things that few Veshnan men dreamed existed and fewer aspired to share. With each passing year, his reputation and influence grew in the corridors of power on Balarium, the tranquil, lovely planet that was the administrative center for the Alliance. He had even begun to dream of having at least one aide with a more enlightened perspective, but after all this time he was so used to each of them that such a radical change would be unsettling. He knew enough not to take offense, though now was hardly the time for teasing. Zatar cleared his throat haughtily.

Chastised, she continued.

"He saved G'ela's life, and Maguna's, and Munshi's, and— "

"But how...?"

"They all went to visit a Terran social club and some of the guests became unruly. Like wemblies guarding their brood, I suppose. So the Terran led them through an emergency exit—sent them 'back to the wind before they could warm themselves,' as it happened, but it was not really his fault. In fact, it was quite prudent, as I understand it. Now, Munshi is shaking from the cold and no other but you understands Terran talk. Our guest is wandering downstairs without a host, and we must not appear to be rude."

Zatar bowed and dismissed her from the room. Immediately, he began searching his wardrobe for something suitable. Red perhaps, since they would be celebrating, even if the feast would be merely for Avoidance of Bother. He could deal with Munshi later. Why she would be so foolish as to venture outside by herself, much less contrive to avoid the Terran militiamen assigned as their escorts, was unexplainable. Simply unexplainable. But then, even though he was the official head of the delegation, it seemed that nobody in this House ever listened to anything he said.

As he changed from his housecoat to more formal attire, uncertainty creased his face. This would be the first time he had met a Terran without an interpreter. It would also be the first time any of them had met a Terran in a social setting, away from the formal trappings of diplomacy. His thirty-day language-immersion course may have taught him the rote responses needed for the stilted greetings of diplomats, but was hardly adequate to the more rigorous demands of small talk. Besides, some people had language talent and others did not. And while he could understand most Crutchtan dialects quite well, the Terran language was utter chaos to him. Terran vocal chords might be remarkably similar to his own, and each day found Zatar recognizing and pronouncing more Terran words than before. But he found himself intimidated by the syntactical bogs and conjugational swamps that were the hallmarks of their strange, guttural tongue. Munshi said the language was really quite simple, and that the staccato barks and growls that Terrans used to communicate were no different than any other language after mastering the inverted grammar and alien idioms. But Munshi was quite gifted.

His dressing completed, he looked in the mirror to see the embodiment of Veshnan manhood—tall and proud, like his forefathers before him, brightly arrayed in festive attire. He adjusted his robes to their best advantage and breathed heavily, forcing himself to relax, knowing that descending the stairs would be the most difficult part of the entire evening.

Of course, meeting the Terran would be easy. Exhilarating, actually, thought Zatar. What would be difficult would be trying to ignore Gh'sienna's mating scent on the way to meet his guest. Veshnan women always found excuses for not taking men seriously, but they hardly helped matters by finding male preoccupations so amusing, especially since they were the biggest distraction themselves.

ROSCOE COOK wandered aimlessly around the makeshift embassy, peering at the curiosities scattered about the living room. Brightly colored tapestries covered the dull walls, depicting scenes of Veshnan life in abstractions that the commander found unintelligible. Strange aromas filled his senses, beckoning his imagination on journeys reaching past the untamed wilderness of outer Terra. Even his boyhood awe at the heroic explorers who first breached the confines of Old Earth and headed off into the cosmos was lost in the wonder he felt touching the artifacts of an alien civilization. Unlike those who left the tantalizing ruins that dotted the forests of Isis, the Veshnans were a living culture. It made the dead relics of his home planet seem as cold and barren as the sands of Ishtar.

In the corner, an open cabinet stretched to the ceiling. Made from an unknown substance that was cool to the touch, it left a salty-tasting residue on the officer's fingers. Its shelves were filled with strangely colored plants, which quivered and hummed as he approached. Beneath his feet was a plush, velvety carpet of deep maroon, which almost swallowed his boots as he wandered around the room. Bending to brush the material with his fingers, he found the carpet soft and supple as the winter fur of a Babylonian schrault. A large, transparent urn sat in front of the window, with multicolored fish squiggling in the water. What appeared to be stringed musical instruments hung from the wall on the room's north side.

Cook walked to the north wall and ran his finger over the strings of a Veshnan lute, producing a wavering, metallic sound like the tremulous whine of a subspace engine in a vat of water. The sound was eerie and unsettling, reminding him of the mood music that accompanied the vid-screen monsters he loved to watch as a child. It stopped as soon as he removed his hand. Feeling suddenly self-conscious, he turned to see a red-robed Veshnan standing at the entrance to the living room. It had the same pale translucence, the same four-fingered hands, the same calm serenity about its bearing, as those he had met in the pub. But this alien was large—almost a foot taller than the others—and its face was more angular, its features more pronounced.

This was, the commander guessed, a Veshnan male.

AT THE cosmic pace of distant stars passing in the blackness, the two males waited in silence for the other to speak. After the first tentative bows and smiles, Zatar began to feel quite foolish and the ensuing silence just compounded the problem. The artifacts and scents of home that filled the senses in the gathering room, so carefully designed to remind all of them of the worlds they left behind, merely added to his sense of disarray.

Curiously, while finding another species in such a place disturbed his sense of balance, the alien visitor was hardly the cause of the ambassador's concern. Slowly, he realized that his shyness arose largely from his reluctance to make a fool of himself by butchering the Terran's mother tongue. This was the way of cowards, he reflected, but found that he could not help himself. The mind that could charm the High Council and send those on the other side of any issue careening into outrage and despair balked at the prospect of floundering in a sea of alien phraseology. He was dismayed, as well, to learn that the well-endowed ego of a High Official of the Grand Alliance did not take kindly to the thought of communicating by grunts and sign language.

The Terran stared at him through circles of color in a sea of white. Terran eyes were paralyzing, thought Zatar, at once compelling and hypnotic. The effect was less pronounced at the negotiating table, where interpreters served as a buffer, but now Zatar felt a subliminal wariness. It was, he concluded, a singular advantage for a predator species, yet he recalled the Terran's almost gleeful inquisitiveness as earlier he watched it dart across the room, moving with surprising agility for such a large creature. Unlike those with proper Veshnan manners, it was not at all self-conscious about its curiosity. And that was, thought Zatar, the mark of a civilized man no matter what the women thought. It was enough to make him wonder how his own species appeared, when seen through Terran eyes.

Silently, Zatar studied the costume of their long-nosed simian visitor. It was a type of uniform worn by other members of the Terran militia force. "Protectors of the Universe," they called themselves—or *khasg'a'rhd'h*, in their own language. It seemed a heavier uniform than he had seen before, of coarser material and cluttered with pockets and flaps. The uniform was also the color of the sky, which meant that their guest was a military officer of some sort. Zatar could not guess its rank merely by looking, but the Terran's face suggested that their guest was one of some importance.

Except for females and children, most of the people he had seen on the planet—and many militiamen, as well—covered their faces with fur. Only those the Terran government had sent to negotiate with him kept their face fur so closely cropped as to be invisible.

And the difference was not congenital, he knew, for Zatar recalled seeing fur grow on many of the Terran negotiators during their long sessions in seclusion together. He supposed that the Terran government ordered its diplomats and senior militiamen to trim their faces, so as not to frighten the representatives of the Grand Alliance needlessly. After all, the first sightings of the long-haired simians had driven the Crutchtans to panic at the bloody First Encounter. The Terran policy of cropping their fur was an act of profound civility for which Zatar was grateful, even if his colleagues dismissed the gesture as the product of his own imagination.

Finally, the ambassador could stand the silence no longer. Resolved to muddle through as best he could, he swallowed his misgivings and began to speak, only to find the venture cut short: the Terran, apparently just as impatient at the long silence, blurted out the last sounds in the world that Zatar expected to hear. His guest spoke tentatively, unsurely, and indistinctly, but the message came through nonetheless.

"Friend," it said; at least that was what it sounded like. Zatar could not be sure, given the thick accent and low-pitched growl of the Terran's voice. Actually, it sounded more like "*f'Rroinght,*" but the context was right, and Zatar judged that it was as close as a Terran could come without choking. What astounded him was that the Terran knew any Veshnan words at all. Even Terra's ambassadors seemed disinterested in learning to speak for themselves, and Zatar had all but concluded that Terrans had little interest in other languages. Choosing his words slowly and carefully, Zatar forged ahead with his effort at cross-cultural communication. But by now he was smiling so broadly that he could only guess what he sounded like to the Terran.

"*Hearth our toward, is hospitality,*" Zatar said in the Terran's language, repeating by rote one of the many greetings he had learned from the language tapes. "Zatar of Ibleiman, *the emissary am I.*" He approached the Terran, prepared to clasp hands in the traditional Terran greeting. Zatar rather enjoyed the quaint custom, though he could not fathom its significance. He assumed it derived from the keen tactile sense noted in proto-simians throughout the galaxy and was meant to engender some sort of temporary bonding between the participants. To his surprise, his guest smiled and bowed in the finest Veshnan manner.

"*Emissary sir,*" the Terran replied in its own language. "*Conferring is contentment.*"

"*Like health, conferring of mine is joyful,*" Zatar responded, returning the bow. To his horror, he realized that his memory was failing him and he was running out of rote responses. Trying not to panic, he tried to clear his mind by listening to the sands whipping against the side of their dwelling. But the thought of the cold, pelting winds merely made him shudder and seemed to keep the words from rising in his brain. Finally, the distraction itself unclogged his mental faculties, and another Terran phrase popped into his head.

"*Pray, your title what grows, plus?*"

Zatar winced; he knew that he had said it wrong, but hoped he had come close enough for his guest to understand. Talking in this strange tongue was quite exhilarating, he realized, but it seemed that much of the excitement came from never being quite sure what he was saying. As far as he could tell, Terrans strung words together randomly, with no discernable pattern, and in the past he often created confusion whenever he tried to follow conventional rules of syntax. He sighed with relief upon hearing a familiar voice come to his rescue.

"His name is *Khu'ukh of Waashkho.*"

It was Munshi. She had changed into more formal attire—a dark blue tunic and long, flowing gown—and her skin no longer pulsed with the cold. The ambassador had rarely been gladder to see anyone in his life.

"But you are doing so well," she said, obviously enjoying herself. "Please, do not stop on my account."

Zatar was not amused.

"*KHU'UKH,*" MUMBLED the ambassador, struggling with the pronunciation and feeling quite ignored as Munshi and the Terran chatted unintelligibly.

"You know what it means, do you not?" asked Munshi. Her

laughing eyes told Zatar that he could ignore the question without loss, but curiosity triumphed over his sense of dignity.

He exhaled loudly, frustrated that his reputation among the High Council offered no immunity from teasing by his own kind. As with most men, his curiosity never failed to provide amusement for the mischievous females around him, who seemed to delight in showing their casual irreverence toward any of his accomplishments.

"I hope the cold has not stripped your sense of irony," she continued wryly. "For the word '*khu'ukh*' denotes the Terran equivalent of an apprentice Crutchtan chef."

Zatar laughed loudly, soon joined by Munshi. Neither noticed the look of concern that clouded the Terran's face, for neither could tell that their good spirits sounded to him as if they were choking. But as the moments passed their visitor relaxed, sensing that his new friends were in no real danger. Soon his eyes resumed wandering impatiently around the room.

"A propitious omen for our Crutchtan friends," Zatar said at last. "But I suppose if we tell them, they will celebrate their good fortune until the stars grow horns."

They both shared another long laugh, until they were interrupted by the Terran. Zatar tried to follow the conversation, but quickly lost its gist—something about returning to school when they were pensioners, he thought. It hardly surprised him when Munshi's translation came out differently.

"*Khu'ukh of Waashkho* suggests proceeding to the library, where we can talk in more relaxed surroundings," Munshi related. "He can stay only briefly today, but promises to return if we invite him. He thinks that quiet conversation may do more to further understanding than all manner of diplomatic yammering."

"Your friend is very wise," said Zatar, bowing solemnly to both in turn. "Tell the kitchen to prepare their finest refreshments. Our guest should feel welcome, and you may tell him that we wish him to stay as long as he wishes and look forward to his return with eager anticipation."

As the three made their way toward the next room, Zatar noticed the rest of the staff peeking from behind every available wall, like children who have forgotten their manners. Women chuckled at the curiosity of their men, he thought, but they were every bit as bad.

Still, he realized that he could not keep them from intruding, and hoped that the prying did not offend their guest.

Walking beside the Terran, he found his eyes drawn, as always, to the exquisitely pointed Terran snout. It was the most striking feature on the otherwise fathomless Terran face. Why any intelligent creature needed such extended nostrils baffled scientists in all corners of the Grand Alliance. Asking its function would be impolite, of course, but Zatar recalled reading that most biologists back home thought it showed a transitional phase in Terran evolution: when the early Terran ancestors first left the trees, they theorized, they needed long snouts to dig for roots and grubs. Their omnivore's mouth supported this theory, but Zatar wondered why the earliest Terrans would use their nose instead of their hands. He agreed with the dissenters: obviously, it had something to do with mating.

As they arrived in the study, Munshi told the Terran that, in his honor, they would be serving one of the few Terran delicacies that refined palates throughout the Grand Alliance found irresistible. Terran Ambrosia, they called it. Soon three large pitchers arrived from the kitchen, and the three new friends sat on soft, satin pillows on the floor to toast each other and exchange insights and impressions about themselves and their cultures.

Khu'ukh of Waashkho smiled and told his hosts that he was grateful for their hospitality. He lacked the heart to tell them that he hated what Terrans called "prune juice."

* * *

IN A SEEDY part of town, a door creaked open and a half-drunken spacer staggered through the threshold.

"Caw! Look whut the cat dragged in."

Cyrus McGee shot his brother a sullen, menacing look with the eye that was not swollen shut. Every bruise on his body pulsed in aching unison. His face was puffed, and dried blood caked his scruffy beard. He slammed the hotel room door and hobbled to his bed.

The room was circular and dark, lighted only by the lamp on Mason McGee's night stand. The ceiling was tiled with grimy mirrors, many of them cracked, some of them missing. Dust covered the floor, and the musty odor of stale sweat filled the air.

Mason was determined not to laugh, no matter how pathetic his brother looked. Cyrus had warned him, in his most patronizing big brother tones, not to leave the hotel alone. Big brother deserved to come back with his face as raw as hamburger. But he knew from painful experience that, once aroused, Cyrus' mean streak lingered for hours. Mason was not about to snicker his way into a fight. He reached into the provisions bag for some ointment to give his brother.

Cyrus snatched the ointment tubes without a word. He sat quietly on his bed and began tending his wounds. Hatred still raged in his heart. He would talk when he was damn ready, and not one second before.

Mason was about to return to his entertainment tapes when a knock came to the door.

"Room service" called a husky, female voice.

Mason grinned ravenously. "Door's unlocked," he howled. Cyrus grunted disagreeably.

A tall, dark woman entered the room and locked the door behind her. She wore form-fitting coveralls and a brightly colored scarf. A generous layer of powder and rouge covered most of the wrinkles on her face. Thirty years old, she looked as tired as Earth, and her eyes were weary and sad. But her deep red lips parted in a lusty smile, and the thick scent of jasmine soon captured the room.

"Sorry bein late, gents," she shrugged, "but we're two girls down t'night an runnin way behind." With a flurry of short, bold strokes she shed her coveralls. Underneath she wore a pink halter top lined with brilliant blue feathers and tight fitting black slacks. Her raven black hair fell in gentle flows across her bare shoulders.

Mason, sitting on his bed and leaning against the cold, concrete wall, drooled like a lovesick schoolboy. No matter how cold and dreary they were, he thought, the hotels on Ishtar knew how to make a man feel welcome.

"What's with him?" asked the woman, pointing at the miserable heap of flesh on the next bed. Cyrus was shaking his head and mumbling—something about Cozzies and turtle shells—but the other two couldn't quite make it out.

Mason dismissed it with a wave of his hand. "Don't never mind him," he told her. "He'll be all right by the time you leave. Just a hard night is all." The two of them laughed.

"I'm sure he'll come around when it's his turn," she leered.

Slowly, teasingly, she walked toward Mason, her eyes fixed on his dimpled cheeks and smooth, whiskerless face, her long fingers dancing along the feathered fringe of her top. The younger McGee swung his legs onto the bed and eased his head onto the pillow.

In his corner of the room, Cyrus grudgingly admitted defeat. Nothing would stop his face from aching, he told himself. Nothing but time. The lizards' turn would come, soon enough; there was no sense wasting the present fretting about the past. He picked up a stool and moved to the center of the room, where the view was better.

My day will come again, he thought to himself. And revenge was sweetest when savored through the bitterness of anticipation. Soon, he was dismissing such thoughts from his head. He could use some cheering up, and their hostess was starting to undress.

Chapter 3

THE GENTLE WHINE of the tracking station's generators faded under the ventilator's steady hiss. To the twelve-man crew of the Quarter Watch it was unnoticed white noise, especially when more pressing matters commanded their attention.

"Christ, what a disaster."

"This is getting ridiculous—eh, Chief?"

"Shut up and deal," said Yeoman Chief Huslander, the shift leader. The Chief was in no mood for small talk. Dropping two hundred credits in one sitting to a tyro was no laughing matter. He had his reputation to think of, quite aside from his money. If he didn't recoup his losses by watch change, he'd be the laughing stock of the base. Even Commander Ashton had never cleaned him out so thoroughly. And, for an officer, Ashton knew how to play cards.

It was a while before anyone noticed the flashing yellow light atop Monitor Six. The computer had caught a hailing signal from a Crutchtan chaser hovering barely past the Neutral Zone. Erupting into purposeful chaos, Huslander's shift raced to their stations. The yeoman hurried to the control desk to acknowledge the signal. One crewman went directly to Number Six to engage the manual controls; the others assumed positions at the support station, trying to get a fix on the chaser's position and watching the remaining screens.

Huslander pushed the yellow switch on his control panel, then hit the terminal's transmit key. Instantly, a message flashed into a receiver on Starbase 117:

ATS 8—BEGIN RECEIPT ALIEN TX: MORE TO FOLLOW.

He logged the time and activated the speaker. "Commander Ashton," he said, his voice coursing throughout the base. "Please come to the control room."

* * *

LT. COMMANDER Jeremy Ashton walked briskly down the central corridor. He was a tall man, with a Ceresian's light brown skin and tightly curled hair. As Executive Officer on the frigate *R. B. Fuller*, he'd let his subordinates call him "Mr. A," at least as long as the skipper was out of earshot. A third-generation CosGuarder, and his family's first Academy graduate, he favored an enlightened, liberal style of command, aiming to lead by example rather than intimidation. Bright and conscientious, he'd compiled an outstanding service record aboard the frigate. But upon promotion to lieutenant commander he hadn't gotten what he wanted more than anything else. Instead of his own ship, he was given command of a tiny, lonely outpost on the edge of nowhere, with nothing but space, stars, and interstellar rubble for light years in all directions. In silent protest he'd grown a beard—short, well-trimmed, and becoming, but entirely non-regulation—and his men loved him for it.

Today, Jeremy's mind was not on his job. He'd requested a transfer again. It was his third request, but before retiring from the service Admiral Folino at the starbase strongly hinted that Jeremy was nearing the top of the promotion list, and promotion to full commander usually meant a rotation of duty. A new posting would do much to lift his flagging spirits, he told himself. In his heart, he knew that everyone had dues to pay, but after five cosmic months in a tracking station—more than a full solar year, by the old calendar—he'd come to hate his current assignment. The change, any change, would do him good, and as long as he was dreaming, he would let his imagination soar. He'd already asked for deep space duty. A sleek, fast cruiser would do quite nicely, he told himself a hundred times. But he would settle for anything, from a rusting old freight hauler to a lowly escort, if it would get him away from here.

He still remembered his tour of duty on the *Fuller*, and every mistake Commander Fletcher had made. Jeremy was resolved to repeat none of them. He would have the finest ship and the proudest crew in the whole fleet, whatever its class. No sweat-shopping the crew, or bullying them at captain's mast. A crew returned respect for respect, and arbitrary cruelty had no place on board a CosGuard vessel. Else, he thought, they were little better than the pirates.

The control room door was open; the station was maintaining condition green today. Jeremy passed the redshirted security guard on duty, who snapped to attention as soon as the commander rounded the bend in the hallway. Moments later, Jeremy stood looking over Huslander's shoulder, reading the aliens' short, routine transmission.

"An inspection transit?" groaned Huslander. "That's the second one this month."

"That's their right under the Agreement, Chief," Jeremy rejoined. He logged the request in the main computer and relayed the message to Starbase 117.

When CosGuard and the Consortium space fleet agreed on the dimensions and location of the Neutral Zone, each thought it prudent to insist upon verification, to make sure that the other lived up to its promises. So the Agreement allowed each side a limited number of crossovers—or "Inspection Transits," in the language of Command Order 142-00437—to the end of the extended buffer zone, so that both sides could assure themselves of the other's compliance. The Consortium made many more requests than CosGuard, mostly because all the violations seemed to occur on Terra's side of the border.

Soon, a reply came from the starbase. Everyone knew what it would be: the Crutchtans were still below their monthly limit of three. But protocol was protocol.

"REQUEST APPROVED," read the message on the computer screen.

"Ah, shit," Huslander muttered in disgust.

Jeremy laughed as he broadcast the approval across the Zone. Everyone on the border would bitch now, because all stations had to monitor the alien ship as long as it remained in sensor range, plotting its position and reporting hourly to the starbase. This turn of events would break up the monotony, but it meant more work for everybody. And it seemed that the one thing worse than having nothing to do was being forced to stop doing it.

Chapter 4

S HE GLISTENED IN THE BLACKNESS, her outer hull shining brilliantly in the sunlight, the dock supports chafing at her sides.

Dwarfed by the creation that had cost four years of their lives and more than one trillion credits, the workmen who had given her life hovered around her arching curves. Agleam to the edge of glowing, the heat shields still needed polishing; tested to the twelfth level of redundancy, the hatches and outlets required more rechecking and the power systems awaited reconfirmation; and even though her massive computers and internal relays had been cleared once a week for as long as anyone could remember, the engineers insisted on one last glitch run before approving her systems as starworthy. Large black figures started to appear on her face; before the giant vessel could leave the dock, her registry markings would need time to set. Now known as *Challenger Prototype Number 3*, when she left at last for Ishtar she would be "**CGS 2001**." Sometime after the dock crew began to work on the next formless mass, someone else would name her.

All around, the stars burned like many-colored embers in the heavens. Below, the quiet blue planet turned silently, as it had for billions of years before its newest masters dreamed of its existence. There was only the blackness, and the stars, and the ship; and beneath it all, the tranquil world spun timelessly, as if tomorrow and yesterday were all the same.

* * *

"THIS IS DEMETER Command Traffic Control, do you copy?"

"Roger, Demeter Command, this is Transport Ten Sixty-seven, repeat, CGT One-Zero-Six-Seven, requesting departure clearance to Ishtar Command. Manifest is DCIC-321J16-CGSF-1017/T1067, Code Blue; will you confirm?"

"Affirmative, Ten-Sixty-seven. You are cleared from Loading Dock Twelve on venture route D-17, vector two to flight path I-3 en route to Ishtar Command, cc: 142-7919.7. Do you acknowledge?"

"Roger, Demeter Command, we are departing...but, Charlie?"

"Yeah, Sam...what is it?"

"What are you sending us off with? My computer comes back gibberish every time I try to check the manifest. And my orders say we're being escorted all the way to Ishtar. What's going on here?"

"Well, it is Code Blue."

"Charlie...."

"Okay, okay. Wait a second, I'll check."

"This stuff must be solid ultrynium. The tractor's at full power already and we're not even moving yet. It feels like I'm pulling a neutron star, and I can't even see all the way to the end of the train."

"Most of it's the usual—food, equipment. Probably some inflatable broads for the redshirts. You know the bit. But you have a dozen frigates right from the store, four to a box.

"And be careful with the last three in Section Two—they're brand new starships, fresh from the mint."

"The new model? The *Challengers*?"

"You got it."

"Why the hell are they sending'em by transport train? Why not have the engineers putz'em over to IshCom and check'em out along the way?"

"Well, what's even dumber is that two of them are coming right back here after shakedown. But who are we to question thousands of years of military tradition? Why do something right if you can fuck it up—eh, Sammy? Just don't break'em, hear? Clay'll have your butt."

"Roger that. See you next month, Charlie."

"Smooth sailing, buddy. And if you make it over to the planet, don't bring back the Flu."

"You got it, pal—and I've got my shots. Over and out."

Chapter 5

H ELLO, ADMIRAL," SAID GEORGINA DYER, Admiral Clay's personal secretary, looking up from her desk.

"Any news today?" barked a gruff voice with the barest hint of a Zarathustran accent.

"All's quiet on the frontier," she replied, "and the day's reports are waiting for you at your desk. The ship rotations were posted at Zero Hour on all command boards, as you ordered, and I printed a copy for your review. And the new starships are finally on their way. Admiral Weatherlee says they'll arrive in eight or ten days at the latest.

"Oh, and Admiral Pendleton wants to talk to you when you get the chance, about some proposed new Central Command directive. Apparently they want all ships to transmit their weekly reports to their home base instead of flagging their position and heading, and filing the rest when they dock, like they all do now. He'd like your opinion."

The admiral grunted an acknowledgment of sorts, but said nothing beyond the usual.

"Thank you, Mrs. Dyer. I'll be in my office."

The door closed with a rush of air. The admiral stalked over the blue carpeting to his oversized desk on the far side of the room and sat down in a soft, padded chair.

Tall and vigorous, Fleet Admiral Porter Clay was an intimidating figure, even to his close friends. His white, thinning hair added a look of distinction to the alert eyes and ruggedly handsome features that found themselves at the center of the Cosmic Guard's most taxing controversy in two centuries. His sharp baritone voice no longer barked commands to crewmen whose most important concern—aside from staying on the good side of the best, if most demanding skipper of his day—was clearing pirates from the trading corridors of eastern Terra. He had risen to command whole fleets rather than single ships, and the safety of the entire frontier now rested in his powerful, oversized hands.

But there were times, and they came often these days, when he longed for the simplicity of earlier days—before aliens and diplomats started complicating his life; before frontier politicians began calling for his head; before marching demonstrators burned him in effigy. He longed for the times when his hardest problems involved checking the flight manifests of freight haulers caught outside approved shipping lanes, and when the only excitement a ship's skipper was likely to have was chasing after pirate raiding parties or rescuing ships trapped in interstellar squalls. Most of all, he missed the days when Central Command forgot about the Eastern Fleet for months at a time and let him run his command as it should be run: with no interference, and without the current abundance of addle-brained experimentation.

These days, CentCom was forever finding new ways to complicate life on the frontier, he thought angrily. The desk jockeys running things obviously did not understand the realities of space exploration. Like this latest bit of nonsense: how could a starship in deep space spend the stationary hours needed to transmit across fifty parsecs or more? And they wouldn't just be solar hours. It would take two full cosmic hours to broadcast a typical report on a low frequency band across the distances ships traveled on a typical mission. If they broadcast often enough, they might as well give the aliens their code book, for all the good it would do. It was lame-brained from the charts to the docks, and he simply would not stand for it.

Today, though, he had bigger problems on his mind. Now that the first *Challengers* were on their way, they needed crews and, more importantly, new captains to command them. He'd put off convening the promotions board for as long as he could, but was running out of time. No matter how much squawking Winthrop Weatherlee would put them through, they had to decide whom to promote. And that meant problems—political problems, that had no place in making command decisions.

What frustrated Clay more than anything was that Weatherlee—Old Blunderbutt they called him in the back rooms of the Eastern

Fleet—had him in a corner this time. As much as Clay hated to admit it, he'd have to pass over his best cruiser commander once again. Weatherlee, the admiral in charge of Demeter Command, had raised hell all the way back to Covington when the last set of promotions had come through, even after they struck the young Isitian from the list. Now, with the peace talks still moving at a snail's pace, the conciliatory stance Clay had taken with the Crutch-tans had the frontier politicians calling for his head more loudly than ever. Even in a less forbidding climate, Weatherlee would never stand for giving one of the *Challengers* to a commander he wanted blackballed, not without a nasty fight. Once again, Clay couldn't afford the heat; and once again, the talented young officer's career—whose progress through the ranks was becoming as interesting to Clay as to his own Demetrian rival— would find itself stalled.

What galled the admiral most was the utter pointlessness of Weatherlee's feud. Ornery as he was, Old Blunderbutt had never before shown the visceral dislike he aimed at this particular blueshirt. From the start, Weatherlee had sought to block the young man's rise through the ranks, all the more so after it became obvious that the lad was the most promising officer in the fleet. Now, each new demonstration of brilliance by the young Isitian forced Weatherlee to reach further and further to justify himself. The Demetrian nearly shot through the roof when the young man's promotion to full commander came through in the aftermath of the Hawkins Massa-cre; when prejudice joined with real or imagined personal grievance, thought Clay, the result was uncontrollable.

Yet for all of Weatherlee's shortcomings, the Demetrian was an able backroom politician with well-placed friends, both in and out of the command structure. Though Clay was often hailed as the bravest line commander of his generation, in his heart he knew he was just the smartest, and now was not the time to mount an assault. For now, the matter would sit: the best cruiser commander Clay had ever seen would remain blackballed by a vindictive superior. With all of Terra raging over firestorms that the frontier politicians fanned for their own partisan advantage, there was nothing anyone could do. Even a fleet admiral's hands were tied by politics, from time to time, and once again he would bow to the inevitable.

But not first thing in the morning, the admiral thought. He relaxed into the soft cushions of his chair, remembering what it was like to be a young, promising skipper with his whole future before him, and wondering whether the fleet commanders of his youth had Weatherlees of their own to contend with. Perhaps the headaches always came with the job, he sighed. The gentle hiss of the ventilator dulled his senses and brought a deceptive peace to his troubled mind. He turned to his console; it was 375 Hours, and the available weekly reports should be in by now. He would make his decisions later. It was time to learn how his men and women spent their time for the last ten days. He turned the screen to the priority index; he would worry about Weatherlee some other time.

* * *

THE OLD EARTH-VINTAGE chandeliers lit the tables with soft, diffuse light. The table orbs glowed dimly, giving a gentle warmth to the room. The rich texture of the wallpaper captured pastoral scenes from Victorian England, of foxes and hounds, and gentry at play. It was the Country Club, the finest restaurant on Ishtar Command, where the gentry of the Eastern Fleet could come to relax in comfort and spend their money at leisure.

In the hallway connecting the annex to the main dining area, Henri looked nervously at Table Forty-seven, where he had placed the three CosGuard officers almost two solar hours ago, when the annex had been empty. But when the shift change brought the dinner crowd, he had no choice but to begin seating patrons wherever he had an available table. To his eternal mortification, that meant seating men and women of refinement next to common spacers.

Worse, he shuddered: they were starship captains, probably freshly returned from deep space and ready to shatter the Club's reputation into a thousand tiny pieces.

Suddenly, Table Forty-seven erupted in laughter, and Henri saw one of their number—the one with the roguish eyes and the piercing laugh; he believed the name was Tanana—slap his thigh. Throughout the annex, more than one head turned toward the spacers, only to turn away with disdain.

By the time the next eruption came, this time on the heels of a large and unmistakable belch, Henri could stand it no longer. With a face as red as his jacket, he retired to the service lounge. He would leave Maurice to greet their guests. Maurice was an Earther, and Earthers were used to humiliation.

"WELL, FITZ, you sure drew the brass ring on that one. Dream as they will, not everyone gets to serve under Miriam Wright."

"You know, Fitz keeps plugging away, but sooner or later he seems to hit the mark."

Ignoring temptation, Brian Fitzgerald stuffed another bite of dinner into his mouth. An unkempt mop of graying hair sat atop his head, and mustard lined the corners of his mouth. His eyes crackled with a blunt and practical intelligence, and behind his hearty sense of humor his friends found him the very essence of sturdy honesty. Like most Demetrians he was strong and stocky, with a ready smile and an irreverence born of hard times and working-class roots. His reputation, though, came from his scrappiness as a battler, and the fact that his starship was hardly the most graceful on the frontier. His maneuvers were often compared to a Ceresian mutluk in heat, and Fitz himself had to admit that he lacked the artistry of a Jefferson McKinley Jones, DemCom's senior wing commander.

But graceful or not, he got the job done, no matter what the grading computers thought of his style. For now, he was too hungry to match insults with Tanana and Chandler, his friends from their days together at CosGuard Tech. And he was too pleased at the duty rotation to feel like doing anything but enjoying himself. Any duty that kept him away from "Whinin' Winnie" Weatherlee for another turn was a blessing. Besides, Looking Glass never looked better. Not since the day that Admiral Clay turned it over to Miriam Wright.

"You think Fitz is of a mind to settle down now?" Chandler asked with a wicked grin. "Now that he'll have a ring through his nose, I doubt he'll want to be joining us for a romp on the planet. I expect he'll have little use for the girlies of Ishtar, now that he'll be taking orders from Commodore Wright."

"Well, I wouldn't want to infect her base now, Tommy," Fitz replied, able to resist no longer. As his choking friends spat their last bite of lunch all over the table, he smugly reached for a glass of wine. He often thought that good food was wasted on line officers. The cuisine aboard the typical starship made plasterboard seem tasty, and starships had the finest galleys on any ships of the line. But he could usually coax his taste buds back to life by the end of liberty, and Ishtar Command boasted better chow than any starbase this side of New Babylon.

After dinner, the three friends walked from the restaurant down the central concourse toward Corridor C. Fitz always marveled at the immensity of the spanning archways of IshCom. A starship's hexagonal hallways and corridors seemed cramped by comparison. After endless months in space even the illusory roominess of a starbase gave a feeling of freedom that land dwellers—"ground-toads" in spacer's jargon—could never understand. Spaceflight freed Man from earthly bounds only to impose others from which he could not escape. Few content with life on land could comprehend existence inside the constraints that space pressed upon the fragile hulls protecting spacers from the blackness through which they sailed.

But today the three friends were not in a philosophical mood. Neither space nor the Guard had much use for philosophy, and they had more pressing concerns.

"You sure, Fitz?" Tanana asked, his wispy eyebrows raised in amazement.

"Yeah, you guys go ahead without me. I have other things to do."

They neared the Corridor C pneumatic tube station, the largest on the base, with shuttles to every corner of the starbase.

"Madame Tarneaux will be disappointed," Chandler said. The last time the three of them got together, she'd kicked them out of her establishment for starting a fight with a squad of drunken security guards. Fortunately, CosGuard captains were her favorite customers—profitable to a fault, thanks to regulations which frowned on commanders sleeping with members of their own crews—and she'd promised them special treatment the next time they called.

"I've got other things on my mind," replied Fitz. "I'll catch up with you later."

After his friends left, he walked toward the fountain in the middle of the concourse. The statue in the middle was hardly worth the bother—the modernist school had such jagged edges, reminding Fitz of the grotesque sculptures of the late 1900s—but running water held a magical fascination for him. He'd spent half his adult life in enclosures where every drop was captured and recycled, and crewmen had standing orders to hold their bladders until they returned to ship. Now even the meager abundance of a starbase fountain held him in thrall, returning him to younger days along the Demetrian shores, where wind and water were details of life that passed unnoticed and unappreciated.

After what seemed an eternity, he rose and walked once more toward the tube, his footsteps lost amid the daily shuffle of those who called the base home. He checked the screen for destination listings and punched in the code for Z-Deck, Northeast Quadrant. His ex-wife had recently moved to IshCom, and he'd never seen her new quarters. Besides, it had been ages since he'd seen their son.

* * *

SITTING BACK IN his chair, Admiral Clay yawned. Official reports might be his last link with the old days, he thought, but they were dry as Ishtar itself. Often, the most interesting thing about them were the listings of equipment malfunctions, and today was no exception. Clay was about to deactivate his screen when a flashing yellow light caught his eye, signaling an incoming Priority II report. His eyes widened when he put the teaser on the screen; it was from the very commander he'd spent the last hour putting out of his mind.

The screen read:

```
CGC 587 <<CONSTANTINE>>
POSITION: Ishtar Orbit, 43-110901/a2
SPEC RPT CODE II cc:142-7920.4
```

"Roscoe Cook," he said, stunned by the coincidence.

He was even more stunned by the report.

A HALF-HOUR later, Clay leaned back and looked up at the sterile paneling on the ceiling, chuckling long and deep. For two years the government had tried to cultivate contact with the aliens on a personal level, and for two years their own people had bungled the job through clumsiness and ineptitude. Now Cook had done it by accident. For the last week he'd spent more time visiting the aliens on the ground than tending his ship, and his insights into their psychology and culture looked to be more valuable than anything

Terra's best diplomats had gleaned from across the conference table. It was almost as if the young Isitian had determined that the quickest way to advance in the modern Guard was by rubbing CentCom's nose in their own directive about showing initiative in all dealings with non-human civilizations. Inventiveness had worked for him in the past, and he showed no signs of stopping. Clay was determined not to let that kind of initiative pass unrewarded.

"Roscoe Cook," he marveled, "you lead a charmed life." Over the intercom, he told his secretary to arrange a command staff meeting for 475 Hours the next day.

"And notify the base commanders as well," he added, with a self-satisfied smile. "We'll be convening the fleet Promotions Board."

* * *

"Admiral Weatherlee!" exclaimed the young lieutenant. "Is something wrong?"

Contempt filled the admiral's face, and the young officer sensed that it would be better for his career to say nothing more. Weatherlee stormed past, almost running into his office door before it opened to admit the admiral to the one place on the base where he could find the solitude to ride out the disgust welling inside him.

Winthrop Weatherlee had seen this day coming for the last week, but knew he was powerless to stop it. Ever since notifying IshCom that the *Challengers* were on the way, he'd smelled the foul odor of another promotion for Roscoe Cook. Now, thanks to the damn aliens, the admiral was again powerless to do anything. He walked to his desk and poured himself a stiff drink of Demetrian rum. The soothing music he had piped into all administrative offices in his command was now grating on his nerves. To make matters worse, the tune that had just begun was an Isitian melody. He plopped heavily into his chair and sat for several minutes, seething with outrage. His heavy jowls pulsed with anger and his eyes burned with cold fury.

Weatherlee's teeth could grind ultrynium whenever he thought of the arrogant young blowhard. Despite his laziness as an administrator, Cook never lacked for friends in high places, though the stars alone knew why. Isitian smugness oozed from his every pore, and the fool never did have any sense when it came to dealing with the aliens. The obnoxious Isitian personified everything that Weatherlee found infuriating about that miserable planet—quoting books nobody read anymore, peppering conversations with pointless parables, and though never so uncouth as to voice it aloud, posturing as the poster boy for the Isitian boast of the best educational system in all of Terra.

Weatherlee turned to his desk console to write. Writing always helped when he felt outraged; it gave him something to do. But today what enraged him was knowing that he might never get the chance to set things right. He dashed off a half-dozen blistering and long overdue memos to subordinates, as well as two or three letters to friends in Covington. Venting his frustrations in a constructive fashion always made him feel better, even if it didn't really solve the underlying problem.

After an hour, he buzzed his receptionist and told the young man to order something from the officer's mess and schedule a staff meeting for later in the day. There was lots to do, he told the lad, and it promised to be a long day. From the tone of the admiral's voice, the receptionist knew that it would be a long day for all of them.

Peering through the open library door, Weatherlee saw the young midshipman sitting at a table. Charts and textbooks were strewn everywhere, apparently at random, and the boy looked lost in thought. Commodore Weatherlee paused before he stepped inside, and he closed the door behind him. He knew he'd embarrassed the young man that afternoon, backing him into a corner and teasing him about his home planet. But the tactics seminar the commodore had come to attend was more than a mere formality before his elevation to admiral. He really did need a live opponent for the simulator, to show that he'd mastered this last hurdle. And he'd actually intended the invitation as a compliment to the boy—who, the commodore sensed, was something of a loner. Just like another lonely midshipmen he remembered from his own past.

"Preparing for our contest tomorrow, I see," he said cheerfully. Walking down the aisle from the entrance, Weatherlee came to sit on the table, four feet away from the young man who'd be his opponent on the simulator the following day.

The boy looked up; to Weatherlee's astonishment, the lad did not bolt to his feet, as any other academy student would have done. Few would have been aware that libraries were one of the few places on campus where most protocols of deference did not apply; even fewer would have dared to remain seated when a superior officer popped in, unannounced. For an instant, Weatherlee thought he saw a flash of disdain cross the young man's face, but he dismissed the thought at once. Midshipmen did not treat commodores with contempt, he sneered inwardly; especially not commodores who were already admiral-designates. The lad's reply came like a blow to the commodore's stomach.

"Not really," yawned the student, leaning back in his chair. "I'm tutoring a friend in Advanced Navigation, and needed to unravel the textbooks they're using in class before I try to explain it to her."

"I'd think you'd have your mind on our upcoming simulator duel," Weatherlee smiled. "I'm sure your own plans aren't quite fully developed. I could have some of my staff help you with a few of the details if you like, since you really haven't had much time to get ready. But Advanced Navigation is a senior's elective. Aren't you studying it yourself?"

"Actually, I placed out of Navigation entirely on the entrance exam," the boy replied; Weatherlee could see a smirk forming on the boy's lips. "And I've already prepared all I need to, for our little exercise tomorrow."

"You know," the commodore smiled, stepping closer to the young man. "I really shouldn't have made that crack about your home. I'm sure that Isis is a wonderful place for a bright and handsome young man like you to—"

"Distractions won't work on this midshipman, Commodore," the young man interrupted sharply; Weatherlee could feel the arrogance in the boy's voice, and saw his pretty eyes narrow with condescension.

"Besides, I've looked over our scenario, Commodore. I'm on defense, which means that my plan is really quite simple: I'll just be disrupting whatever it is you're planning to do, and striking wherever you leave yourself open. So my advice to you is to

worry more about your own plans than about mine, because I'll be doing my level best to blow yours up, once we get going. And as combat tends to make a hash of everything anyway, I suspect your plans will be largely worthless, once they close the doors and we start having at it."

"Midshipman Cook!" snapped Weatherlee, his eyes cold with hate.

"In any event, my friend's midterms are the day after tomorrow. She has lots to digest between now and then, and I need to see what kind of misinformation they have in these books of yours so I can explain what she needs to know for her test—and what she really needs to know on board a ship."

"You arrogant little snot."

Furious, Weatherlee turned on his heels and left, slamming the library door behind him. As he walked out of the building and into the crisp air of early spring, the commodore felt a knot growing in the pit of his stomach. He hated the Academy. He still bristled at the memory of countless humiliations he'd endured as a young man struggling to show everyone his appointment hadn't come only through his father's connections, on Demeter and beyond. Weatherlee knew he'd earned his place there just as much as anyone else, but nobody ever let him forget about his father's political clout in the capital.

He hadn't come back to the Academy to be humiliated again.

Chapter 6

THE GENTLE BUBBLING of the small aquarium gave a melancholy richness to the sad music that filled the cabin. Shelves overflowed with curiosities from a half-dozen worlds. Pastel paneling softened the busy collection of plants and flowers hanging from the walls. Beside the sleeping chamber hung a Demetrian tapestry in earth tones of browns and greens, a silent reminder of a presence that still haunted the room and its principal inhabitant.

Janet Mendelson rested on the sofa in the anteroom, her dried eyes staring at the ceiling. Her head lay on a pillow, and her graceful, well-conditioned body gently rose and fell with each breath. Her soft brown hair was braided today; time always passed more quickly if she had something to do, and fussing with her hair took her mind away from more painful concerns. Tears no longer streaked her pretty, youthful face, but her eyes were still puffed and red. The hurt had faded, though she knew it would return before long. In its place was anger and resentment—anger at the regulations that made her current anguish all but inevitable; anger at the system of regimentation that dominated her life; anger at herself, for the sweet delusions she'd allowed herself these past months. But most of all she felt betrayal, and a gnawing sense of helplessness that stripped away all of her lovely illusions.

Seeking comfort in memories of more innocent times, her mind drifted to happier days as a skinny tomboy on New Babylon. Before long she was fighting tears again, this time trailing her brother and his friends as they raced to the schoolyard, too young to understand the cruel taunts hurled at her but old enough to know that they were meant to hurt. Her parents' stern words to the boys actually made things worse, and eventually she learned not to tag along when they went outside. She never understood how the brother she adored could stand by, laughing as his friends tormented the little eight-year old girl who only wanted to play.

Inevitably, her eyes weakened again, as her face remembered the touch of a hand that she knew she would miss forever. She buried her face in her pillow, and began to cry.

LT. COMMANDER François LaRue was sitting at his desk, writing a letter to his sister when the intercom sounded. Like most cabins on the cruiser, his quarters were slightly cramped, but the Ceresian carpet on the floor softened the otherwise austere furnishings, and an oil painting of a farmhouse in the hills gave the room a touch of home. By reflex, he activated the speaker.

"LaRue," he said wearily.

"Commander Cook wants to see you in his office," said the disembodied voice of a young female ensign.

"On my way."

He left his quarters and walked down the corridor, trying to compose his thoughts. Commander Cook was impossible, he thought as he entered the elevator. In the cosmic year they had served together, they'd disagreed on almost everything, and Cook gave him little support in the inevitable battles with the crew for respect. Finally, the cauldron was coming to a boil. LaRue had warned against granting leave to too many crew members at once, but the stubborn Isitian had insisted. Now, with orders just arrived to proceed to Isthar Command, they had ninety-eight crewmen and officers—all but two dozen of the entire ship's complement—frolicking on the miserable planet below, doing God knows what, while the rest of them had to scramble to get the ship ready to depart on what, for all they knew, could be a mission of great importance. He knew that any attempt to blame himself for the inevitable delay would reflect badly upon his commanding officer. But Cook had powerful friends—how else to explain his cavalier attitude toward the Command Manual?—and LaRue worried that he himself would be made the scapegoat.

The elevator left him around the corner from the Captain's Quarters. Entering the adjoining office, LaRue was startled to find the commander just returned from Ishtar and still clad in his thermal uniform, busily rummaging through the unkempt piles of papers, books and binders on his desk. Star charts cluttered the worktable to his right; a single map of his home planet hung crookedly from the otherwise naked wall to his left. Behind were sketches of a half-dozen or so forgotten faces from Terra's past. All around the room were shelves filled to overflowing with books and technical manuals and knick-knacks from all corners of Terra.

"François," said Cook, looking up from the knotted maze but continuing the search. "I don't suppose you've seen my Krutzmann—that leather-bound book on comparative biology?"

"No, sir," LaRue replied dryly, wondering whether his commanding officer had the audacity to summon him to help search for an outdated, mold-bitten book. A printed book, no less.

"Well, never mind," frowned Cook. He pushed a button on his intercom.

"Library," answered a low-pitched voice.

"Fred, this is the Skipper." Cook still foraged about his desk, but without the determined fervor of before. "Would you order a printout of the following textbook: Johannes Krutzmann, *Biology Across the Heavens*. I have no idea what the tracking code is, but it should be listed in the reference section."

"Certainly, sir. You want it run to your quarters?"

"No," replied Cook; a look of defeat crossed his brow. "I'll be by later to pick it up." The leather-bound Krutzmann was one of his prized possessions, and he wanted to give it to the Veshnans before departing. Now they would have to settle for a computerized printing, which took the soul out of the masterwork. Much like a paint-by-the-numbers Rembrandt, he thought.

"Damn," he sighed, sinking deeper into his chair. Absently, he picked up some papers, letting them fall to the table. "One of these days, I've got to get organized here."

"You wanted to see me, sir?" LaRue interjected haughtily, wondering if Cook had forgotten about him.

Instantly, the commander's bearing changed. He leaned forward in his chair. The confused haze was gone from his face and his fierce, intelligent eyes burned with curiosity. Without warning, a commanding presence had filled the room and the air crackled with purpose.

"You took the IshCom transmission, François. The one calling us back to base, I mean. Do you know what it's about?"

"No, sir. The orders were to proceed at once to the Base. So, I instituted procedures to— "

"Well, if it's not an emergency," interrupted Cook, "they can damn well wait until the rest of our people check in." He pushed another button on his intercom.

"Ensign Schmidt?"

"Schmidt here," came the reply.

"When's the next call-in for our leave parties?"

"About another cosmic hour, Skipper."

"Don't bother trying to find anyone else. Plug the computer into the call-in channel and tell all hands to return immediately. And make sure the message is clear—we're leaving in two hours, whether everyone's aboard or not. Then put the Molly boys on stand-by for the signals."

"Molly" was short for Molecular Transmitter, the quickest and safest means of traveling between points less than fifteen-hundred miles apart. Cook never quite trusted the technology but there was no practical alternative, at least when traveling between a spaceship above and the ground below. Besides, he hated to appear old fashioned; it wasn't very Isitian.

"Got all that, Schmidt? I don't want another Xanadu on our hands."

"Aye, aye, sir" Schmidt laughed. The last time they'd stopped at Xanadu, everyone waited until the last minute to molly back to the ship. The backlog made the transmitter blow a circuit and delayed their departure for two days.

"Who's manning the bridge now, Schmitty?"

"Xing has the Chair. And Davidson's on controls, sir."

Cook paused to think. All three women had done double duty during the crew's liberty—it was odd, he thought, though not really surprising: throughout the Cosmic Guard, the women always volunteered to stay behind whenever their ship moored at Ishtar. He hated to push them further, but time was short and there was much to do before they sailed.

"Tell Davidson to chart a course to Ishtar Command, estimated departure time in two cosmic hours. I'll have Cardinale check her plot when he returns from the planet, or I'll do it myself if I have the time. Meanwhile, Xing should start the Checklist; I'll be there in five minutes to relieve her, and once a few more officers return to the ship I want you three to stand down for the next week—and however long we stay at IshCom. You've all earned it."

"Thank you, sir."

"Over and out."

LaRue held his tongue but could not believe his ears. Cook knew him too well not to notice the disapproval on his face. "I know that look, François," Cook smiled mischievously. "You're keeping something to yourself again, aren't you? That look of horrified disdain gives you away every time."

LaRue said nothing but began to fidget uncomfortably.

Cook clasped his hands behind his head and rocked back in his chair. "So tell me what you think, François. Talk to me. Don't make me beg."

"Commander Cook," he began, in stilted, formal tones that often slipped into his provincial accent. "May I speak freely?"

"Of course you may, François."

"I do not wish to question your judgment, *Commandre*," said LaRue, his accent becoming noticeable. "But our orders were to proceed 'at once.' How can you keep Command Base waiting? How can we remain here two hours more?"

"François," Cook replied patiently, but with an underlying intensity LaRue always found unsettling. "Do you really want to leave half the crew on Ishtar, only to wait a day or two at the base until somebody remembers why they sent for us—or even notices that we've arrived? No matter why IshCom wants us, we'll still have to come back to the planet for anyone we've left behind. Leaving now is a waste of time. Besides, we're less than an hour away from the base, so we can be there *toute suite* if they really need us."

"*Mais oui, Commandre*, but our orders— "

"*Sacré frommage*, François," Cook tried not to laugh as LaRue winced at his butchering of the idiom. "I admire your devotion to duty—and your opinion is noted for the record, if you like—but don't worry about it. It simply isn't worth the bother. Now, return to your quarters and take some time off. You deserve a rest."

LaRue bowed in deference to his dismissal, and backed clumsily toward the door. But he paused before leaving, not quite sure how to proceed next.

"Something else?" Cook asked.

"About Lt. Mendelson, *Commandre.*"

A look of fury flashed across Cook's face, passing as quickly as a tropical rainstorm.

"Whatever personal problems she is having— " LaRue began.

"I'm sure she'll appreciate your concern, François," the commander said pleasantly, but with a hardened edge to his voice.

"But to let an officer of her caliber sulk in her room over some personal concern cannot but impede the smooth operation of this ship."

"Thank you François," came the cold reply, "but I will decide what impedes the operation of this ship. And I have given her permission to stand down until further notice. Anything else?"

"No, sir," said LaRue, timidly shaking his head and wondering why his resolve disappeared whenever he and the commander aired their differences. He withdrew quietly, leaving Cook alone in his office.

Slowly, Cook rose from his chair to pace absently about his office. At last, he stopped in front of a bookshelf next to the door to his quarters, the one that held most of his personal library. He reached for a figure used as a bookend on the third shelf, where he kept his natural history materials, and stood for several minutes looking at it. It was a gift from a friend now lost to the past: a small castle, made from the sands of Demeter.

With a burst of resolve, he replaced the trinket on the shelf and left the office, heading for the bridge. There was work to be done, even before the rest of the crew returned. And with Mendelson out of action, Ensign Jacobs would be helmsman for the trip to IshCom. Cook chuckled as he walked. This would be the young ensign's first solo at the helm; the captain hoped it wouldn't be the last sail for the lot of them.

Chapter 7

WHAT THE TERRANS CALLED the Caucus Room had no windows, but was admirably furnished. Six stuffed chairs arrayed next to an artificial fireplace lent the room a coziness otherwise lacking on the barren world they had chosen for the current round of peace talks. On the walls were tapestries, imported from as far west as Earth for the purpose of impressing their visitors with the richness of Terran artistry. Over the mantle was a reprint of a painting by an Old Earth master, depicting a Renaissance lady in all her mysterious beauty. The walls were painted a soft ivory, to accent the fine woodwork crafted to mimic the warmth found on friendlier worlds. As if to atone for their choice of planets, the Terrans had spared no expense to make their guests feel at home.

Unfortunately, most of the touches that the Terrans lavished upon their guests passed unnoticed. Rather than dangling their legs over the end of the "Terran sitting implements," the diplomats of the Grand Alliance sat on the floor near the fire, taking what warmth they could from its artificial flames. They found it hard enough to tolerate sitting Terran-style through the talks—it did, after all, tend to cut off circulation to their posteriors as well as their legs—without subjecting themselves to such abuse when the courtesies due from guests did not demand it. Though tapestries were a major art form among the Veshnans, the abstract patterns of design that hung from the bland walls were disconcerting, like peering through a distortion lens, and the delegates, each of whom felt disoriented enough already, avoided looking at them whenever they could. What appeared to be a Terran painting looked flat and lifeless, like a poor photograph with faded colors—although Zatar thought he could feel the eyes of the Terran female follow him around the room whenever he moved. But however uncomfortable they felt upon entering the room, they always managed to lose themselves in discussion whenever they retired to caucus, and this time was no exception.

"What do you want of me, Zatar?" asked an exasperated Munshi. "Should I permit you to make a fool of yourself when it is within my power to spare you embarrassment?"

"If I choose to play the fool," snapped Zatar, "what right have you to interfere? You, who chose to venture alone into their midst and almost to your own death! And do the Terrans really care if I butcher their tongue? Did they take offense? Did my effort to reach beyond ignorance find them laughing like children at another's clumsiness, or beating their breasts like a waddlewort closing on his prey?"

Several of the other Veshnans began to smile—men took to anger so easily, for all the good it did them—but the ambassador's glower soon froze their smirks on their faces. It was impolite to bait a brood male during a nest mate's rutting season, and today's talks did come at a most inopportune time. It was understandable that Zatar was in no mood for teasing. Besides, none of them wanted to be the new target of the keenest mind and sharpest tongue of the High Council's Procuracy. Patiently, they waited for Zatar's anger to pass, and soon he returned to the topic at hand.

The Terran ambassador, the one they called *Gr'Raun-te*, had offered a dramatic concession, one that rendered obsolete their tepid compromises of the past. For the first time, Terra was willing to cede sovereignty over the disputed space, all the way to the Terran edge of the Great Divide—which the Terrans, with characteristic inscrutability, called *ny'Otrl'Zhog'hn*, or "The Area of Indifference." What they asked in return were the twin rights of exploration and exploitation, in nearby portions of the great Crutchtan Cloud. Zatar was certain that they would be willing to restrict their movements even more, accepting limits on their penetration into Crutchtan space. But G'Rishela, the Imperator's representative, demurred nonetheless, for reasons which remained a mystery.

It was that maddening Crutchtan stoicism, thought Zatar. They never committed themselves to anything, never showed the slightest emotion, until they were certain of their course and confident of their advantage. If that didn't change quickly, they would lose the momentum this new initiative could give them, perhaps squandering their chance for peace as well.

Zatar looked at the Crutchtan seated by himself near the fireplace, whose face was a study in stolid impenetrability. The Crutchtan's eyes stared ahead impassively while listening to the others airing their disagreements. All the Crutchtans he had ever met displayed the same expressionless calm, thought Zatar, as if expressing interest or passion would be a show of weakness. In the course of his duties as procurator for the High Council, he had watched the Crutchtan delegates sit motionless, listening to passionate arguments on the most difficult issues facing the Alliance, all the while keeping their own counsel until the very end, when they finally decided on the proper course of action. Then, of course, they were among the most forceful of advocates for their own cause, but their very reluctance to commit themselves often led to misunderstandings with their allies.

Intellectually, Zatar could understand their ways. Mildly telepathic, the Crutchtans instantly sensed the intentions of others of their kind. When faced with a crisis, they never needed to reassure each other by word or conspicuous deed, for each could sense the good will of the others—or their malevolence, if that were the case. It let a Crutchtan think matters through thoroughly before venturing to speak. While an admirable trait sorely lacking in most of the Universe, it often caused consternation in their dealings with other races.

"I suppose none have a thought about this latest impasse?" the ambassador said at last, his voice thick with dignity.

G'ela cleared her throat. "I cannot understand the Terrans' dismissal of our exchange program. It can only foster understanding between all the races, by giving science the chance to study new life forms."

Zatar cut her short. "We are not talking about your cadaver proposals, G'ela," he snapped. "We are still talking about the border dispute. And that idea may take a long time, in any event. The Terrans are still primitives in many ways. According to the anthropology texts our friend *Khu'ukh* has provided, they still bury their dead.... "

Suddenly the Crutchtan's head snapped up, as if stirring himself from lethargy; Zatar suddenly remembered that their allies also buried their dead, but continued undaunted.

"And they and have a rather mystical attachment to the bodies of their loved ones. I'm afraid it will be hard for them to adopt a more practical approach to the needs of science.

"Now, does anyone else— "

The Crutchtan learned forward, toward the rest of the group. The light from the fire illuminated one side of his face, giving a reddish glow to his leathery brown skin. The slits of his pupils, which had contracted to almost nothing while he was deep in thought, now dilated to full circles, and on either side of his neck his gill slits, vestiges of an earlier stage of evolution, flushed with the green of churning Crutchtan blood.

"You have been curious as children," he said, in the hissing, image-rich tones of his native language. "You have been wondering why we of the g'Khruushtani so quickly reject the ideas of the longnoses; why we do not jump with child-like glee at the prospect of agreement with the strange ones from the West; why thoughts of peace with these newcomers...."

Zatar sighed wearily. Crutchtans kept their own counsel longer than he found comfortable, but when they finally did speak they tended to ramble a bit, and often took a while to come to the point.

"...and why we approach the ten-fingered simians with the caution of songbirds, and not the boldness of raptors."

The Veshnans leaned forward, listening intently. Although only Munshi could speak the Crutchtan language—and with difficulty at that—all but G'ela could understand it.

"Friends of the g'Khruushtani, this is the reason." Still seated on the floor, the Crutchtan seemed to rise until he towered above the smaller Veshnans nearby. But he had merely straightened his back, as Crutchtans often did before beginning a lecture, or one of their epic ballads. He placed his hands together in his lap. The lights in the room flickered briefly, as the dust storm raging outside toyed with the city's power system. The Crutchtan continued without a sideward glance, as if the fury of the Terran weather were of trifling significance compared to imparting understanding to his friends, now that he knew his own mind.

"When the Sheregal roamed only the hills of home, the g'Khruushtani were like the children of Spring. We knew but of hope and gladness, with the ocean of dreams nourishing our spirit as the river of life nourished our fields.

"But the Sheregal would not remain in the hills, though game was plentiful and flavorful fruits abundant. Their wandering spirit watched birds soar beyond the horizon, and they heard the call of distant hills and fertile valleys. So they left their own river behind them, and trailed a river of death flowing thick with blood, following the setting sun to the land of our fathers.

"And I tell you, friends of the g'Khruushtani, and I tell you Truth: the Sheregal were not done until the sea itself flowed with the blood of innocents, and the heavens cried with the screams of murdered children."

"But surely," said Munshi, in her finest Crutchtan, "the Terrans are of a different world. And as wise a race as the g'Khruushtani cannot let prejudice cloud their eyes. The resemblance is strong, that I will grant. When the longnose males let the fur pour from their bodies, a Terran mother could not pick the Sheregal from among her own offspring without difficulty. But the enemies of our friends were savages, without the spark of humanity. And the last Sheregal vanished into the jungles of time in the long-ago past. The Terrans are not the same, and the g'Khruushtani cannot treat them the same. They seek peace, not war, and they worry over children of their own."

The Crutchtan leaned forward and gazed intently at Munshi, then at each member of the party in turn until his eyes came to rest upon Zatar. His eyes bulged wildly, and his head nodded slowly, in the Crutchtan manner of showing amusement.

"My friends mistake parable for prejudice," he said at last, "for we know that the longnoses are not the enemies of legend. But they are simians nonetheless, with the same driving curiosity and burning passions. Perhaps in time we can live as neighbors, sharing friendship as friends share food. But even now the Terrans cannot keep their word—for as we speak, Terran ships continue straying beyond the Great Divide."

"Though against the wishes of their government," Zatar interjected, speaking in his own tongue.

G'Rishela bowed in the Veshnan manner. "And what does this tell us, Zatar? That any agreement we reach will bind their leaders, but not their people? And where will this lead us? If we accept their proposal, my grandchildren will live to see the Terrans scattering throughout *g'Khruushte*, pounding at our doors and demanding more, ever more. If they pass the Divide today with our blessing, they will be with us forever. And they will never leave of their own accord."

Zatar turned his eyes to the fire. Silently, he watched the flames dance playfully along the heat-resistant plastic that the Terrans had fashioned to look like a piece of a dead tree. He searched his mind for a response to the Crutchtan but the words wouldn't come. None could tell whether G'Rishela was right or wrong, and Zatar could not bring himself to disagree.

Chapter 8

O N LEXINGTON BOULEVARD, across from the Senate Commons, a gracefully-aging two-story building rose on the edge of downtown Covington's Old Center area. Bright flowers sprouting in large, white boxes beneath the upper windows lent a splash of color to its gray exterior. On the cornerstone, barely legible from the passage of time, the Old English lettering fashionable in the era of its birth was still decipherable: "O.E. 2397," it read; "Burstein & Cohen Building." For the past thirty years, the structure had been home to *Ricardo's*, the most exclusive and expensive restaurant in the city. It was the eating place of presidents and admirals, businessmen and diplomats, hosting leaders from every corner of Terra. The exquisite menu was prepared by Roberto, the finest chef in all of Central Terra. All came to see and be seen by their peers, and to enjoy the personal attention of Ricardo himself, who took it as a personal duty to make everyone welcome. Welcome, at least, in direct proportion to the guest's influence in Covington society.

For his trouble, Ricardo was one of the wealthiest, most influential men in Covington. He knew most of Terra's moves and shakers by their first name. All of them appreciated the aging restaurateur's discretion, as well as the many services available to the powerful that were not apparent from the stately exterior or gracefully decorated dining rooms.

The ubiquitous host and owner was usually the very model of unctuous charm, laughing urbanely at the jokes of the mighty and overseeing the smooth functioning of his staff with a discreetly iron hand. Today, he was near panic. Alarm paled his dark features, and gone was the fierce, patronizing tone with which he disciplined his staff. In its place was the echo of a small, bewildered mind, terrified at the prospect of encountering something it could not control.

"It can't be him. He always calls first, to make sure we have everything ready by the time he arrives. You must be mistaken—yes, yes, you must be mistaken."

"No mistake, Boss," said the manager. He led Ricardo to the window overlooking the park, where the poor man almost fainted from disbelief.

"No," Ricardo said haltingly, as if altering reality were as simple as denying his senses. He could feel his stomach rising as he spoke. "He wouldn't just come. He never comes for breakfast—he likes Frederick's deserts—he likes the—specialties—we prepare when he comes to dine. And he's never—come without giving us time—to prepare something special. Something truly memorable. Something— "

"Well, whether he would or not, he's here."

"But his box is occupied! And he's coming up the steps!" exclaimed Ricardo. The office quickly erupted in an undirected flurry of activity.

"Quickly now—hurry! Tell Frederick to drop whatever he's doing. And tell Pierre to move the couple from Booth Twenty-six."

"But— "

"Never mind. Tell them anything—tell them their meal will be on the house. But we need their booth and we need it right away."

"But— "

"Hurry!"

"SALLY, YOU light a hundred hearts and spark a thousand smiles just by blinking your eyes." The rich baritone voice made the young woman blush, as the speaker's blue eyes twinkled coldly. The woman cast her eyes down toward the plush, velvet carpeting. Her reply was almost drowned by the background murmur of the patrons. Even at eight o'clock in the morning, *Ricardo's* was filled to capacity.

"Oh, Senator," she giggled, her face flushing until her skin almost matched her blouse. She blushed easily; it was one of the reasons the Senate's most powerful committee chairman always flirted with her—that and the fact that she was the prettiest of Ricardo's waitresses.

Like his father and brothers, E. Emerson Hollenbach was a big man. In most gatherings he towered a full head above the rest of the crowd. He wore his massive bulk like a mantle of command, with the easy assurance of one with no self-doubts. Over the years he'd learned to take full advantage of the psychological edge his physical size gave him. In politics as in life strength prevailed over weakness, and Hollenbach learned early in his career that there were ways of intimidation subtler than brute force. Force was too messy, too easy to trace to be much use in modern politics; even worse, it often gave its victims an incentive to fight back. If Old Earth history taught anything, he often reflected, it was that resentments caused by overt force took forever to fade, and were rarely worth the trouble. And Hollenbach, like most Earthers, was an expert in the field of resentment. It wasn't so much the overt snobbery that offended him. It was the condescension toward the "unfortunates" that stiffened his back, and gave him such pleasure in displaying every ounce of power at his command. His delight in psychological dominance gave him an edge in the primitive power struggles that Covington's stately corridors concealed from public view. Ironically, he found among the chief pleasures of being one of the Senate's most powerful politicians was the chance to watch sycophants like Ricardo squirm whenever he did something unexpected.

"Senator Hollenbach," gushed Ricardo, emerging from behind the wooden door to his office and wearing his warmest smile. "How good of you to join us this morning. My, but you look hungry! Might I suggest an appetizer of Eggs Ricardo in white wine sauce while we prepare something more memorable? Or one of Roberto's omelets, perhaps? Or maybe you would like...."

Hollenbach smirked as Ricardo fawned over him. In all the years he'd patronized the restaurant, what amused him most was Ricardo's desperate longing to be noticed. The man hungered for respect, and Hollenbach half-suspected that his host would kill for the chance to be part of something important. Now, the senator himself would be using *Ricardo's* to accomplish the most daring coup in Terran history, and its owner—who loved intrigue more than a miser loved money—would never even know.

"I'd like my usual stall, Ricardo. The one overlooking the river. Have Sally bring me some coffee, and I'll leave breakfast to your discretion."

"Yes, Senator Hollenbach. At once, Senator Hollenbach."

Ricardo clapped his hands, sending a half-dozen employees scurrying in a dozen different directions. He tried not to notice the man and woman being escorted from Number Twenty-six by one of the waiters, an uncomfortable-looking man with a thin moustache who smiled sympathetically at the outraged sputterings of the displaced couple.

"Oh," Hollenbach added, almost as an afterthought. "I'm expecting some friends to join me. One I expect shortly, the other may be detained. Please show them to my table directly."

"Of course, Senator Hollenbach. And may I say...."

* * *

NORTH OF COVINGTON, near a bend in the Mendenhall River, was a large parabolic dish carved into bare rock. Through a collection of communications satellites in orbit over the planet, the device linked New Babylon to the rest of Terra, and served as Terra's window into the capital. Through a planet-wide network of relay stations, radio towers and cable links, every bit of news that enterprising journalists from Ishtar to Isis could uncover found its way into the mammoth computers buried deep inside the rock. From there, it was beamed skyward for instant dissemination to the planets and colonies that comprised the Terran League. But with the Senate in Winter recess, the Crutchtan border quiet, and nothing but continuing prosperity on the economic front, there was little news to liven a cold January day in the Earth Year 2551. Aside from routine government announcements about trade balances and space traffic, and the typical human interest filler that dominated the subspace channels from time to time, the only item of note was the monthly brunch hosted by the Greater Terran Media Society in the Old Center area of downtown Covington. There, the banquet room of the Broadcaster's Club was filled to capacity and buzzing with excitement. Duncan Heathcoate, Demeter's senior senator, was about to address the gathering.

Unlike most of his Senate colleagues, Heathcoate enjoyed press banquets. He frequently spoke at these monthly gatherings, though he'd never before accepted an invitation that conflicted with a vacation. Gregarious and good-natured, as handsome at age seventy as he was controversial, the Society found his oratorical skills useful in preserving the importance of their brunch on Covington's social circuit. Relaxed and calmer than in days past, he was still given to the occasional reprise of his youthful tirades about the threat posed by alien powers to the east. He had, in recent years, also taken upon himself the role of elder statesman for the Tory movement, becoming as committed to promoting the traditional Tory concepts of free trade and planetary sovereignty as he was to venting his customary outrage over the inadequacy of Terran security. And though some saw in him the same fool they'd always seen, others heard his pronouncements as the words of a sage entering the twilight of a distinguished career.

As the chairman of the Greater Terran Media Society finished his introduction, a smiling Duncan Heathcoate, his silver hair neatly in place, rose and walked to the dais, nodding his head and acknowledging the applause.

"Mr. McSweeny, members of the Press, fellow guests," Heathcoate said at last, in the velvet voice that knew no equal. "I remember the first time I addressed this group, as a wet-behind-the-ears freshman Senator some time ago. It was summer—one of those hot days Covington gets from time to time where the sun seems to bake the air itself. Everyone had left for the beach and I had to address a room where the busboys and waiters outnumbered the guests in much the same ratio as the press outnumbers the senators during our all-night debates at the end of each session. It was then I learned that the press values a good vacation almost as much as a good story, and I've been putting that lesson into practice myself ever since."

The audience laughed and applauded; Heathcoate smiled good-naturedly and continued.

"If you will excuse the pun, the burning issues back then were fear and security—that is, Terra's security against possible invasion by forces we could not understand, and whose intentions and capabilities we could not know with any degree of certainty; the fear felt by men and women everywhere for the future of their children in a Universe filled with the unknown; and the fear felt by all of us that contact with alien races and alien cultures would change us in ways we cannot predict, and from which we may never return.

"Well, aside from the weather, not much has changed in thirty-seven years...."

* * *

"THAT WASN'T the agreement!"

"Those are the terms."

"I'm warning you, Emerson...."

"Three committee chairmanships, and my personal control over all CosGuard procurements, now and in the future. That is our final word on the subject. Take it or leave it."

Nicholas Schiller was furious. He'd come to this meeting in good faith, expecting to resolve a few loose ends. Now he found a whole new list of demands, including a crucial one rejected long ago. Placing anything as sensitive as military procurement in the hands of a cutthroat like Emerson Hollenbach was simply out of the question. Schiller's people all agreed on that—but that was a long time ago, before the lure of possibilities began to tug at them, and they realized what it would mean to hold the reins of power again. It had, after all, been twenty years since the Tories last occupied the Executive Mansion. They'd forgotten how intoxicating power could be, and how desperate they were to taste it again.

His eyes darted to Hollenbach's silent companion, only to see a bland smile and no sympathy at all. Then Schiller stared into Hollenbach's unforgiving face to find wry amusement. Earth's senior senator had a reputation for ruthlessness; Schiller had known that from the start. The corridors of power were littered with the ruined careers of those who stood in Hollenbach's way. And through all of it, Hollenbach kept increasing his influence, rewarding his friends and tormenting his adversaries, accumulating so much power and so many debts that nothing could be done in the Senate without his cooperation—or his passive complicity. When the first feelers went out, and Tory operatives relayed the word that Hollenbach was sympathetic, Schiller hadn't believed it, not for an instant. He even tried to warn them: Hollenbach would never make common cause with political enemies he'd fought all his life. There had to be something in it for Emerson Hollenbach. Now, he knew what it was; but now, it was too late to do anything about it.

Still, Schiller thought, Hollenbach was also the Senate's best head-counter. If Hollenbach said it was possible—and was willing to stake his political life on the outcome—then that was as sure a thing as anyone could ask for in interplanetary politics. They had no choice, he concluded bitterly; they had to go along.

"I'll see what I can do," Schiller said at last, his eyes flashing with anger. He smiled a tight, humorless smile of his own. "But it won't be easy. There aren't many of our people who count you as a friend. And you're not exactly making yourself seem trustworthy."

Hollenbach chuckled. "I'm sure you'll do your best. Especially when you consider that the alternative is letting Sarkisian run our defenses further into the ground. Remember, he doesn't have to call another general election for six years, and you'll never gain enough seats in the regular biennial elections. Not with the current combination of safe, Federalist seats and contested Tory districts up for grabs as far as the eye can see. If you and your friends want to help that silver-haired Demetrian nitwit take over, your only chance is a no-confidence vote—and you fools will need all the help you can get."

The cold rain outside obscured the view of the river. Schiller pushed his food around his plate aimlessly with his fork. He had quite lost his appetite. Soon, the waitress approached with the bill, summoned by an ebullient Hollenbach.

"Is it afternoon already?" Hollenbach asked, with mock incredulity. He downed the last sip of his wine with a practiced flair. "Well, Sally—I must say you've been a delight. And patient to a fault, with three old men sending you this way and that. Oh, and give the bill to Mr. Schiller. He's buying today."

* * *

FAR TO the east, along the Terran frontier, the cold Ishtari winds buffeted the concrete bunker that housed the Veshnan consulate.

"Tell the Ambassador that I welcome his candor, and that he may rest assured that nothing that we discuss will be revealed—except, of course, directly to the head of my government."

Seated in a dimly lit room in ambassador's sitting room, Jonathon Osborne Grant waited as the lone translator, a Veshnan female he knew as Munshi, translated his remarks. Gazing into the eyes of his counterpart, Grant looked for a glimmer of anything he could recognize as empathy, but saw nothing. The Veshnans, he knew, had as full a range of feelings as any human, but their facial expressions seemed lost in the milky whiteness of their skin, and he found himself unable to fathom the workings of an alien mind. Even an alien reputed to be as intelligent as Zatar, he found, seemed unable to grasp the simplest nuances of human emotions. All their races really had in common, it appeared to him, was the bareness of sterile logic, and common self-interest.

Grant had labored long and hard during these talks, reading everything about the aliens he could find. Still, there was much that baffled him. There were suggestions that the Crutchtans enjoyed limited telepathy, but that hadn't prevented misunderstandings from nearly sinking his mission. And he simply could not understand why, given the pronounced matriarchy of the Veshnans, they had chosen a male to lead their delegation. Beyond this were all the questions about the alien Consortium itself—how it was organized, its power structure, how so many diverse cultures had been able to resolve so many questions touching the vital interests of all with no appreciable conflict for countless millennia. Most puzzling of all, the Consortium had existed when Man was still living in caves on Earth. How in God's name could Terra have pulled almost even with them in so short a time, and what did that imply for the future of the human race?

Grant was so lost in thought that he almost missed the Veshnan ambassador's reply.

"Zatar says that he welcomes the opportunity to discuss matters frankly, without the need for the niceties of form. Among our people, it is well recognized that delicate matters are best handled by those who are not—as Terrans often say—playing to an audience."

"We seem to make progress only to see it stall. Whatever direction we take, we find obstacles that seem more formidable as we discuss them. It has become apparent to me that the Crutchtans are disinterested in reaching a quick agreement. What I have to know is whether there is a reason."

"Such as?"

Grant smiled. "If I knew that, we wouldn't need to be discussing it, would we?"

From Zatar's immediate response—an ominous, choking sound that he had come to recognize as alien laughter—he could tell that Zatar was following portions of the conversation. He never knew how much of the language his opposite had mastered. But however much it was, Grant thought ruefully, the Veshnan's knowledge of Terran language and culture far surpassed his own meager insights into the alien's mind.

"Zatar asks if you have a specific question."

Grant's eyes narrowed, and he looked directly into Zatar's. He had long noticed that the aliens would all avert their glance if a Terran met their eyes. Apparently, Zatar had noticed the same thing, for the Veshnan continued to smile and return the stare until this time it was the Terran's turn to blink.

"Are the Crutchtans planning for war?" he asked at last. "Is that why they are reluctant to sign an agreement?"

The question seemed to provoke a lively exchange between Zatar and Munshi. Grant could follow none of it and found himself speculating about what it all might mean. He was oddly reassured when the answer finally came, apparently despite the translator's better judgment.

"Zatar remarks that your question is most ironic, for it is one which the Crutchtans themselves have often asked about Terra. As to the thrust of your question, Zatar has instructed me to tell you that war is the last thing the Crutchtans desire."

"What do they want, then?"

Munshi smiled blandly, as Grant had learned that Veshnans did whenever they knew they were about to say something that made little sense.

"The Crutchtans wish only to be left alone."

"But— "

"To be left alone," Munshi interjected, the slightest edge to her voice. "Nothing more, and nothing less."

Chapter 9

WHERE IN BLOODY HELL...."

From his seat at the forward control panel, Mason McGee listened to his brother's voice trailing off into the distance and breathed a sigh of relief. Their ship was big as brigantines go: fifty meters long, with the central hallway stretching from the bridge past the living quarters to the rear decks. Offshoot hatches allowed access to the holds on either wing, and Mason was wondering whether it mightn't be wise to tend to the cargo, now that his brother was on a rampage.

He looked out the porthole. The stars hung like silent beacons in the distance, and a glowing nebula lighted the skies toward the galactic center. As much as he loved space, with its eternal calm and limitless vistas, he always hated coming to Ishtar. They needed someplace to sell their ore, that was true, and the heavens knew that they could use the change in scenery. But every time they headed back home he swore that he'd rather take the lower prices of the outpost stations and be overcharged for their provisions than watch the wretched planet take its toll on his brother.

Cyrus was ornery and mean by nature, thought Mason— independent to a fault, and hard enough to live with in the open reaches of space. Bring him to Ishtar and he lost what little sense he had in the first place. The woman they shared at home was nice enough; she might not be much to look at, but she was a good worker and a source of comfort who never caused them grief. But come to the Wasteland, where the women were just as ugly but twice the trouble, and Cyrus lost all sense of proportion. Between the free-flowing liquor and the overpriced whores, his older brother never failed to leave the planet bloody and out of control. It would take Cyrus a week to dry out, another week to reconcile himself to his gambling losses, two weeks more to come to what remained of his senses. In the meantime, Cyrus would rage like an ion storm in full fury, all because of some barren hunk of sand and rock that was better left alone.

Suddenly, the door flung open. Cyrus stormed into the room, almost tripping over the below-deck hatch. His eyes, wild with drink, flashed with anger.

"You!" Cyrus screamed, wobbling as he stood and reeking of drink. "You're the one who's been inna my provisions. You took my fligh'gear, and you were th'one who tried'a talk me into sleeping away half the return trip."

Mason put the ship on automatic pilot, then stood to face his brother.

"Get off the bridge, Cyrus," he said slowly enough so his words would register in his brother's rum-soaked brain. "I didn't touch your provisions and wouldn't want to anyway, even if you are too drunk to know the difference." He pulled a handblaster from the side console and set it on heavy stun.

"Get off the bridge," he repeated.

Cyrus reeled, the weight of comprehension proving too much for his dulled senses. After a few moments his rage receded, and he turned slowly and made his way back into the main hallway. Quickly, Mason secured the door. Breathing a sigh of relief, he returned to the controls.

Two more weeks, he thought. Two more weeks before they got home. He hoped Cyrus would calm down by then. He usually did, once the store of rum ran out. All the same, he pressed the buttons on the internal control panel, locking all doors and hatches but the one to Cyrus' quarters, and to the kitchen. Mason would keep them locked until they arrived home.

* * *

SOME DISTANCE away, in the shipping channel between Ishtar and Demeter, an old man yawned, struggling to stay awake. The instruments whirred and clicked, and near the end of his turn at the wheel the sounds always lulled him to sleep. But it was no matter. He'd made the run hundreds of times, and the stars never changed. There was still the huge, glowing cloud abaft and to port, where the mining colonies were as thick as the whores on Ishtar. Ahead, the cloud dissipated, the reddish glow turning a wispy blue. And as the radar kept sounding, his thoughts turned to the greeting that awaited at the end of the run.

Blip.

It should be summer along the Demetrian Riviera when they arrived, he smiled. The girls would be prettier, but Demetrian whores were fussier. Less likely to indulge a withered old spacer—at least, not for less than a premium price. And a lot more trouble, what with their fancy clothes and all. Not like the spacer's girls on Ishtar.

Blip.

In the back, he could hear Shamus stirring. It was nearly his time to take the chair. The two of them had roamed across half the galaxy, he smiled, thinking back to their younger days. Made it far into alien skies, too. Lots farther than most.

Blip.

Of course, that was before they knew about the aliens. Or, at least, about how close the lizards were venturing west. Now, the spacers all had to keep to this side of the Hodges System. And it was a pity, he thought. Some of the prettiest skies were east of Hodges.

"Damnation!" cried a voice from the ramp.

The old man turned around to see Shamus, his partner, whose eyes were wide with fear. "Ye dodd'rin' old fool!" Shamus screamed. "Ye can't hear the radar a-soundin' trouble?" He dashed from the ramp, heading straight for the ship's radio.

Turning back to his instruments the old timer finally saw it, clear as the heavens.

There were three of them.

At this distance the ship's computer couldn't identify them, but both men recognized the readings at once. And they knew they'd never be able to change course in time.

Brigantines.

Shamus tuned the radio to the emergency channel, hoping he'd entered the right password and trying to keep his voice calm. It wouldn't help them if nobody could understand the message.

"This is Freighter-9042, call name *Demetrian Mist.* We have a Code-One emergency in this sector. Repeat—Code One emergency. Over."

"This is Ishtar Command," came a woman's voice over the radio. "We read you, *Demetrian Mist.* State the nature of your emergency."

"We've spotted pirates. And they're heading right for us."

Too impatient to tolerate his partner's sluggishness, Shamus shooed his old friend out of the pilot's seat and began trying to change their heading. Lugging a half-dozen cargo trailers in tow, the ship would take at least ten astrokilometers to slow and come about, and the pirates looked to be forty klicks away. If help didn't come soon—

"Freighter-9042 to IshCom, status inquiry."

"Roger, *Demetrian Mist.* I'm checking for ships in the vicinity. Keep this line open and start transmitting a distress beacon."

"Roger, IshCom. Please hurry."

Shamus turned from the helm console to the trailer controls, on the left-most panel, and began to enter the security code to jettison their cargo train. He hated the thought of decoupling. The payday that awaited them on delivery would have left them sitting pretty for half the year, and given them plenty of cash to spend on Demeter once the paperwork cleared. But if it came down to their hides, they'd leave the cargo for the pirates and be off, as quick as a Ceresian gigolo.

* * *

AS THE TRAMP FREIGHTER struggled to free itself from its cargo, at a dry dock back at the starbase an alarm tone exploded deep inside the cerebral cortex of CosGuard's newest captain. Struggling toward consciousness, Cook groped to shut it off. His head was a symphony of pain, repaying him dearly for the hours of abandon he shared with the crew on his full last day commanding the *Constantine.* The clock by his bed read 350 Hours; he'd slept half the day—nearly five cosmic hours—and vaguely recalled that he still had a lot to do. He couldn't remember what any of it might be, but he knew he had a full day in store. And he had the sinking feeling that in his stupor he'd quite forgotten to call Vera, his old classmate, to tell her that he was in no shape to leave the ship and wouldn't make it back to her place until today. Actually, he slowly realized, he hadn't called her at all since the day he'd learned of his promotion, when he felt the need for an old friend's company, and invited himself to her place to celebrate.

Still clothed in his standard blues, Cook staggered to the shower in his cabin and fumbled at the activator until the warm water began to flow. He leaned against the stall, grateful to have mastered his first major task of the day. Gradually, he shed his clothing, leaving it in an inert pile in the corner of the shower, and stood transfixed by the streams of water from the dual nozzles. After what seemed like several hours he opened the hatch, dragged himself back into the cabin, and fell onto his bed, face down and dripping wet, where he remained until his yeoman came to call him to duty.

"Commander—I mean, Captain Cook," said the startled young woman. Tactfully, she tossed a bedsheet over his bare bottom before gently shaking his shoulder to wake him. As Cook began to stir she took to tidying the room a bit, throwing soiled fatigues and socks into the laundry shoot.

"You're needed in security," she said, as matter-of-factly as she could. "Some of the redshirts got rather out of hand last night, you see, and Lt. Moll would really like you to conduct the captain's mast. You know...before you turn over the ship to Mr. LaRue."

Cook grunted an acknowledgment of sorts, his groggy mind fighting its way toward consciousness. As his yeoman chattered merrily away, reminding him of the duties of a outgoing skipper, his two major tasks of the day gradually began to crystallize in his foggy brain.

First, he told himself, he would speak to Mr. LaRue about overdoing discipline upon assuming temporary command. This was a good crew, and good crews need nurturing, not an iron fist. The sooner LaRue understood this, the quicker his own command would follow. He started to sit up until he was interrupted by his giggling yeoman. Her face flushed beet red, as she quickly turned her eyes toward the far wall.

"Wrong again, Cook," he smiled at her wearily, too tired to care about his loss of dignity. As carefully as he could, he leaned over to recover the fallen bedsheet.

"The second thing I'll do is see Mr. LaRue."

AFTER A TASTELESS breakfast in the cafeteria, Cook made his way from B-Deck to Security, where he declared an amnesty for all infractions of the day before. The cheers still ringing in his aching head, he went down two more levels to Engineering, to say goodbye to Chief Engineer Seth Montgomery. The old-time Cozzie had been a favorite of Cook's, with a Demetrian's contempt for pomp and an endless supply of stories. The two had passed many an hour sharing a whiskey bottle and bemoaning the luck of the draw that had infected the ship with such a stickler of a first officer. They'd had a falling out the past few months as Cook's personal life intruded upon their friendship, and Cook wanted to square things before he left. But Monty interrupted Cook's apology with the observation that real friends had little need of such formalities, and such things were usually understood. "Especially," Monty said, his eyes twinkling, "when the insulted friend is proven right."

Cook laughed along with his friend, hoping that Monty wouldn't be too disappointed when he learned that CosGuard's newest starship skipper still had a few blind spots in affairs of the heart. He declined the offered drink; his head was still recovering from the last batch of "one more rounds" he'd had the previous night, and his stomach was already having trouble adjusting to the near-zero gravity that Monty kept in the engine room to make traversing easier. Instead, Cook spent his time listening to his friend tell about the starship skippers he should watch out for.

"The sorriest batch of losers in the heavens," the engineer snorted, a mischievous gleam in his eye. "Egos a parsec wide and mouths to match. Particularly that jackass from Demeter."

"Jones?" smiled Cook. Jefferson McKinley Jones, the senior wing commander at DemCom, was reigning champion at the semi-annual maneuvers six times running. Cook's sole encounter with the man—Jones literally patted him on the head after the *Constantine* had staunched a Red Fleet breach that would have cost Blue the encounter and Jones his sixth gold medal—had not endeared the esteemed Commodore Jones to the young Isitian.

"That self-important twit was a squirrelly frigateer when I knew him, befuddled as a fly in a glass ball. His idea of battle is two ships dead in space, firing amidships until someone's shields buckle. The pompous bastard couldn't tell his butt from a black hole then, and I hear he ain't changed much since."

Cook heard about men he already knew—Drexler from CentCom, Addison from Ceres, McIntyre from Looking Glass—and even shopworn stories about the old days, when Captain Porter Clay, with "Fighting Joe" Ferrigan and Little Dickie Blodgett, finally drove the pirates out of the Demeter sector. In the end, he quickly conceded that he'd fallen in with a hopeless cast of scoundrels , and led Monty on a last inspection of the ship's powerful engines. The nine large cylinders, each three stories high, had seemed so huge when he first took command; it was hard to believe that they would be dwarfed by the fifteen monstrous engine blocks of a starship. All too soon, time came to bid his friend farewell.

"Next stop," Cook called over his shoulder as he leaped toward second-story catwalk leading to the main corridor, *"la maison de l'Escargot*—and then, you'll have a new skipper."

"Still trying to talk some sense into François?" Monty shouted in return. In the low gravity Monty kept in the engine room, Cook sailed through the air like a diver, deftly coming to rest between the handholds on either side of the gangway atop the 'tweendecks companionway.

"Nice shot, Captain!"

"So long, Monty," Cook laughed. "Maybe you'll find someone who can beat your next skipper at no-grav bandyball."

* * *

THE VOICE on the public address speaker boomed monotonously, announcing the routine departures and arrivals to those assembled at IshCom Central, the mammoth starbase's civilian terminal, filling the gaps with items of interest to the starbase.

"Shuttle to Ceres, departing from Dock C-7. All passengers please report to Departure Gate A. Last call for New Babylon Express, departing from C-6 enroute to Ishtar Main in 10 minutes; Departure Gate B closes in seventy-five ticks—repeat Gate B closing in seventy-five seconds—mark!

"The following announcement is posted on all Eastern Fleet bulletin boards by order of Admiral Clay: 'All CosGuard personnel wishing to place their names on the rotation list are reminded that the deadline for submitting transfer applications is Zero Hour on cc:142-9000. Officers and enlisted personnel currently on off-base assignments are reminded that applications must be received by their home base before the deadline in order to be considered for the next rotation in duty, unless written permission is secured from Eastern Fleet Headquarters in advance. There will be no exceptions.'

"Local Trunk Daily Three Fifty-five has arrived from Ishtar and environs, disembarking at Gate E. Base Security, report to Dock C-12, Code Seven. Commodore Turner, please call Eight-Three-Four...."

The arching ceiling of the terminal lobby loomed like a cathedral dome. On either side of what locals called Little Chicago, snack shops and boutiques lined the corridor and the lobby itself teemed with an endless crowd. Every day, all kinds of people flocked to the bustling stalls and shops. It was, after all, one of the few ports of call along the frontier offering the amenities of twenty-sixth-century life. Because IshCom was the only starbase this side of Demeter accepting civilian traffic, IshCom Central was port of choice for half the spacers in the Ishtari outlands—namely, the half that had nothing to fear from being recognized. This meant that the terminal saw its share of riff-raff, and the command staff forever complained to Central Command about the drain on base security that the open port policy caused. It came as a shock to new arrivals whenever a temporary space dock shortage caused diversion of a CosGuard ship to the civilian facilities, to see that their new base played host to half the flotsam of the frontier. But the square's carnival atmosphere made up for any inconvenience they felt, for nowhere else on the frontier did two such diverse cultures—the military and the free-wheeling pioneers—co-exist in such proximity, with so little friction.

Duffle bag slung over her shoulder, Ensign Connie McKenzie hurried down the middle of the square, marveling at the energy of the merchants lining the terminal hallway. After the week-long trip from Demeter, the bright colors of the shops and tantalizing aromas of the food stands teased her senses. On all sides, the merchants hawked their wares. Seen through the porthole of their ship, IshCom seemed immense and sterile, hanging in the blackness like a hollow shell. From the inside it buzzed with life, like the market street of any city.

Much as she wanted to, she could not stop to answer the merchants' call. In rigid formation, she and the other new arrivals from Demeter moved through the square, ushered through the chaos by a squad of guards from the CosGuard Security Office, led by a handsome young lieutenant. His assignment was to take the newcomers to Orientation as quickly as possible. With practiced ease, his steely voice parted the river of people, hurrying the newcomers to the tube station en route to Central Processing. The guards he led, all clad in CSO tan and sporting black garrison caps, flanked the arrivals to form the small phalanx that moved briskly through the crowd. Occasionally they brushed past a civilian a little too closely and knocked him to the floor. But the guards moved too quickly for tempers to get out of hand; and in any event, they were too big and strong to challenge.

They neared the end of the corridor, approaching the mammoth arch of the Little Chicago Concourse. Connie felt anticipation surge through her body and felt the giddiness of starting a great adventure. She had already given four years of her life to the Cosmic Guard, studying engineering and astrophysics, principles of navigation and elements of modern weaponry. She'd had fun along the way, and some of her friends, like Paul Jackson, would always be more than just a mysterious smile on her lips. But Paul was long gone, to the Western Fleet and Zarathustra. She was on her own now, to make a name for herself along the eastern frontier.

"Hello, Connie," said a familiar voice, belonging to a too-familiar figure coming to hover close beside her as they rushed along. She cringed at the very sound of his voice, and the lovesick look on his face every time he talked to her made Connie want to retch.

"Hello, Dexter," she said dryly, wishing she were really on her own. Completely on her own.

"Isn't this something? I mean, it's so big. Like DemCom multiplied by two. I bet you could fit the grounds of CosGuard Tech inside a single concourse here. And the people—look at them all. Why, this place is almost a city all by itself."

"It is a city, Dexter. All starbases are cities. This one is bigger than most, that's all."

"But the engineering that went into building this thing! They built it from scratch, you know, from asteroids and rock, smelting the metal in temporary stations built specifically to process the raw materials. And it's a half light-year from Ishtar itself, so for the five years it took to build this place they had no real landfall to speak of. And Ishtar isn't much to begin with in the first place, you know?"

"Who cares, Dexter?" she replied. Quickly, she cut in front of the yeoman on her left and pushed toward the outer reaches of the formation, where she hoped to be left alone. With all the friends she had at the college, and all the people she knew who could have drawn the same first duty, she got stuck with Dexter—a myopic non-entity with tangled hair and a crush on her a mile wide. Life could be so cruel, sometimes.

* * *

STRIDING INTO the command center, Admiral Clay cast a stern glance from the monitor screens on the left to the radio controls on the right. He was pleased to see the room well-disciplined and tightly controlled. Every technician was seated and focused on the instruments, and there was none of the mindless chatter that often made the Command Deck seem so chaotic. Every voice was either asking or answering a question; a crewman sat at every screen. Everyone in the Cosmic Guard knew just how deadly a pirate raid could be, and the coded security announcement calling him to the bridge had made clear that another attack was underway. The admiral didn't like the turn things were taking the last few weeks; he didn't like it one bit.

"Admiral on the deck!" announced the officer of the day, a dark, pretty lieutenant commander whose name Clay couldn't remember.

"Situation?"

"Brigantines moved to attack a lone freighter along the Ishtar Spike, Admiral. Fortunately, the freighter was sticking right to the middle of the shipping lanes. We had a squadron of escorts patrolling the affected sector. They scrambled and put the bandits to flight."

"The freighter?"

"It was hauling a train of six cargo trailers. The pilot decoupled almost at once and took flight. But the pirates didn't seem interested in the cargo—they started after the freighter. The escorts arrived before they could close. Now they're helping the freighter recouple with its cargo."

"They took after the naked freighter?" Clay squinted.

"Yes, sir."

"But the situation is under control?"

"Yes, sir."

"All right, Commander—carry on."

Clay left the Command Deck and walked down the wide corridor toward his office. Guards from the Security Office snapped to attention as he passed, but he was too preoccupied to nod an acknowledgment, as he usually did when young Cozzies tried to impress him. This was the seventh pirate attack they'd seen in the last three months, he thought. All against lone freighters.

He decided to issue another advisory, this time strongly advising against solitary travel, and urging all commercial shipping to form into convoys before entering interstellar skies. He knew he'd get resistence: the shippers always resisted advisories, and usually ignored them. It delayed their delivery schedules and added to their costs. But he knew he'd never be able to make a mandatory directive stick: the threat was still too amorphous, too random, too unfocused. He'd be overruled by Central Command by the end of the day, if he tried to impose another Convoy Directive. Just like he was at the outset of this latest round of attacks.

Arriving at his office, he strode into his private chambers and locked the door behind him. Gazing at a picture of himself as a young skipper, he smiled sadly before taking a seat and beginning to write out his notes for the report he'd file later in the day. He'd spent his youth battling pirates, he reflected. He'd chased them away from Demeter and cleared the shipping lanes all the way to Central Terra, but they never really disappeared. The past few months it seemed that they'd returned as bold as ever, raiding ships closer and closer to base, harassing the lanes from Ishtar all the way to the frontier.

Briefly, he thought about scheduling a command conference for the next day, to discuss their options. Maybe a simple redeployment would give them more assets to use along the commercial corridors. With the aliens behaving themselves, they certainly could spare some ships from the frontier. But he dismissed the idea as soon as it formed in his head.

They'll just think I'm an old granny, the admiral chuckled. Attacks had always tended to come in streaks, and whenever pirates got bored, they'd take to buzzing convoys, just to amuse themselves. Still, he thought, it had been nearly a year since they'd seen Chadbourne Wilkes and his band of cutthroats. Wilkes was not often given to lying low, and he was hardly the type to retire quietly. Clay couldn't avoid thinking that while the raids were doing no real harm, they seemed a lot like an enemy probing for weakness.

Finally giving it up, he decided that everyone else was probably right, and he really was just an old granny. He quickly sent along his advisory, and turned his attention to resolving the logistics snafu that kept routing half of their food from Looking Glass back to the Hodges Binary, and most of their replacement parts back to Central Command.

* * *

THE GENTLE TAPPING at the open door caught her attention, and Janet looked up from the dark blue duffel bag and disorganized piles of clothing on her bed. Instantly, Cook knew he was in trouble. Janet's eyes blazed with cold fury, making the hair on his neck prickle with embarrassment. But he had rehearsed his speech and there was nowhere else to turn. Tentatively, since admittance had not really been given, he stepped into the anteroom of her cabin.

"Lieutenant," he began. He was not prepared for what awaited him.

Like a coiled spring freed of its constraints, Janet stepped to the table beside her bed and retrieved a cream-colored piece of crumpled paper in her left hand. Before Cook realized what was happening, she charged toward him, tossed the paper in his face, and returned to her bed to continue packing her bag.

"I suppose this is your doing," she said archly, not even looking up from her task. "Not that I'm surprised. It seems I never have had much of a choice in the matter, whenever you're concerned."

Cook looked at the paper. They were orders, transferring her to his new command. What remained of his stomach left him, but he had the presence of mind to close the door behind him.

"Mendelson," he began, already on the defensive and looking quite uncomfortable.

"Save it, Captain," she said sharply, looking him squarely in the eye.

"I'm afraid I've bungled this thing quite badly, Lieutenant. I told headquarters I needed to get your approval first, but I can see they paid no attention to me. I'll have your orders changed at once."

Janet's eyes narrowed hatefully. "Starship assignments rarely come more than once. I'd be a fool to turn this one down—as you probably already realized. So once again you have me at a disadvantage, *sir*," she smiled bitterly, almost hissing the last word. "But we both know it's easier to transfer to a starship from another starship. Don't count on having me stay on your new ship for very long. Now if you'll excuse me, I have a lot of packing to do. I don't want to be late for my new assignment. I hear the commanding officer there is rather full of himself."

Impassively, but with grim satisfaction, she watched Cook squirm in discomfort as he searched for a response to break the tension. Finally conceding defeat, he lowered his eyes and withdrew in silence, leaving Janet all alone. Her face, smooth and pretty even in anger, softened as the rage left her. She felt darkly triumphant, but victory brought her no joy.

Slowly, she looked around the room. Piles of clothing were everywhere. Everything she owned in the Universe was scattered on tables and chairs in the small chamber that had been her home for the past cosmic half-year. Her breathing became shallow and rapid and she felt her throat tighten. She'd sacrificed everything she knew to be part of the Cosmic Guard—her friends, her home, her family. Now that her career was rocketing toward the heavens, she felt cheated and misused. It had once been her fondest dream to draw duty on a starship; why, she wondered, when it was finally coming true, did she feel that her life was falling apart?

Her eyes caught sight of a pale green lump, sticking out of one of the boxes on the floor, the one she had designated for trash. She reached inside and drew out a small stuffed animal, a gift from a friend in better times. It was a grubnush in caricature, a small, bear-like creature that lived in the forests of her native New Babylon. Blinking back tears, she looked at its comical face and thought of moonlit walks through endless gardens, and carnival vendors and ferris wheels. Slowly the realization fell upon her that the soft mass of cloth and matting still held too many memories for her to abandon, no matter how bitter she felt today. Frustrated and furious, she flung the toy animal against the wall. It thudded softly and fell to the floor, and silence filled the room again.

Janet fell forward onto the bed, her head buried amid the piles of clothes, and closed her eyes. Her body ached with loneliness. A tear left her eyelid and trickled down the side of her face, and she began to cry.

* * *

His goodbyes almost finished, Cook headed down Corridor A, past the elevators and down the walkway. He gave the security door his clearance code, and the door opened with a rush of air. He stepped through the gate and onto the deserted bridge.

Unnoticed when the bridge was in use, a buzz cracked the stillness, as power coursed through the powerful electric brain that controlled the ship even in dry dock. The viewing screens were blank now, black rectangles in the shadows of the ship's darkened command center. Over the last cosmic year they had shown him much, as the ship explored unknown star systems, chased pirate raiders across the heavens, and slipped through the cold beauty of space like a dream on wings. Casting a glance from one side to the other, Cook smiled sadly, for the bridge had been his home for what seemed to be a lifetime. He hated to get mawkish over material goods, but the *Constantine* was hardly a trinket he could discard without a second thought. The ship had sustained him, nurtured him; he had mastered his craft on this bridge, and leaving for good was harder than he would have predicted in the giddy rush of promotion. For all the trappings of command, he concluded, at heart he was just a senti-mentalist. It was yet another drawback to being an Isitian.

"Everyone's asking for you at the party, son. Uncle Neil's making his usual fool of himself, practicing his Roscoe imitations, and your mother is waiting to serve dessert."

Roscoe smiled, but said nothing. The brook trickled over the shallow rocks, and a small squirrelline chattered noisily in the trees overhead.

"Is something wrong?"

"No, Dad. Everything's fine."

The father stepped onto a sturdy-looking rock overlooking the water, and sat down. "You know how proud of you I am, Roscoe. I've probably never told you, but you have been a constant amazement since before you could talk. There is no hope I've ever had for you that you haven't fulfilled. I wanted you to know that, before you leave."

"Dad," said the young man, after a long silence. "Mom has barely spoken to me for the last two weeks, and Grandpa Tom is getting old. I'm afraid that—"

"That he'll be dead before you return?"

Roscoe nodded and looked away.

"That's a possibility every time you depart after a visit. And not just with your grandfather, but with everyone you leave, for however short a time. It can be hard to say goodbye, but you can't live your whole life being afraid of seeing someone for the last time.

"You have many gifts, Roscoe. You have to master them. But most of all, you have to live the life you choose for yourself. Your talents can take you anywhere you want—they can open the Universe for you to examine. And the Space Institute on Earth is the finest school for space studies in all of Terra."

"Better than New Alex Tech?" Roscoe said mischievously.

His father laughed. "I'll deny saying it—and who'd believe the word of a Lyceum man anyway? But yes. And simply visiting Earth will be an education in itself.

"Now, let's get back to the house, Scooter. Your mother will skin both of us alive if we make everyone wait much longer."

Laughing, the two of them raced up the hill and through the woods. As always, the son won the race; but these days, he won even when his father tried his best. When Roscoe returned to the party his good spirits had returned. And he didn't even wince when the guests, taking his father's lead, all began using the hated nickname of his boyhood.

COOK HAD ONE final task to complete before leaving the ship. The weight of memories held him down, and Cook sat silently for several minutes. Then, he made his last entry into the ship's log.

```
CC:               142-8355.7
FILE:             Log
ACCESS:           Command.
SECURITY:         Standard
OPERATIONAL STATUS: Normal
LOCATION:         SB 114, Ishtar Command
Having received orders on cc:142-8100 effecting transfer to new
assignment, I hereby relinquish command to Lt Cmdr LaRue.
   Capt R Cook
```

He copied his last entry into his personal diary and placed the disk into his duffel bag. Quietly, Cook gathered his belongings and took the private elevator to the hangar deck, where a single security guard stood watch over the mooring lock. Misty-eyed and alone, he left the ship.

Chapter 10

C APTAIN COOK? HE WAS HERE a minute ago, sir. Why don't you check Engineering? He was complaining about the mess down there before I lost sight of him."

"Thank you—uh— "

"Atkins, sir. Crewman Technician Atkins."

"Carry on, Mr. Atkins."

"Aye, sir."

Slinging his duffel bag over his shoulder, Jeremy Ashton started back toward the elevator once again. He was hungry and tired, and his temper was worn to threadbare. The news that there would be no ship of his own waiting for him at trip's end had not sent him off in the best frame of mind. He was still in a foul mood when he caught the IshCom shuttle from Looking Glass. En route, an ion storm put them five days behind schedule. Finding nobody to meet him at the spaceport, and nobody in the captain's office when he finally did manage to find his new assignment, seemed a fitting climax to a voyage that had seen an endless succession of last straws. To be left stalking a phantom the width and breadth of the ship had not helped his disposition.

Out the door and into the hallway he stormed, his load growing heavier by the minute. Protocol demanded that he report to the commanding officer before settling into his quarters, but the captain was proving as elusive as a desert mirage. Jeremy was starting to wonder if the skipper of this ship might not be a mass hallucination. Everybody claimed to have just seen him, but no matter where Jeremy turned, the captain had already left. Perhaps this was some Eastern Fleet desk jockey's idea of a joke: assign a crew to a starship and see how long it takes them to realize that they don't have a commander. Or maybe it was a loonie CentCom psychologist's attempt to measure the human animal's capacity for mass self-delusion.

Whatever the explanation, Jeremy was out of patience. He stopped near the portside artery to collect his bearings. Crewmen passed on all sides, some leading freight dollies loaded with equipment crates, others bulling past as he stood, barely pausing for a hurried "'Scuse me, sir" before vanishing out of earshot and beyond the range of a tongue-lashing.

Jeremy felt lost and disoriented. The ship's halls and walkways were more disjointed than on his old tracking station. They ran this way and that with scarcely a reason, and the circular arch of the radial corridors made getting around seem a hopeless quest. The lack of hallway markings only added to his confusion. Engineering was two levels down, he tried to remember. Or was it three?

"Damn starships ought to come with maps," he said. He turned the corner toward the main elevators and immediately saw the ceiling twisting and falling away from his face. The next thing he knew, his spinning head was fighting to clear itself. He was sprawled on his back and looking up at the ceiling panel, his bag on the deck floor near the wall. Scattered on the floor was a host of program trays for the main computers, in the middle of which was a young man shaking his head and raising himself on his elbows to survey the damage.

"Loller of a whack," said the other man, shaking his head to collect his wits. Jeremy couldn't quite place the accent. Its owner wore old, ragged sneakers and dark blue fatigues without rank markings, obviously a tyro ensign or an eager beaver desk jockey lieutenant out to earn his line badge before curling up behind a desk for the rest of his life.

Jeremy was up in a flash. "What sort of maniac dashes round corners without a hail of warning?" he snapped.

Still muttering, he limped to his bag, angrily kicking the trays to the side with his foot as he walked. "I suppose you have good reasons for running around this ship like a rut-mad bull."

"Nope," came the terse reply. "Just too dumb to know any better."

Two redshirts, quickly coming to help, ignored Jeremy and dashed to assist the young officer to his feet. He waved them away with a laugh and rose under his own power. Suddenly, the young man didn't look as young as before. His eyes blazed with curiosity about this testy newcomer, and a crisply confident manner instantly transformed an otherwise disheveled appearance into a commanding bearing. Jeremy had the distinct sensation that he had just flushed his own career out the sanitation airlock.

"I'll just bet you're Commander Ashton." The air of finality to his voice seemed to admit no discussion of the matter, but Jeremy's throat was too dry to utter a sound.

"Come on—help me deliver this crap and I'll give you the ten-credit tour. Then you can roll up your sleeves and help us start putting some order into this mess we have for a ship."

"And you're— "

"That's right. I'm Captain Cook. Welcome aboard."

Moments later, an amused Roscoe Cook was still waiting for his open-mouthed first officer to extend a hand to meet his own.

"...AND THEN," continued Cook, leaning back in the oversized chair behind his cluttered office desk, feet propped up and hands locked behind his head, "by the simple inertial force of spending all that money for all those weapons, both sides lost track of the whole point to the competition, and sped past the point at which each was safe. Aside from their relative technological advancement, you know, it was a bit like the good old days of the Peloponesian Wars, in which Athens and Sparta...."

Jeremy did not know quite what to make of Captain Cook. The chronometer read 775 Hours. The captain had been talking non-stop for the last hour, and it had been ages since they'd stopped talking about the ship. Cook's office was cluttered with boxes and half-open crates, and the remnants of several days' worth of galley leftovers. His desk was buried under mounds of papers and folders, except for a small clearing to one side where he propped his feet.

"...and they kept piling weapon on top of weapon, until finally one economy collapsed under its own weight. Kind of like the beached whales of Old Earth, caught short in the tide. But in the end it was all for the best. Probably quite lucky, for us, you know. If they'd kept it up, we might not be here today. And it's one of the grandest ironies of history: the technological spill-off from that arms race was what led to gravitronic physics in the first place, a hundred years later. But think of the dislocation and upheaval it caused at the time! It's as if New Babylon and Demeter...."

But for all the clutter, and despite a maddening eagerness to turn the most meaningless small talk into a graduate school seminar, Jeremy found Cook's intellect intimidating and mind the sharpest he'd ever encountered. In the back of his mind, he seemed to remember hearing something about a hotshot cruiser commander named Cook, though for the moment the specifics escaped him. The young captain made Jeremy fidget in his chair like a dull schoolboy who hadn't done his homework. And he found the most arresting feature about the captain to be his eyes—alert, demanding, yet filled with a wry humor that Jeremy could never quite follow. Even clad like a common laborer, the captain seemed to fill the entire room, though he obscured more than he revealed about the inner workings of his own personality.

"Well, Mr. Ashton—what do you think?"

Jeremy's heart froze in his chest. So much of the captain's monologue had gone over his head that he'd allowed his mind to wander. The barest trace of a smirk danced across Cook's lips, but he pretended not to notice his first officer's discomfiture.

"Come now, Jeremy—we must pick a name for the ship someday, and I'd rather let the crew start calling her by name as soon as we can. 'The Ship' sounds too groundtoadish for my tastes.

"So, what are some good names?"

* * *

"WE ARE going home?"

Zatar smiled broadly and nodded. Seated on the floor, he sat on his favorite pillow, the deep purple one with the velvet lining. As G'ela jumped and clapped her hands, Blendisi raced from the room, eager to summon the others. Zatar and Munshi exchanged amused glances. G'ela was always so excitable, but all of them would feel like dancing before too long. Soon, the whole group was crowding into the gathering room, chattering like a herd of nebbini, asking a dozen questions at once.

"When are we—"

"...how much space...."

"Does G'Rishela know— "

"Do we have...."

"—leaving?"

"May we write home to—"

"How soon—"

"— time to pack?"

At last Zatar rose to his feet through the crushing crowd and signaled silence. The jabbering continued for several moments, but gradually faded until all were quiet at last. Those who could find seats took them. Zatar looked to see his pillow taken by a grinning Ml'lusha, who sought to placate him by a coquettish arch of her smooth, soft neck. Zatar sniffed archly and remained standing.

"As you may have heard, the breakthroughs of the last several weeks have now reached an impasse. The Terrans have agreed in principle to a moratorium on settlements in the disputed region, but neither the duration, nor the interim limits on scientific research in the area have been agreed upon. And after the hard progress of the recent past, tempers were beginning to flare anew.

"Then, from the depths of nowhere, came a solution. The Terrans suggested adjourning the talks to permit both sides to gain perspective, and our Crutchtan friends proposed resuming on Gr'Shuna."

"Of course the biggest surprise was that both sides agreed at once," Munshi added, "without exchanging a single snarl."

"As for when," Zatar continued, in the grand manner of a senior procurator of the High Council, "that depends upon how quickly we can pack, and how much regret we are willing to leave behind.

"For myself," he added, his eyes twinkling, "I would gladly leave my belongings behind, if we could leave today."

"Meaning?" asked a voice from back near the entrance archway.

"Meaning that our ship is on its way, and we can leave when it arrives, as long as takes you less than a month to get ready."

Zatar laughed aloud as the room quickly emptied. The females of his species had endless fun at his gender's expense, and satirists had long immortalized the failings of men: the lack of energy when there was work to do, the endless naps, the stoic flatulence, the constant obsession with mating. But in their own way, Zatar thought, women were every bit as amusing. They did everything in flocks; and it took them forever to pack.

* * *

JEREMY SHIFTED uncomfortably in his chair. For the twentieth time in the last ten minutes, his mind had gone blank. He knew that anything he said was going to sound stupid. Better to say nothing, he thought.

"Well?"

Jeremy panicked, his resolve to stay safely silent vanishing in a crisis of self-doubt. "How about *Valiant*?" he blurted without thinking. Instantly, he knew he had marked himself forever a fool in the captain's eyes: the *Valiant* was Commander Cosmo's ship on the old *Cosmic Avengers* adventure series. His spine prickled with embarrassment, and he struggled to keep his outward composure.

Cook sighed wearily. This exercise was proving to be a major disappointment, he thought. They were no closer to christening the ship than when they'd started, and all they'd done was waste time that could have been spent helping make the ship starworthy. For the twentieth time in the last ten minutes, he consulted the computer console next to his desk.

"Six merchant ships are named *Valiant*," he said. "Three haulers, a freighter, and two trading schooners—not to mention the thousand or so pleasure boats.

"Let's give it another go."

"RAMSEY."

"Here."

"Steer."

"Here."

"Topolewski."

"Yo."

From atop an empty packing crate in the hangar bay, the tall, bearded greenshirt kept reading the names from the duty roster until he reached the end. As each crewman's name was called, he stepped out of the larger group, and to the yeoman's left.

"Zingerman."

"Here."

"All right, ye zoo animals," he bellowed in a mellifluous Demetrian brogue, looking out over the assembly of new redshirts. "That ends the Low Watch assignments in Engineering, Hangar Deck, and Life Support. I know we're spread a mite thin, but it's the best we can do till the tyros show, so let's do the Skipper proud. The rest of ye—High Watch starts sooner than I'd care to hear myself, so ye'd best be gettin your rest while ye can."

"I hear the Skipper's a tyro, too, Chief," called a voice from the back of the room. "D'ye think we've a chance to get this tug moving afore the forests return to Earth?"

Yeoman Chief Gregory Connors cut short the laughter with a scowl to make the devil shake from the cold. His full beard gave his face an animal fierceness that friends knew was more bluff than bluster, but it always had the desired effect on the redshirts.

"I'll not be hearin a word against the Captain," he warned. "Not unless ye want me to make your life so miserable that ye'll be beggin him for brig time. Scuttlebutt says we got us a rare'un. I hear they don't make blueshirts better'n Cap'n Cook—as a spacer or a skipper—and until he proves me a liar I'll bust any groundtoad's butt that says otherwise. Ye'll not put the Skipper in the same league as the snotnosed ensigns we'll be gettin any day now.

"And that goes for all o'ye—like him or not, he's the Captain. And till he marks himself a hacker's mate, I'll not stand for any disrespect. Am I understood?"

Conners let his harsh scowl soften. "Leastways, not while we're still in port," he added with the barest trace of a smile.

The crewmen mumbled a grudging assent. Lampooning the skipper was a time-honored Cozzie tradition, akin to hazing the new officers or flirting with the bluebirds, but everyone recognized the truth to what the Chief had said. As long as the ship was still in port—a "star maiden," in CosGuard parlance—there was too much to do to allow themselves the luxury of disrespect. That could wait until they were out in space, where grumbling in the ranks was an honored way of life. Besides, enough of them had heard the grapevine assessment of their Skipper to give him the chance to disappoint them, before the ship's wags focused all guns amidships.

"All right, ye twit'rin chirpie birds," said the Chief. "Low Watch starts in less than an hour, and Chief Andersen is less of a dawdler-lover than I am. When we get permanent duty assignments, the two of us'll be exchanging blacklists, so I suggest ye try to stay on his good side or ye'll be the sorriest lot o'laundry drones in the Fleet. High Watch is at liberty until 250 hours, and we'll be keepin dual shifts until notice.

"Any questions?"

A half dozen hands shot up. Conners laughed roughly, and dispatched the questioners with a wave of his large, calloused hand.

"Good. Dismissed—and I'll see the heartier souls in the Galley."

* * *

THE TWO MEN sat in the captain's office, alone with their thoughts. The room was silent, except for Cook's squeaky chair. His mind raced with possibilities that his better judgment vetoed instantly. Names like Krautheimer, Kettleston, and Titsworth might confer immortality on deserving if little known scientists, philosophers, and poets, but they were unlikely to ring through the heavens without provoking snickers of scorn from their peers. And of the two hundred or so names CosGuard reserved when the first starships started coming on line—names like *Aurora* and *Constellation*, *Antares* and *Magellan*, *Columbia* and *Majestic*—by now, some hundred-ninety starships later, all the good names were gone.

Cook snorted in disgust. All his life, he'd suffered from other people's lack of imagination. He refused to squander the one chance he'd have to name his own starship. Suddenly, he noticed what looked to be an idea glimmering across Jeremy's face.

"Something?"

Still unsure of himself, Jeremy paused, until Cook's consternation forced the issue.

"Well?"

"How about *Enterprise?*"

Cook mulled it over silently. The name had a sporty ring about it, with the perfect hint of purpose to quash any notion of frivolity. The more he thought about it, the better it set in his mind. With hopes high, he turned to the computer, and his heart sank.

"One CosGuard frigate, a military cargo carrier, thirty-seven merchant haulers, a hundred twenty-two freighters, a few hundred schooners, two dozen garbage scows—and that doesn't count the forty pages of pleasure boats, or— "

"Captain...."

Cook shook his head. "Good name. Pity it's been used before."

"Captain..., " Jeremy began again, for the fortieth time in the last half-hour.

"I won't hear of it, Jeremy," Cook snapped. "There is enough beauty and grandeur in the far recesses of the English language to find one name for a single crystalline hunk of ultrynium. We will find a proper name if it takes until the Cosmic New Year. You remember, of course, what Makinen said...."

"Who?"

"Neoclassical poet, twenty-first-century Earth: 'Poetry weds Science, and Man's imagination soars a thousand years.'"

"But— "

"That's enough. Now think."

Jeremy saw that arguing was useless, and leaned back in his chair trying to look thoughtful. He was not prepared when Cook suddenly bolted upright and banged his desk with his fist. Jeremy's head hit the floor as he fell backwards, his chair shooting toward the far wall. Cook paced resolutely behind his desk, tapping it several times with his fist. Seconds later, when he turned from the computer to face his standing but embarrassed first officer, triumph flamed in his eyes.

"*D'Artagnan*," he announced proudly.

"I beg your pardon?"

"We'll call the ship the *d'Artagnan*." Cook smiled self-contentedly, sitting back in his chair. "I like it—it has panache—élan. A certain *joie de vivre*."

Jeremy winced.

"Well?"

"You're the captain," Jeremy said diplomatically. Part of a first officer's job was to protect the captain from his own follies, but naming a ship was not covered in the rule book. Besides, he felt foolish enough, even without revealing his ignorance.

Cook, however, was not completely obtuse. "What's wrong with *d'Artagnan*?" he sighed.

Jeremy scratched his beard, looking very uncomfortable. "Well," he said sheepishly, "it might help if I knew what a— what a— "

"*D'Artagnan*."

"Yes. It might help if I knew what one of those things was."

Cook nodded knowingly, smiling the charitable smile of one trying terribly hard not to seem patronizing and failing miserably in the attempt. It made Jeremy feel like a dullard, and a particularly useless one at that. "From the old historical novel, *The Three Musketeers*,"

Cook explained professorially. "Late nineteenth-century romantic period, written by one of Old Earth's most prolific writers and set amid one of the various French-English conflicts of pre-Napoleonic Europe."

By now Jeremy was hopelessly confused.

"D'Artagnan," Cook continued patiently, "was the hero—a dashing, swashbuckling sort, ready to cross swords with any enemy who dared cross his path, ready to storm the parapets of Hell to rescue the woman he loved.

"In short," he dead-panned, "he was kind of an Old Earth Commander Cosmo."

Jeremy couldn't keep from laughing—and once he started, he found it nearly impossible to stop. Tears welled in his eyes, and when he looked to see Cook's own eyes twinkling merrily, he started laughing all over again.

Cook merely chuckled, his controlled exterior never revealing how refreshing he found it to find a first officer with a sense of humor. The captain hoped that his ability to laugh would help his new first officer bear the news that he'd have the responsibility for drilling the bridge crew. And for the tyro officer's small craft proficiency tests as well.

"*D'Artagnan*," Cook repeated, setting his first officer off again. "Perfect name for a starship." He engaged the computer and entered the name on the ship's registry, then turned to face Jeremy again, his eyes gleaming with mischief.

"You know, Jeremy," he smiled, leaning back and locking his hands behind his head. "Beards are a tad non-regulation."

THE SHIP'S new name was quickly posted on bulletin boards throughout the ship. The crew's reaction was unanimous.

"What kinda sissy-face name is that?" drawled a dark, young yeoman named Hogan, walking down the portside artery on the conning deck. He was short and stocky, his North American accent as thick as his waistline. "Ask me, it sounds like some weird I-*sissian* spider."

"Naw," said the taller greenshirt beside him, another Earther named Andersen, the ship's second yeoman chief. "I asked the librarian. It's from an Old Earth book by a guy named Dumb-Ass, about some puff-shirted dandy strutting around in tights and a cape."

They stepped aside to let a crewman pass. She was pushing a gravity cart loaded with electrical equipment for the molecular transmitter. Like most of the female redshirts, she was solid and sturdy; the willowy types on ships of the line tended to be officers. But she had a pretty face and dark, sensual eyes. She winked at Anderson as she passed; they'd served together before, keeping close quarters on a convoy frigate in the Valhalla sector. It was a welcome treat to find an old friend on a new ship; CosGuard lore held it an omen of good fortune.

"Know her?"

"In a manner of speaking," replied Andersen, but discussions were cut short when Yeoman Chief Conners appeared, turning the corner from the inner corridor.

"Chasing red again, Chief?"

"Ah, rot!" muttered Conners, flashing a grimaced smile as he stopped to exchanged greetings. "It never fails. Give me an old ship, an' a crew that's put some sweat into her. That's what we need. A crew that's pained themselves over a hunk o'metal will scarce take her for granted. Then ye can come on with the peach-faced tyros an' never come to grief. But take one fresh from the mint an' half the crew turns into lounge lizards. I'm runnin myself ragged, tryin to get the duty roster straightened out, an' half the redshirts on board won't leave the recreation area unless I fetch'em myself. Been here less'n a week an' I'm sick of it already."

"Cheer up, Chief," said a grinning Hogan; he never could resist needling his superiors. "Remember—the tyros are due any day now."

"You like the name *d'Artagnan*, Chief?" asked Andersen, trying to head off another outburst. The last thing Conners needed now was a reminder of problems on the horizon.

"A name's a name." Conners scratched his beard pensively, trying hard to convince himself. "Besides, Skipper's job is spacin, not siftin through registry books. Ain't his fault he couldn't find a better one."

After a few more pleasantries, Conners excused himself and continued down the hall. He knew his problems were only beginning. The ship was in chaos and the crewmen were already scattering like pollen in the wind. To top it off, he'd spend the next tour of duty trying not to flinch whenever a pub-house rounder asked the name of his ship. The Skipper should've thought twice before sticking them with a moniker like that one, he thought; the wags would have a field day. But he consoled himself with the prospect of greeting the tyro ensigns. Knocking the lot of them down to size after officer's school inflated their ego enough to dwarf a red giant was among a greenshirt's most treasured duties, relished by yeoman throughout the long history of the Cosmic Guard. And a good hazing was all he needed to lift his flagging spirits.

* * *

```
CC:              142-8905.7
FILE:            Log
ACCESS:          Command.
SECURITY:        Standard
OPERATIONAL STATUS: Repairs in Progress
LOCATION:        SB 114, Ishtar Command/Dry Dock
```
Engine cable installation is progressing normally, but we cannot test the engines until the main computers are activated, making the Simulator operational. Computer glitches will continue unabated for the foreseeable future, as a large portion of programming from the contractor was scrambled before the final copy was entered onto the program discs. Only life support and security programs are intact, but outlet terminals are available for simple functions when programmed manually or connected to the starbase mainframe. Molecular transmitter will operate in theoretical realm only until we resolve the glitches; initial test turned metal block into a mangled mess resembling the artistic grotesqueries of the late Primitive Abstractionist period of Old Earth.

Lack of experienced personnel impedes progress on all fronts, but the trickle of trained technicians has accelerated to a full-fledged dribble and the rest of the officers should arrive at any time. Nevertheless, I plan for the ship to be starworthy by the end of the current Cosmic Year, despite the deteriorating discipline caused by overwork due to Fleet delays in filling my personnel requisitions. Once our full complement arrives, many problems should vanish. However, I plan to sequester the ship and crew until repairs are completed and the ship is ready for final pre-launch inspection. While this may cause additional

```
morale problems, on-base distractions appear to be causing
greater problems, albeit of a different sort.
   Capt R Cook
```

Cook pressed the entry button on the portable computer dangling in the air above him and recorded the entry. It was the sixteenth log entry he'd made as captain of his ship—one each day, every ten cosmic hours since he'd formally assumed command. And, he'd remarked to himself more than once, each one said the same thing: problems, problems, problems. There seemed to be no end in sight, and the problems kept coming. Yawning, he placed the machine in its stand on the wall by his bed.

Suspended above his bed by the antigrav relay, Cook stretched himself and stared at the ceiling, using the handholds on the wall to steady himself as he floated over his bed. Old Captain Boyle had warned him about mint-fresh ships: more bugs than a jungle on Demeter, he'd said; and you'll wait forever for your crew. Cook was coming to appreciate his first skipper more with each day he spent pouring over progress reports and specifications.

Ship-shaping the *Constantine* was bad enough, what with the engine adjustments and navigation overhaul she needed before they left port. But the headaches his old cruiser caused could not compare to the migraines that *d'Artagnan* delivered daily. First the elevator doors started sticking, randomly trapping crewmen as the lift cages floated on endless journeys through the bowels of the ship. Then the food processors fritzed out—no great loss in itself, but it forced Cook to send out for meals for the crew. Cook hated assigning a half-dozen or so redshirts to waste time better spent working on the ship, waiting for the commissary to finish fixing "three hundred forty-seven to go." If they didn't ready the galley by the time the rest of the crew reported, he'd have to make restaurant detail a full time duty, and that was a step that he was reluctant to take. He wouldn't lack for volunteers, of course, but he'd already noticed a tendency for those assigned to food procurement to gain weight at an alarming rate.

But the small glitches and petty problems they faced were dwarfed by the sheer size of the job ahead of them. The ship was twice the size of a cruiser—fully four hundred meters across—and every cubic inch had to be brushed up to CosGuard trim. Cook felt lost in a sea of details with no end in sight. To top it off, he had only three officers to supervise a half-complement of crewmen. The more he thought about it, the worse it made him feel.

Sick of the problems, and realizing that it would be quite some time before his mind would relax enough to let him sleep, he took the port-a-comp from its stand again, and decided to call the file dossiers of all his senior officers onto the small screen. Except for Mendelson, of course; he already knew her better than he should, and well enough to write her biography. Still, hers was the first name he called onto the screen, and he lingered over her file for several minutes before moving on. Though only Jeremy Ashton and Bruce Van Horn had reported for duty, the rest of the senior staff was due any day now. No matter what state of chaos prevailed in the rest of the ship, Cook thought, he would know every one of them inside out before they met.

Chapter 11

MASON MCGEE PLOPPED ONTO his bed and kicked off his shoes. The gray walls felt roomy beyond measure, and he'd almost forgotten the simple treat of feeling real gravity beneath his feet. The soft whisper of the ventilator lulled his senses and he imagined himself on a sandy Demetrian shore, with the breeze wrapping around him and the warm sea lapping gently on the beach. He was twelve when his parents died and his brother pulled him off into space, but he remembered the feast a real planet gave to the senses. Some day he'd return, he pretended, though he knew the tug of space would always haunt him.

"So howwuz the trip, Macey? Bring back a trinket or two for the house, or did ye let Cyrus curse ye for squand'rin the family fortune?"

Mason turned his head to see Janey, the housemate he and Cyrus shared. They'd gotten her from a Ceresian trader bound for home after making his fortune supplying the frontier with all manner of contraband. Mousey brown hair hung lifelessly from her head and her plain, round face had known little joy. But her eyes always perked up whenever she and Mason were alone, and he could remember long nights together, sitting and watching the stars spin overhead. Frontier life was hard enough on a man, he thought, It must be unbearable to be the only woman for parsecs around, with no company but two dust-bitten spacers who were rarely home, and who did little but complain when they were there.

"Hello, Janey," he smiled, beckoning her to sit on the bed beside him. "Think I'd forgot about you?"

He reached into a sack on the floor beside the bed and pulled out a large blanket of finest Rositer goarstwool. He'd gotten it at the IshCom bazaar from a dealer specializing in scalping the spacers. It cost a small fortune, and if Cyrus had been sober enough to see it, he'd have whooshed it out the airlock just to teach his brother not to waste his money on frills. Mason didn't mind being overcharged, not when he could watch his woman's eyes light up like fireworks.

"It's—it's— "

She gave up trying to find words. She'd been snatched from home as a teenager and never finished school, so she found it hard to express herself. But she flung herself into Mason's arms and gave him her warmest hug, the kind she never gave his brother.

"Now if you don't like it, I'll take it back right now. The ship should be ready to go in another day or two."

"Don't ye be a-funnin me, Mason McGee," she laughed, suddenly tickling Mason's ribs, and sending him into fits of laughter himself as they wrestled on the bed. "Not unless ye wants t'see how cold it can get, alone on a rock in space."

* * *

THE MILKY WAY splits the night sky over Covington almost in half, rising from the northwest horizon and arching across the heavens like a translucent mask. In Spring, Old Sol, the star of Old Earth, sets too early to cast its faint glow on Terra's capital before nightfall, and by midnight the distant star Deneb shines fiercely on the eastern horizon, like a beacon calling through the eerie silence of alien skies. Halfway to overhead and slightly to the north, too dim to be visible through the vast expanse of space, the reddish clouds that dominated the discussions of diplomats far to the east swelled beyond the consciousness of most Terrans early in the year 2551, looming large in the minds of a select few.

Hollenbach was breathing heavily. The walk up Woodhouse Ridge was taxing to a man of his girth, and his breath was visible in the night air. Above, the moonless sky was alive with stars; below, the city lights lined the river, and on Capital Hill the Senate bathed in the floodlights that would keep the double dome aglow until dawn. Hollenbach found the view from the ridge enchanting, as he paused to recover his wind. He wondered why he came to enjoy it so rarely.

But his mind soon returned to the matter at hand. Two o'clock in the morning rarely found him in the mood for contemplation, and the meeting awaiting him needed all the concentration he could muster. Duncan Heathcoate wasn't the brightest man in the Senate, but he'd learned the art of discretion well. Over the last few weeks,

Hollenbach had wondered whether he'd underestimated the man he privately chided as "Old Bluff and Bluster." Schiller was smart, but Schiller didn't know the Senate. If the Tories realized how precarious their hold on power would be—Hollenbach could deliver a majority, all right, but with just two votes to spare—they'd have leverage that Hollenbach had tried very hard to prevent. Someone with savvy had gone over the possibilities very carefully, and a sinking feeling in the pit of his stomach told Hollenbach that the someone would be standing before him quite soon.

The wind shifted to the north, bringing a strong gust down the crest of the hills overlooking the Mendenhall. Hollenbach shivered; he'd worn a thin jacket, and the wind knifed through it as if through paper. But he didn't shiver alone for long. He was busy cursing himself for listening to the local weathermen when a familiar voice called to him.

"Emerson?"

Hollenbach looked to see Schiller standing twenty yards away, at the top of a gentle swell in the earth. A few feet beyond, a faceless companion stood in the darkness, his silvery hair catching the distant city lights like a ghost. The companion said nothing, but Hollenbach knew at once who it was.

* * *

MUSIC BLARED over the speakers in the repair shop, only to die in the sound-absorbing panels of the walls. Wires and knobs littered the floor and an open tool box teetered on the workbench, its grimy contents scattered around the room. Mason McGee tapped his foot in time with the song, oblivious to all but his work and the music. He'd even failed to notice when his brother had left.

Outside the repair room hatch and past the closed bay door, Cyrus hung weightless in the air. Their ship rested lifelessly behind him, held in place by mooring cables; the heat-shield tiles of her outer hull were discolored by long use and the rigors of space. He could hear Mason clanging away in the distance, repairing the Bradbury Converter—the small device that regulated the exchange of energy from the ship's engines into artificial gravity. On a small ship they needed only one, and if his mind had been on business, Cyrus would have thanked the stars that Mason had talked him out of buying a bigger ship. A bigger ship meant more cargo, but it also meant more things to go wrong, and it would hardly profit them to haul twice as much, only to have the ship starworthy for half as long.

But Cyrus' mind was wandering far beyond the asteroid he shared with his brother and their woman. He looked out the hangar bay porthole, toward the stars of the East. He and Mason knew every parsec of space in these parts. Most of it had already been picked over by prospectors long before they arrived on the scene. It took longer and longer to find a good strike that wasn't already claimed by somebody. There were still bounders aplenty who would as soon kill a man as steal from him—and he should know, Cyrus chuckled to himself. After all, he'd done it himself in his younger days. He didn't have the energy anymore; besides, it would mean arguing with Macey, who was acting more and more like a woman every day.

But he and Macey had found a strike; it fairly swam with nickel and copper and titanium, with lode upon lode of gold besides. The asteroid belt with all these riches spun around a yellow star. Ten parsecs from this star—just a few day's journey, if their ship was in proper trim—was another one. Around that star spun a world with flowing water and air so sweet you could taste it.

Cyrus' jaw hardened as he looked through the milky cloud that filled the distant heavens. Anticenter from Deneb, which hung brightly to port, and barely a month away, it was all he'd ever wanted: a warm place on a planet as peaceful as sleep, with riches to be plucked at leisure whenever he felt like working. But their second night there, they were torn from their beds by a bunch of devil-eyed monsters with slimy hands and screeching laughs, to be shipped home like naughty children caught stealing candy. The lizards let them keep the ore stored in the ship's hold, but the forty tons of gold they left in the other system went begging. It was the fortune of a lifetime, and Cyrus had no doubt that the lizards meant to keep it all themselves.

Hatred turned his soul as black as space. He stared into the distance, his eyes fast on a starless point that never varied in the distant cloud, a point he could pick out of the sky from anywhere in Terra. It was the same point that held his endless fascination, whenever he found himself with nothing to do.

* * *

THE SECURITY OFFICER walked slowly down the corridor leading to the bridge. The *d'Artagnan* was his first assignment on a starship and he was eager to learn all he could, as quickly as possible. He had to know every inch of his ship, and there was no place better than the bridge to get started. Though they were made of standard cloth, he could almost feel his new lieutenant's bars shining on his epaulets. He'd been so proud when his promotion came through; his parents even called by subspace relay all the way from Earth to congratulate him. And now, he could finally put his training to use—and on a starship! In his wildest fantasies, he never imagined drawing such a plum assignment his first time out. After leaving the Academy, most CosGuard Security Office trainees found themselves on some obscure rock guarding a science station, or banished to an outpost along the frontier where the only excitement was counting the days until the next duty rotation. Starships usually fell to those who had been around a lot longer. And though his first assignment—security on a subspace radar station out of New Calais—won him a citation for anticipating and repelling a pirate raid on the base, he had no illusions that this was the reason for his rapid advance.

No, he told himself, the reason he pulled this assignment was dumb luck. His reassignment to IshCom, for reasons lost to a computer glitch that left him with nothing to do on the grandest starbase this side of Demeter, had made him the only security officer available. And since *d'Artagnan* needed a security officer, the same CSO computer that pulled him away from New Calais for no reason assigned him to the starship—also for no apparent reason. He could only smile at the irony, but he was hardly one to sneeze at fate.

The command hatch opened and the young lieutenant stepped onto the bridge. Instantly, he could see that something was not quite right. The lights should have been dimmed, but they were as bright as day. Star charts flashed haphazardly on the small screen beneath the main viewer at the head of the bridge. As he stopped to listen, he heard annoyed murmuring coming from somewhere nearby, punctuated by grunts of exasperation.

Quietly, he moved ahead to investigate.

"Aw, crap!" muttered an angry voice. The lieutenant 's head snapped toward the direction of the sound. He saw a pair of legs sticking out from beneath a console station in the middle of the room—Navigation, if he remembered correctly, though ships could be awfully confusing. The legs were clad in dirty fatigues and sporting a well-worn sneaker on each foot. The left sneaker was held together with duct tape.

"Excuse me," the young officer said, his voice firm and commanding. "But the bridge is still restricted to— "

"Who's that?" demanded the voice at the other end of the feet. "Never mind—go get me the toolbox. It's over by the Auxnav."

"The what?"

"The toolbox."

"No, I mean—the 'onyx valve?'"

"No, no—the interface, the auxnav interface."

"The 'inner phase' of—of what?"

"No, no, no. The auxiliary—who is that, anyway?"

Seeing the captain scuttering out from beneath the navigation console, the CSO lieutenant felt like a hopeless imbecile. Here he was, charged with protecting the most advanced machine in human history, and he hadn't the slightest idea what anyone was saying when they talked about the simplest bits of equipment. Worse yet, he'd demonstrated his incompetence to his new commander. Cook rose and dusted himself off, fixing the junior officer in a glare of such severity that the young lieutenant felt his face flushing like a ripe tomato, and his bladder preparing to empty. But Cook's mien soon softened into one of mild curiosity.

"You're the new security officer, aren't you—Burdick, isn't it? Yes, Burdick."

Burdick's throat was dry as dust, and he found it impossible to swallow. "Yes, sir," he managed at last, in the scratchiest of voices.

"Doesn't CSO teach you people anything about ships?" Cook sighed, more to himself than to the tortured young man who imagined himself standing in judgment. "I swear—how can they put you into space if you don't know the first thing about— "

Cook looked to see his young security officer near tears.

"Well, never mind about that," Cook said, scratching his nose. "I guess you'll learn soon enough."

"Yes, sir," nodded Burdick, his voice barely audible. "I am a rather quick study."

"I imagine so. And by now I guess you've probably adjusted to the different uniforms. CSO tan doesn't go with the decorum, you know. Too bland. Blends right into the walls."

"Yes, sir," Burdick laughed weakly.

"All right, then," Cook smiled. He pointed to a small box behind the second tier railing on the starboard side of the bridge. "The toolbox is up there, by the auxiliary navigation console."

"I'll get it right away, Captain."

As his security officer scurried toward the toolbox, Cook leaned back to sit on the main navigation console and wiped the perspiration from his brow. Reprogramming the navigation computer was a big job, and he wished he could trust his new navigator to do it—Talbot, he thought; or was it Talley? Whatever—he'd be arriving the day after tomorrow. Cook glanced over his shoulder at the hopeless mess on the navigation screen. He might not know everything in this Universe, but he did know that there was just one Deneb. Not sixteen. If those idiot engineers would use their heads in the first place—use Rigel and Deneb as fixed points of reference instead of Demeter and New Babylon, whose stars were too dim to be much use in the depths of space—he wouldn't have to go through this every time he got a new ship.

He breathed deeply as the young man returned with the toolbox. Once he'd stopped, thought Cook, it was hard to get started again. But he had to do this sooner or later. And since he refused to argue the point with his navigator, it was better to do it sooner. The file on this Tally-something pegged him as a chronic complainer. The last thing Cook needed now was the added grief of a temperamental navigator.

"Here you are, Captain."

"Thank you, Mr. Burdick," Cook said, lifting himself off the main console. It was time to get started, he thought; and he would keep at this until he was done. Or until he was sick of it, whichever came first.

"Carry on, then. And Burdick?"

"Yes, sir."

"Could you tell Chief Connors to come to the bridge? We have some things to discuss, and he could give me a hand here while we do it."

"Aye aye, sir. Right away!" Burdick said, and hurried off the bridge.

Cook lowered himself onto the floor. They should put padding under the consoles, he thought. That way, people could work on computer innards without rubbing their backs raw. But such concerns faded quickly, for he had other things on his mind. Things like turning the navigation computers into something useful rather than accepting Standard CosGuard Issue. Or finding a way to tell Yeoman Chief Connors that there would be no hazing the tyros on his ship.

Chapter 12

"THIS IS RIDICULOUS."

Cook exhaled loudly. He was leaning back in his chair, feet propped up on his desk and holding a folded sheet of paper.

Untouched on a tray on a side table was a breakfast of reconstituted eggs and toast, and a cup of lukewarm coffee. A digital scanner was on the work table next to the wall, and display disks were evenly divided between the floor and the half-open binder box on the floor. He woke up in a foul mood. Insomnia kept him up reading half the night, and that usually meant a rough day for anyone he was around the next morning. The mail that greeted him had not helped his disposition.

"Problems?" asked Jeremy, entering the room, wondering what new problems faced them today. The captain seemed a font of boundless energy, but as nearly as Jeremy could tell, most of that energy was focused on sending the ship's executive officer chasing in a dozen different directions.

"I haven't been on Isis in fifteen years," Cook complained. "Aside from an occasional reference to my Uncle Cornelius in letters from my parents, nobody tells me anything that's going on there. What do I know about local politics? They don't even tell me which district I vote in these days, for crying out loud."

Baffled, Jeremy walked to the captain's desk and took the paper from Cook's hands. His eyes widened in surprise when it dropped to the floor and unfolded into a sheet nearly eight feet long. It was a ballot, sent him by the Northland Province Elections Commission. By law, everyone in the Cosmic Guard received an absentee ballot whenever his home planet held elections. Isis had the minimum number of senators—one fixed-termer, one special-termer elected whenever the president called for elections—and this was the year Isis selected her fixed-term senator. The Isitian ballot also presented a confusing array of candidates and ballot proposals and was taller than he was. The tiny printing on the ballot's twelve columns did not seem designed to help anyone to make sense of it all, and apparently nobody thought to distribute the ballot by district. By the looks of it, every office on the planet was listed. Fortunately there only seemed to be two parties, and a brief scan of the top of the ticket revealed a name that even Jeremy recognized.

"There's Irene McGinnis," he said. "I remember her from the hearings on that big scandal a few years ago. She has quite a reputation, as I recall. I was quite impressed with her."

"No, no, no," Cook said, trying not to sound impatient. "That's not the way we do things on Isis. She's already had her turn. Besides, she's the wrong party. She's a Nuthatcher."

Jeremy looked again. The only parties on the ballot were the Liberals and the Conservatives.

"Well, you see," Cook tried to explain, "we don't like to give anyone more than one turn in Covington. Politicians are like naughty children. They're easily spoiled and must be constantly watched. Give them too much and it goes right to their heads. Makes them think they're big shots. So tradition is quite specific. Nobody goes to the Senate more than once. Anything beyond that is simply not very Isitian."

"But hasn't she already served two terms? And what in God's name is a nuthatcher?"

"On Isis, tradition is not carved in stone," Cook said testily. "And the Cooks vote for Mugwumps, not Nuthatchers. Nuthatchers are a subspecies of unenlightened visigoths. Corneilius Cook would never let me hear the end of it."

"So what's the problem?"

"There is no problem."

Cook voted straight Mugwump, too proud to admit that McInnis—Old Ironpanties, as she was known on Isis—was the only name apart from his uncle's that he recognized as well. All the while, he grumbled about the fact that he didn't know enough about the issues or candidates to vote for "None of the Above." Like most Isitians, he also voted to reject all the proposals and initiatives, since voting for them only encouraged similar nonsense in the future. It made no difference anyway, he muttered to himself. In interplanetary politics everyone on Isis was a Federalist: they stuffed the last Tory and put him in a museum long ago. And it hardly mattered that the Mugwumps made a hash of things whenever they came to power. The Nuthatchers were just as bad, but at least this way they'd face a Mugwump mess in the end. Those messes were usually more convoluted, of course, but at least their hearts were in the right place. As he finished, he noticed that Jeremy was trying not to laugh, and doing a very poor job of it.

"All right, what's so funny?" Cook snapped. Immediately, he felt a surge of guilt at his lack of good temper. He knew that Jeremy wouldn't like his next assignment, but if there was one thing he'd learned on the *Constantine*, it was how to delegate assignments that he didn't want to do himself.

Of course, some jobs were easier to delegate to people he didn't like. Jeremy was such an improvement over his last first officer that Cook hated pushing the advantages of rank too far. That reluctance wouldn't stop him from doing so, he admitted to himself. But at least he had the decency to feel guilty about it.

"IT'S AN OUTRAGE."

"That it is, Chief."

"It's a bloody outrage."

Chief Connors put down his wrench and shook his head. Though progress had been steady, the emergency hatch was proving more difficult than he'd anticipated. He took his handkerchief from his pocket to wipe his brow and motioned to the redshirt beside him to keep working. Taking his lead from the Chief, Yeoman Sillers holstered his own wrench; it was time for another break.

"It's disrespectful, that's what it is. Disrespectful of tradition and common sense."

"Aye on that, Chief."

"And ye know what really galls me?"

Connors led Sillars away from the rest of the repair crew. There was no need to sow any more dissension on board. The captain had taken care of that with his sequestration order: no visitors or departures until the ship was starworthy, even if it meant working through the Cosmic New Year. The cream colored walls muffled the sound in the corridors, but the screams of the old time Cozzies still echoed through the ship. Connors stopped as soon as they were a proper distance away.

"What galls me," the Chief whispered conspiratorially, "is the way these tyro blueshirts go struttin 'round these hallways like they was desk jockeys out of Covington. Barely three weeks here, and they still don't know their butts from a black hole—yet they have the temerity to tell me about pullin my weight. As if I've been loafin at the throttle while they be takin their own sweet time a-gettin here.

"I tell ye, Sillars—if one more o'them snotnosed groundtoads tries to tell me how to do me own job, I'll throttle'em myself."

"Calm down now, Chief. It ain't as bad as all that."

"Chief Connors?" A cry came from down the hall. It was Crewman Recruit Larsen, the silk-shirt college boy from Demeter. He'd signed up on a lark, because he was tired of school and wanted to see the universe, but Connors liked him all the same. He sang a good song, and for a college boy he talked with an intelligible accent.

"What is it this time, Larsen?"

"We're ready to test the hatch, again."

"Go ahead, Crewman; let's see what we've done to her this time."

A buzzer rang in the hallway for an instant, only to die like a strangled goose.

"Chief— "

"I heard, Larsen. See what ye can do. I'll be along presently." He turned a stern face toward Sillars.

"Ain't as bad?" Connors muttered, turning his fury to the matter at hand. "One of them tyros—a bluebird name o'McKinsey, I think it was—come up to me while I was mindin a whole field-full o'redshirt recruits on their way to help unglitch the engine coils, and wanted me to folly her to the Molly room. Seems she had a stackfull o'computer disks that needed cartin off somewheres— "

"To her cabin, no doubt, eh, Chief?"

"—an' she didn't want to soil her wee dainty hands," the Chief concluded acidly, not at all amused by Sillars' inability to see past his own lust. "Why, if the Skipper hadn't— "

"Ready again, Chief. Shall we have another go?"

"All right, Larsen. See how she behaves this time."

The buzzer sounded again, this time wavering like a sputtering motor in need of lubrication. Seconds later, the noise crescendoed to a high-pitched squeal, then stopped with a screech that made the hair on Connors' beard stand on end.

"Ah, crap!"

"Larsen—try inverting polarity on the phase-in and speedin the drive on the grapplers."

"Aye aye, Chief."

"Well," whispered Sillars, "Cook had a meeting with all the new officers. From what I hear tell, he laid into them pretty good. All but forbade them from issuing any orders at all, and told'em square off that they'd be giving commands to greenshirts at their peril. Put'em right to squawking, it did. Then he sent the lot of them into the pits to help put the engines in proper trim. I'll give him this—he's not above taking'em down a peg or two himself. And he's not one to play favorites."

"Ah, rot," muttered Connors.

"Come on, Chief," Sillars laughed. "It's not as bad as all that. Besides, we've got us a hatch to unglitch."

The two yeomen returned to the stubborn emergency hatch, barely in time for another test. "All right," barked Connors, "let's see what we've got, here. You know how important proper hatch seals are to a spaceship, don't ye lads? If the hull ruptures, we've got to be able to close off enough of the ship so that we aren't all sucked into space like rubbish out the airlock.

"Larsen— "

"Aye , Chief."

"Seal the hatch."

The young crewman flipped the control lever on the upper sidewall. The warning buzzer sounded and the two grapplers—one from below, one from above—glided together like clockwork until they meshed exactly in the core of the hatch. A gleeful cheer rose from the throats of the whole repair crew. Ramsey, the old-timer from Gaea, broke into a little song about "Coming home with the lassies of Riley's Station," and Connors and the others broke into a little jig of a dance.

All too soon, the celebrants recalled the next job on their agenda— the next emergency hatch, two corridors farther along the port beam spoke—and started collecting tools from wherever they had left them.

"All right, Mr. Larsen," announced a smiling Chief Connors when the crew had finishing policing the area. "You may reopen the hatch." The smile soon froze on his face.

"I can't, Chief . The damn thing's stuck!"

Connors' voice was lost amid the groans and curses and toolboxes falling around him. "Ah, rot," he said through clenched teeth.

* * *

"I don't want to hear it, Jeremy."

"Captain...."

"Jeremy, just handle it. I've got too many other things to worry about."

"But— "

"Handle it."

"But if you never— "

"No 'buts' about it, Jeremy. It will be *your* responsibility to whip the bridge crew into shape," Cook said, in a blandly pleasant tone of voice that Jeremy was coming to find infuriating. "I leave the details to you. You're the executive officer. So...well, execute."

"But— "

"Now, if you'll excuse me, I'm needed elsewhere."

Cook strode out of his office, leaving his first officer as frustrated as when they began. These meetings were solving nothing, Jeremy fumed, and they were doing nothing for his own morale. They hadn't had a full staff meeting in two weeks, and every time Jeremy tried to brief the captain about some new problem, Cook ran off somewhere. He didn't really blame the captain; ship-shaping was a long, thankless task. But it was even grimmer when the man at the top seemed so unconcerned about the difficulties he piled onto the shoulders of his senior aides. He'd rest more comfortably if he thought that Cook really cared about the troubles that faced them.

Sullenly, he sank into the visitor's chair. Jeremy had been so full of complaints when he entered the office, and was brimming with ways for the captain to resolve them. He wondered why his resolve melted away whenever the two of them started talking. He looked at the wall behind Cook's desk. Looming over him were old style sketches of men he didn't recognize, drawings from the captain's sister that Cook had finally finished hanging the day before. And Jeremy felt foolish seconds later, when a cold chill ran down his back.

It seemed that the captain's wall hangings were all staring at him.

* * *

THE STARSHIP'S galley functioned as a third lounge, but unlike the officers' lounge on the conning deck, and the redshirt lounge one level below, the galley provided a meeting place for all ranks. To center of the galley was Corridor A, onto which faced the ship's main services—including Sick Bay, Supply, Science Center, Library, Central Computer, Molecular Transmitter, and the like. Beyond the innermost corridor was the bridge, the very hub of the conning deck.

By informal agreement, tyros of all ranks took charge of Dining Room Two, gathering to share what passed for food aboard the *d'Artagnan*, and to exchange stories and laughs over the plights facing them as "Green-tailed Groundtoads," living among all the seasoned Cozzie veterans. Each of the old-timers seemed to know everything worth knowing about running a starship, although no two of them could agree on much of anything. At a table at the far corner of the room, beneath a portrait of Wellington Carswell—the CosGuard scientist who pioneered the early weapons systems that led to the development of the first molecular blasters—were two young officers in standard blue uniforms, sitting beside a redshirt, all fresh recruits, all tired to the teeth by overwork and double shifts.

"How long before we can transfer out of this hell-hole?" asked Tom Gerlach, a tall, handsome young ensign on his first posting. He ran a hand through his closely cropped blond hair, then rubbed his tired blue eyes and yawned. He personally constituted half of the CosGuard Academy graduates in the current crop of ensigns.

"I don't know," said Connie McKenzie, sitting beside him. "But time seems awfully long when you start counting the seconds. You know, I'm actually looking forward to spending two relaxing hours in the Supply Office. When I graduated Tech school, I thought I'd resign my commission rather than get stuck with a boring job like that." She sipped her coffee; grimacing, she reached for a packet of sugar.

"Well what really bothers me," continued Gerlach, "is this patronizing, heavy-handed way the captain runs things. He won't give us anything to do, except for the shit-shoveling crews and other jobs no long-termer would take without a fit of bellyaching."

"And then," continued Connie, "he has the nerve to stop us from making sure what little we do get to do gets done right. Am I making any sense?" she giggled. "I'm too tired to talk straight."

Martindale, the tyro redshirt, shook his head. "I think you're being way too hard on the Skipper. The stories I hear about the way most ships treat newcomers—and female officers in particular—are enough to spin your fannies. Connie—how would you like to spend your first two weeks on board as chamber maid to a crewman you've insulted. And you know what the most popular hazing for bluebirds is?"

Connie shook her head.

"Typically, the yeomen assign the prettiest girls to stand beside the urinals in the men's room, and clean them before—and after—every crewman conducts his business there. And then she's expected to thank the crewman for his patronage, and ask him to come again."

Connie winced. "Christ! And they let them do things like that?"

"That's to teach the new officers humility. To show them that they're really no better than anyone else on board, the one thing they never learn in officer's school. Hazing for the redshirts is usually less severe, but the purpose is the same."

Connie sat back in her chair. Humility wasn't the only thing they didn't learn in Tech school. And if the closeness of this call weren't enough, she soon heard a voice in the distance that made her skin crawl.

"Connie—Connie!"

She looked to see Kirkland Dexter running toward her, waving a piece of paper in his hand. Briefly, she looked at the ceiling, wondering whether the miserable snip would literally dog her to the ends of the Universe. Worse, her companions actually seemed to enjoy her predicament.

"Hello, Dexter," Gerlach said in his heartiest voice, careful to ignore the fury in Connie's eyes. "Why don't you join us?" Dexter was a pest, he thought, but essentially harmless. In small doses his effect on McKenzie was worth the aggravation.

"Hey—thanks, guys. You know, I've been so busy since we arrived that I haven't had much chance to socialize."

"Here, have some nice, reconstituted chocolate cake," said Martindale. "I've had all I want."

"Gee, thanks," said Dexter. Martindale had eaten exactly one forkfull, and for a good reason. CosGuard Chocolate bore the same resemblance to the real thing as shoe polish bore to shoes. Dexter stuffed an oversized bite into his mouth, never stopping to let his taste buds register their verdict with his brain.

"But you know what—I've seen the list!" he mumbled. Cake crumbs fell down his chin, onto his standard blues.

"What are you babbling about?" Connie asked sharply.

"The list! The assignment list. Captain Cook posted the assignment list on the bulletin board not five minutes ago. We have our first permanent assignments, now. Imagine, no more waking up in the morning—or however they describe it on the Cosmic Clock— not knowing where you'll be spending the day, or what foul-mouthed yeoman will be watching that day, waiting for you to screw up. I tell you, we're really moving up in the world."

"So, Dexter," Gerlach said, winking slyly at Connie. "What are the assignments?"

"Oh, I've got it right here." Dexter handed the paper to Gerlach, who snatched it greedily. He laughed as his two friends scanned the list eagerly, hunting for their names, and smiled at their redshirted companion, whose name he didn't remember.

"I don't see us here, Dexter."

Dexter giggled louder than before. "I removed your names. I wanted to see how you'd react."

"Dexter! " Gerlach menaced.

"Relax—I wouldn't play games with you guys for no reason. You know all those bridge drills we all hate? Where Mr. Ashton keeps yelling at everybody in spitting distance and we never seem to beat the simulator?"

Gerlach and Connie both nodded in suspense, almost afraid to believe that what they thought might be true.

"Well, you sure impressed somebody, because Gerlach, you've been accepted as a Weapons Officer Apprentice. And Connie— you're the ship's new apprentice navigator."

Dexter watched as his companions hugged each other and cheered. He smiled in his odd sort of way, adjusting his thick glasses as they started falling down his nose. One of these days, he told himself, he had to see the ship's doctor about his myopia, but right now he just didn't have the time. Finally, his friends finished their initial round of celebrating.

"This calls for a toast," said Gerlach. "Let's see if we can bribe the galley crew to break open the beer." The others laughed.

"What's your assignment, Dexter?" Connie asked smugly.

"That's the best part," he giggled in reply, nodding like a grinning jack-in-the-box. "I'm the new Systems Officer Apprentice. We'll all be working together on the bridge. Isn't that great?"

Connie and Gerlach were too stunned to reply;. Martindale was too busy laughing.

"ENEMY DESTROYED! Hah!" Weapons Officer Karen Palmer jumped up from her station and circled around her chair in a victory dance. At forty, she was older than the rest of the bridge crew, with blond-streaked hair and piercing blue eyes. Today, for the first time, glee had chased the anger from her face. It was the first kill they'd made at Difficulty Level Two, and it couldn't have come at a better time. Commander Ashton usually held his temper in fine trim for an hour, but after that all bets were off. And they'd been living on borrowed time for the last three simulations.

"Lt. Palmer," Jeremy laughed. "Let us know when you're ready."

"Can't we take a break, Jeremy?" asked Lt. Commander Ronald Talbert, the ship's navigator. "We've been at this for a long time already, and we're starting to lose whatever sharpness we had in the first place."

"Systems?"

"Computer gives us an eighty-one, Mr. Ashton," said Chief Andersen, the yeoman assisting them on the bridge while the captain made up his mind on permanent assignments. "That's the best score we've ever gotten."

"All right, take ten. But don't any of you leave the bridge."

"Unless— "

"Right you are, Miss Palmer. Unless you're needed in the head, as Chief Connors would say."

Jeremy wandered off the bridge. The captain's chair was the hardest bridge station by far, and he needed some air and something cool to drink. The water fountain in the hallway leading to the bridge shell would do quite nicely, he thought. He had to clear his head before facing another round in the hot seat.

When Jeremy had gone, Talbert spun the navigator's chair halfway around, then rose to stretch his legs. He was a tall man, with dark features contracting into a permanent scowl. His jet black hair was combed straight back, and body hair seemed to ooze from every pore not covered by his standard blues.

"I won't repeat this in front of Ashton," Talbert said; in Jeremy's absence he was the highest ranking officer on the bridge. "But I could strangle that witless Isitian."

"How so?" asked Underwood, the communications officer. A technician through and through, he could not understand why he had to participate in these endless bridge drills when there was still work to do on the communications systems on board. He hesitated mentioning this to Mr. Ashton, who seemed to have enough troubles of his own these days.

"I'll tell you, Lieutenant—that maniac has ruined the navigation computer. Completely ruined it! He reprogrammed the damn thing so that it doesn't respond the way it should. Fixed it, he says. But now it's all wrong. It's set to different guideposts. I have to relearn everything."

"I'll tell you what I don't like," said Palmer. "I don't like the fact that we're up here slaving our butts away while he's gallivanting around the ship without a care in the world. The only time I've seen him up here is once after drills. And all he did then was pace around and about the bridge, listening to the computer telling him when the guns were fully charged—over and over and over again. Then he left, right as time neared for our second session of the day. It's bad for morale. I mean, what does he think? That he's too good to drill with us on the bridge?"

Janet Mendelson had vowed never again to defend Cook to his detractors, and had succeeded since coming aboard. When put to the test, she found that old habits were hard to outgrow.

"Actually," she said matter-of-factly, "he is."

"Oh, really?" scoffed Talbert. "And I suppose pacing around an empty bridge is supposed to give him some sort of mystique—like the ghost of the *Canada Royal*?"

"He's getting a feel for the rhythm of the ship," Janet said, to the disbelieving groans of the others.

"Right."

"I know I can't explain it," Janet responded defensively. "But he was something of a musician in his younger days, and that's how he senses the way the ship will respond, and how to time his commands. That's why he's having Jeremy conduct the bridge drills. Cook has better things to do with his time. He prefers to be visible— "

"I can imagine some of those better things," Talbert sneered. "Though I always thought it took two to tango. And he must be so lonely with his dance partner busy on the bridge all day."

Janet blushed a furious red, and struggled to maintain her temper. "I've never said that Cook wasn't a jerk—although, Mr. Talbert, I can already tell that he will not be the biggest jerk aboard this ship. But I'll tell you this: he is the best captain any of us will ever serve under."

"The voice of experience, Missy?" Talbert said wickedly. Titters echoed across the bridge and burned in Janet's ears.

"The voice of experience is telling you," she shot back angrily, "that when Captain Cook finally does come to the bridge, you, Commander Talbert, will have the most difficult time of any of us. The captain is hard—mark me, very hard—on his navigators."

Janet slumped back in her chair. She had no stomach for Talbert's salacious smirk. Besides, Jeremy was due back on the bridge any time now, and she wanted to practice their last maneuver. Even if she had brought them smartly within striking distance, it had been far too sloppy.

The voices around her soon faded from her awareness, leaving her alone with her thoughts and her professional pride. The captain was hard on his navigator, she mused bitterly, replaying the last "Hard a-Starboard" to see where she'd gone wrong. But he was even harder on his helmsman.

"The CONSTANTINE isn't where she belongs!" barked the image on the monitor screen. "Explain yourself, Commander!"

Cold and austere, Commodore Jefferson McKinley Jones had a reputation for tactical brilliance, but he was not the most patient commander in the fleet. He'd won the gold medal at the semi-annual maneuvers five times running, and didn't like having his orders ignored. Especially when his deployment instructions were being disputed by a hot shot newcomer. The Jones temper was legendary, and his fiery blue eyes looked like they could burn a hole through space itself.

"We are the only ship in this sector, Commodore," Cook replied earnestly. "If the enemy attacks us here, they'll open a breach ten klicks wide, along our entire flank. In my opinion, this is precisely where the enemy will strike—because it's precisely where we've given them an opening."

"Those morons from Looking Glass couldn't strike an asteroid if they were sitting on it," Jones snapped. "I have McIntyre's whole attack wing pinned down OVER HERE—and THIS is where I want you."

"With all due respect, Commodore...."

"No, Cook—you get your sorry Isitian ass here, on the double. And bring your damn ship with you."

Janet couldn't understand why the Skipper was being so stubborn. The skies in front of them were clear, and most of the action was far to the east. The wing commander's orders seemed perfectly reasonable to her, and Skipper had already pushed his orders to the limit.

"Commodore— "

"Now, Commander," the commodore snarled.

"Commander Cook—activity on portside, Screen Number Two," came an accented voice from the systems desk. The executive officer turned to face the command seat, panic in his eyes.

"We are under attack," said François LaRue.

Janet glanced at the screen and gasped. Across the entire sector, hundreds of ships from the Red Fleet had appeared, heading right toward their position.

"Commodore...," began the Skipper.

"Hold them as best you can," Jones fumed. "We'll be along as soon as we disengage here. ST. GEORGE out!"

"Mr. LaRue, sound battle stations. Helm, come about—heading 770, ten degrees north. Weapons—charge the forward shields and stand by the starboard guns.

"Mr. Cardinale—"

"Sir!" replied the navigator, moving to the edge of his chair; Cook rose from the command chair and tapped him on the shoulder.

"Stand down."

"Commander!" the young officer protested.

"Helm—take us due north, 250 degrees."

Without thinking, Janet lifted the ship from its directional plane, taking it well above the Red Fleet's vector of attack.

"No disrespect intended, Lieutenant," Cook said, physically ushering his navigator from his station, "and I apologize for any inconvenience. You may remain on the bridge—sit at the command chair, if you like. But things will be a bit dicey for the foreseeable future—we're going to have to move very quickly— and I won't have time to be giving you orders."

"Sir—!"

"Command seat—NOW!" barked Cook.

As the Skipper plopped into the seat beside her, Janet felt her heart racing. They'd never practiced it this way. And there was no way they were going to be able to stand against all those ships.

"Just follow the plots on your screen," Cook whispered to her, "and hope for the best."

"I just hope you know what you're doing," she replied softly. "We never trained for this, you know." She saw the navigation arc plotted—a tight line that would bring their ship racing along the top of the enemy fleet. She adjusted her instruments and took a deep breath.

"No promises, Missy," said Cook, his eyes fixed on the moni- tors, his fingers racing over the navigation controls. "I haven't trained for it, either. Nobody ever trains for this sort of thing, when it comes right down to it. I'm making this up as we go along.

"Weapons—blank all shields except those on the keel, and charge all forward guns."

"Aye sir."

"Helm—slow to C-2."

"Guns amain, Commander."

Soon, the CONSTANTINE swooped down to confront the ad- vanced line of the Red Fleet, and Janet felt herself becoming one with the ship. Her world was the Skipper's voice, and she found herself bending along with the effortless arcs he plotted and re- plotted on her screen. Soon, the rest of the crew began bouncing off walls and ceilings as the two of them sent the ship darting and weaving like a whole swarm of bees, bringing the enemy *attack wing nearly to a halt as the lone Blue ship scored hit after hit. Before long they had thoroughly disrupted the Red formation, luring two squadrons of Red attackers away from the main body of their fleet to deal with the source of the annoyance, grinding the entire Red attack to a halt.*

But the battle didn't last long. The CONSTANTINE couldn't stand forever against an entire attack wing. Five minutes later, the grading computers scored a kill, relieving the CONSTANTINE from further participation in the maneuvers. A minute later the Blue Fleet arrived to begin their counterattack.

Except for the ship's navigator, and the Skipper, the bridge crew of the CONSTANTINE was ecstatic. They'd managed to fend off the entire enemy fleet single-handedly. At least for a time. And, after all, their deaths were only theoretical. It wouldn't matter that some desk jockey muckety-muck would later disqualify them for consideration for the gold medal for the best performance by a ship of the line, because their ship didn't survive the engagement. They'd proven themselves—to each other, and to the rest of the fleet.

And none of them would ever look at the Skipper in quite the same way again.

* * *

"SWING THAT lantern this way, Crewman. We need better light to check the connection."

Chief Andersen waited as the redshirt clambered over the connector cables. The engine coils were always the trickiest part of a ship to unglitch. Even on a frigate, the coils never worked quite right until the ship had been in space for at least a month, letting the crew figure out what was wrong under conditions of actual use. And the eight-foot high, straighter-than-a-preacher coils on the smaller ships were child's play, compared to those on a cruiser or starship. Omni-directional steerage may have made Terran warships more maneuverable, but it made their propulsion system hopelessly complex. Instead of beaming the engine's subspace energy waves forward in single-directioned simplicity, cruiser coils—or their twenty-foot high cousins on the larger starships—circled the ship in arcs of coiled power, spiraling outward from the outer edge of the interior plating to the final abutments of the inner hull, interlaced with multidirectional links to the power release valves of the outer hull. This let the helm send the ship in any direction at full power while maintaining a constant forward view. It was a masterwork of engineering but a technician's nightmare, and the failure of the lighting system wasn't making their job any easier.

"Crewman?"

"Here you go, Chief." Crewman Apprentice Delaney stopped to wipe his brow. Even with the lights out, the inner hull was like a steam bath. The poor ventilation made the work seem harder, and beads of sweat poured from their bodies like steam from a kettle. With a third of the crew split into inspection teams, readying the coils still promised to take forever. It was the single most hated job on a starship. It was also the most important, for only with the system functioning perfectly, with all relays operational, could the ship perform as it should in space. A starship with plugged power valves was like an eagle flying with a sprained wing.

"What's it look like on the other side?"

"Same as before, Chief," breathed Delaney. "Ramsey and Esshaki keep double-checking the B-12 relay, but the lattice gauge still shows a blockage. Either the gauge is wrong, or it's fucked up somewhere along the line. All the same, I'd hate to trudge all the way back to Supply, only to find out that we've wasted another day's work and have to start all over again from 90-starboard-20."

"I know what you mean, Delaney," Andersen sighed. He leaned against the cable to rest. "I'm getting sick of this myself. Even single shifts are hard enough to bear out here in the mines, and we've been pulling two watches a day for longer than I care to remember. If we don't get some relief—and soon—I swear I'll— "

"Halloo— " called a voice from the darkness, farther down the coil. Andersen estimated its owner to be about fifty yards away, past the bend in the coil.

"Halloo—anybody down there?"

"Over here," shouted Andersen. "And I hope you've brought something cold to drink. We're almost sweating away to nothing."

Footsteps echoes through the coils, as Andersen could see the lantern beam nearing. It seemed to be a solitary visitor, though approaching from an odd direction; as far as he knew, there was nobody working ahead of them on this side of the ship.

"Taking a break?" called the voice.

"You'd best believe it," Andersen growled. "It's the only thing we've done right all day."

The approaching voice was laughing, and soon a bare-chested young man rounded the last turn and finally came into view. Andersen's jaw dropped to the floor in disbelief; it was the captain, a lantern strapped to his waist and his hands holding opposite ends of the blue T-shirt draped from his neck.

"I know what you mean, Chief," Cook panted. "Those days seem to occur here with alarming regularity."

"Captain!"

"As you were, fellows. It's too hot down here to snap to attention." Cook leaned on the cable next to Andersen, catching his breath as best he could. "Sorry I don't have anything to drink with me. But I have a radio phone up ahead. I'll call when I get back up there."

"Captain—what in God's name— "

"In the meantime, I need one or two men from your crew, Chief."

"Of course, Skipper, but— "

"There's a glitched relay switch up there," breathed Cook. Sweat dripped from every pore on his body. "Fused itself together like ore station slag. It's created an electro-magnetic anomaly. I think that's what caused the lights to fritz out, and it's probably wreaking havoc on all the electrical equipment you're using here. I brought a replacement down with me and tried to fix it myself, but the damn thing won't budge an inch. Well, at least it's no respecter of rank. If I can borrow a couple of your men for a while, and maybe a cutting torch as well, we may be able to get everyone back on track."

Slowly, the rest of Andersen's team gathered to see if the voice was really the captain's. Ignoring Andersen's intimidating glower, and in an unsteady voice, Metz asked when they could expect improvement in the food in the galley; Cook replied: "About the time the whales return to Ishtar." Emboldened, Fishman wondered aloud when they could expect a few more female crewmen to grace the ship, so the enlisted crew could enjoy the same "advantages of home" as the blueshirts; "Probably when we're all done sweating," laughed the captain. As the others traded gripes and quips with their Skipper, the exhaustion that had dogged them for the past few days all but vanished. For the moment, and even deep within the mines, the darkness lifted from their spirits. Their double shifts ceased to be an endless purgatory, and seemed instead what they had always been: a minor necessity dictated by their limited numbers and the size of the task that faced them. The captain's quick wit and saucy irreverence gave them the best refreshment they'd had in weeks—a hearty laugh with someone who understood and shared their troubles.

Ten minutes later, when Cook left with Doyle and Derderian to repair the fused power relay, none of the men even winced when Andersen called for them to resume their duties. They worked with a will they hadn't shown in days, and as the reams of sweat poured from their brows they felt not weariness or fatigue, but exhilaration.

Chapter 13

THE HOURS TURNED into days, the days into weeks. Slowly things began to take shape, as each small improvement inched the great ship closer to readiness. The progress, too slow for anyone but the captain to notice, gave no lift to the crew's foundering morale. Yet even the diehard whiners had to admit that the captain pushed himself harder than any of his subordinates, and he was pulling the whole crew along by the sheer force of his example. Though Cook no longer spent time lecturing on philosophy or Old Earth history to his first officer, or helping his chief engineer improve the networking of the ship's computers, he made rounds each day, spending at least an hour walking the decks, talking to crewman on all decks, laughing along with all ranks and stations and letting them air any complaints or grievances they might have.

Even so, some on the *d'Artagnan* spent the better part of the day wondering when it all would end; foremost among them was Roscoe Cook himself.

```
cc:        142-9835.7
FILE:      Log
ACCESS:    Command.
SECURITY:  Standard
OPERATIONAL STATUS: Repairs in Progress
LOCATION:  SB 114, Ishtar Command/Dry Dock
Twelve of the fifteen main engine batteries are now operational,
and preliminary tests are proceeding on schedule. However,
unexpected problems in the engine coils will probably force
postponement of full tests for at least a week, making it unlikely
that we will meet our target goal of starworthiness by the end of
the current cosmic year, or meet the necessary inspection
requirements for participation in upcoming maneuvers. Engine
coil difficulties seem to stem from design defects in several
```

pieces of new equipment. I have forwarded a full report to Fleet Headquarters, so that the contractors can correct flaws before the prototype begins full production.

Full crew complement of 650 is now on board, although I estimate that we could use at least another 150 hands to help ready the ship, and expect to keep the crew on double shifts for the foreseeable future. Chief Engineer Van Horn anticipates that....

The bell sounded on the communications console next to Cook's desk. The signal—long, two short, long again—told him he had an incoming call from the base. He pressed the intercom button, impatient at the interruption.

"Yes?"

"Lt. Nkwete calling from Fleet Dispatch."

Wearily, Cook leaned back in his chair, stricken with guilt. Vera Nkwete was a close friend from his Academy days, but they'd lost touch over the years. He'd been reluctant to call her when the *Constantine* came into port, but knew she'd feel hurt if he didn't. Besides, with his promotion he felt the need to celebrate, even if it meant bringing more complications to his life. Now, though, his office was still in chaos, and most days he still couldn't quite see the top of his desk through the clutter. His shelves still had stacks of info-disks waiting to be filed, and he barely had time to keep up with the minimum amount of paperwork that regulations demanded. However pleasant they might be, he sighed, he had no time for distractions.

"Captain?"

"I'll take it right here, Yeoman. Thank you."

Cook sighed as he waited for Vera to appear on the screen, and purged himself of all feelings of irritation. He could imagine the course their conversation would take, and knew that he deserved every syllable of abuse he had coming.

"Hello, Vera," Cook forced a smile as her image appeared on the screen. With each passing second, as she delayed responding and gazed silently into his eyes, Cook became more and more uncomfortable. Finally, he could stand it no longer.

"Vera— " he began, only to be cut short.

"Do you realize how long it's been, Roscoe?"

Cook nodded sheepishly. "It's been nearly a week, I know...."

"It's been fifteen days since you last called," she interrupted haughtily. "Fifteen days of waiting for you to trouble yourself to pick up the vidphone, or have your yeoman do it for you if you couldn't be bothered to place the call yourself. And do you know how long it was before then?"

"Well— "

"It was another ten days, Roscoe. You know, it is very difficult for me like this. But the least you could do— "

"Vera," Cook said, as she began to cry. "I know I've been positively awful, ever since— "

"Ever since you and your damn ship came into port," she said sharply. "I don't understand. For the life of me, I don't understand how any human being can devote so much time caring for an unfeeling, unhuman—machine."

"Vera— "

"No, I'm sorry for troubling you," she snapped."I'll talk to you later. Goodbye."

Cook stared at the blank screen for several minutes before returning to his console to finish his log entry for the day. Before long, he was on his way to the Molecular Transmitter, to help the Chief Engineer restore some order. Over the past few days, repair crews had all but reduced the regulator to its components, looking for the tiny breach in the wire insulation that was causing the system to short circuit whenever they tried to test it. After that, the corridor hatches needed inspecting and their sick bay needed another overhaul to get the medical computers operating again. And he wanted to spend some time wandering around the ship, seeing and being seen by the crew.

As he left, a sliver of light from the hallway door fell across the now-darkened room onto his desk, and beyond it to the wall behind, lingering for a moment on the ancient faces adorning his office until the door closed, and all was dark once more.

"ENEMY FIRE APORT."

"Shields are holding, Mr. Ashton."

"Helm, hard a-starboard; weapons, commence firing."

Jeremy's heart beat heavily as he awaited the outcome. This was their toughest challenge yet—twin frigates, with the computer calibrated to Difficulty Level Two. His mind raced furiously, planning for each contingency, but things seemed to be going well. This was the best they'd ever done on a Level Two simulation. He looked at the side-screen at the captain's chair and felt a surge of triumph: it showed a direct hit on Enemy Number One, knocking it out of action.

"Second frigate approaching astern," said the young ensign at the systems station.

"Navigation, " Jeremy shouted, "plot an arc south of port, heading 750; helm, prepare to swing us around…and, execute."

As the second frigate came into view on the forward screen, Jeremy started to relax for the first time in this simulation. Facing a single enemy was so much simpler; he could now switch full power to the forward guns and not risk another pass by the enemy ship exposing the *d'Artagnan* to another enemy broadside.

"Range, two klicks and closing fast."

"Helm, slow to C-2; weapons, all power to forward guns. Fire when ready."

From the edge of the captain's chair, Jeremy watched the ship's powerful guns blast away at the overmatched enemy frigate, his knuckles turning white as his hands dug into the arm rests. Seconds later, it was all over.

"Sensors show enemy weapons gone, and her shields buckling."

"Thank you, Ensign Dexter," Jeremy smiled. "Lt. Underwood, radio the frigates that we are standing by to accept survivors, and sound the all clear; Lt. Palmer, keep shields up and guns amain. Helm, come to 010 and swing us past the enemy, sublight at quarter power.

"Well, Ensign?"

Dexter punched a blue button to the left of his main screen, then flashed the broadest grin Jeremy had ever seen.

"Computer gives us an eighty-five, Mr. Ashton—an eighty-five!"

Jeremy smiled broadly, and accepted congratulations from the rest of the bridge crew. All were elated, except for the helmsman, who remained oddly subdued. It was their best score, against the toughest simulation they'd faced yet, and Jeremy felt it deserved a proper reward.

"All right people!" he bellowed. "You think we're ready for the Captain?" The cheer that came in response gave him the answer he wanted.

"Mr. Underwood, page the Skipper. Tell him we await his presence on the bridge. In the meantime, the rest of you have ten minutes to relax. Get some food if you want, but be back here at 675 sharp. It's taken us this long to get the Skipper here and we don't want to keep him waiting."

The bridge cleared in a minor stampede, leaving Janet and Jeremy alone. Jeremy stepped from the captain's chair and stepped forward to the helm station, where Janet was busy replaying the last simulation. She was a quiet one, Jeremy smiled, and her reluctance to share her insights on the captain wasn't the only thing about her that was driving him crazy.

"It went well, I thought."

Janet looked up and nodded, though less enthusiastically than Jeremy had hoped. "Yes, I guess it did."

"You find it difficult, working with someone else in the hot seat?"

Janet switched off her station and turned to face Jeremy. "Difficult? No, it's not difficult. It is different, though. And in some ways, it's a welcome change. Besides, you're a refreshing change from the XO on our last ship."

"How do we stack up— "

"To the bridge crew of the *Constantine*?" Janet smiled and tilted her head. Her smile brightened her whole face, thought Jeremy, and her slender uniform complemented every curve. "Everyone here is much more accomplished...."

Jeremy's smile was cut short when Janet finished her sentence.

"But the *Constantine* would cut us to ribbons." The sudden look of dismay on his face made Janet laugh, which only added to Jeremy's consternation.

"Oh, don't worry about it, Jeremy. We'll all get better. But you really should have checked with me before calling the Captain."

"How so?"

Janet bit her lower lip and grimaced girlishly. "He won't like being called yet."

Before Jeremy could ask what she meant, the others began returning to the bridge. Jeremy walked to the systems station, to check his instruments before the captain arrived. When he turned back to look at Janet, he saw her smile at him, then shake her head and turn to her screen. For a moment it made him feel better, until foreboding seeped into his consciousness, and he suddenly realized how little he knew about the captain, even after all these weeks.

* * *

"SO THE SKIPPER's finally going to make his grand entrance," Gerlach whispered. The regular bridge crew was already at stations, busying themselves with final adjustments on the equipment. The rookies all gathered on the sidelines to watch. Three yeoman on the bridge freed the younger officers from running errands.

"I still don't understand why everyone's making all this fuss," said Connie. She felt a tenseness in the air, a current of concern about drilling under the eyes of their commander. Some of the regulars had even changed into fresh standard blues during the break. To her, it all seemed a bit much. After all, if the captain didn't think enough of them to drill together, she couldn't see the point of making a special effort to impress him.

"Well, Connie," responded Dexter; "this is our first chance to show the Skipper what we can do. Everyone's probably worried about the impression we'll make. After all, it isn't every day that you have the opportunity to make a first one. Impression, I mean. Besides, from what I've heard about the Skipper…"

Connie tuned Dexter out, letting him babble to his heart's content. She was more interested in exchanging words and glances with the handsome Academy ensign to her left. All conversation halted as the captain strode onto the bridge and all hands jumped to attention—except at the helmsman's station, where Janet first looked about, then slowly rose, trying not to appear conspicuous.

"As you were," Cook smiled. He was dressed in dark blue fatigues and carried a cup of coffee in his left hand. "I appreciate the effort, but the bridge is no place for strict formalities. I'd rather have you stay at your posts, especially if we're in the middle of a battle. For the future, don't bother snapping to attention as long as we're on the bridge. I'm sure we'll find it less distracting that way."

Looking slightly bored and mildly amused, Cook glanced about the bridge. He noticed the smartness of the uniforms and the keyed emotions displayed by the crew. It pleased him, but he was careful not to show it. There was no need to ruin a promising collection of bridge officers by giving them a prematurely high opinion of themselves.

"Mr. Ashton," Cook said, an edge of disbelief to his voice, "I understand you people have something to show me."

"Yes, Captain. I think you'll be pleased." Jeremy noticed that Janet was rolling her eyes; it did nothing to ease his anxiety.

"Well, let's hope so." Cook sipped his coffee casually and smiled blandly. He stepped to the captain's chair and placed his cup on the arm rest, then turned to face the forward screens. "All right, let's see what we have.

"Oh—and Mr. Underwood, I don't think we'll be needing you right now. I'm sure you have other things to do. Yeoman Bernacki can fill in for you here."

"Thank you, sir," said the startled radio officer; as Bernacki approached the station, Underwood hurried from the bridge, grateful for small favors. The bridge hatch closed behind him just as the tall greenshirt settled in to the console.

"Will we really be needing the rookies, either?" smirked Talbert. "I understand most of them are Techies."

"Now, now—let's not be elitist, Mr. Talbert," Cook smiled coldly. "Not all of us are fortunate enough to be in the bottom third of an Academy graduating class, now are we?"

Nervous laughter coursed over the bridge, and Talbert blushed in embarrassment. The senior officers turned to man their stations. Cook glanced briefly at the rookies, seated on displaced galley chairs on the starboard side of the bridge, then circled behind the captain's chair and walked slowly toward the helm station. Pausing for a moment just behind the helmsman, he took a deep breath before turning again, bringing him back to where he had started.

"Let's start off with something easy," he said, scratching the back of his head. The easy indifference of his manner suddenly convinced Jeremy that it had been a terrible mistake to invite him to the bridge. Almost at once, Cook confirmed all misgivings, sending prickles down the backs of everyone on the bridge, except for the helmsman, who was busy adjusting her controls

"Mr. Ashton, set the simulator for us to face off against a starship, one-on-one—Difficulty Level Three. And deep space, too. No need to complicate things until we're warmed up." Cook ignored the worried glances that darted across the bridge.

"Are you there, Mr. Ashton?"

"Sorry, sir. One-on-one at Level Three."

"Engage the screens; helm, ahead at C-level 4."

The main viewers came to life, showing stars on all sides of the bridge. At each station, lights began to dance along the consoles, as the computer fed information as it became available.

"Enemy starship bearing 010 by twenty degrees north," announced Jeremy. He was beginning to perspire; they had never faced a cruiser simulation before, much less a starship.

"Range, Mr. Ashton?"

"Sorry, sir. Fifty astrokilometers, closing rapidly with shields raised." Suddenly, Jeremy realized that anxiety was affecting his performance; forgetting the range reading was a midshipman's mistake.

Cook lifted his coffee cup to his lips, then cleared his throat. "Charge all shields, prepare to charge forward and starboard guns," he said. He spoke quietly, the calmness of his manner contrasting sharply with the frantic concentration of his crew. "And Mr. Ashton, you may blank the tactical grid screen; I find it useless and rather distracting."

The rest of the bridge crew exchanged looks of puzzled shock; the tactical grids were their only means of orienting themselves with the outlying space. Cook smiled blandly.

"No—on second thought, belay the order. The rookies might find it helpful, after all. Miss Mendelson, slow to C-2 and prepare for bank to port; Mr. Talbert, plot a portside arc past the enemy ship, heading 855, south forty-five degrees."

Talbert worked frantically at the navigation console, trying to hurry the computer along so that he could put something on the navigation screen. After several missed entries, the figures finally flashed on his calc-screen and he rushed to put the plot on the board.

"All enemy guns amain," said Ashton; "her shields are at full strength and she's slowed to fighting speed, to C-2."

"Bank dead to port and increase speed to C-5," Cook said serenely, noticing the hesitation everyone but Mendelson showed at the unusual order; increasing speed in mid-melee was highly risky. The physical distention of faster-than-light travel made speeds greater than C-3 dangerous in battle, and almost never tried.

"Miss Palmer, charge forward and starboard guns, and prepare to charge the portside. And Mr. Ashton—no editorializing, if you please. Helm, come inside the navigation arc by six degrees." For the first time, the captain's voice showed signs of irritation, but it passed quickly. Cook began to stroll slowly around the bridge, sipping his coffee and looking over shoulders at the bridge stations as he passed.

"Range—twenty astrometers; enemy speed steady."

"Helm, cut to C-1; barrel roll left and continue south apace."

Baffled by the unfamiliar order, Palmer and Talbert both turned to look at Janet; Jeremy was too busy working his scanners, but found the subdued tone of Cook's voice disquieting. All three found the pace too brisk to follow: though never raising his voice, Cook's commands came in sharp, staccato bursts, too quickly for them to follow what was happening elsewhere on the bridge. As the captain came to stand aft of their respective stations, looking over their shoulders as if they were naughty schoolchildren, each of them felt acutely embarrassed, though none could quite say why.

Cook ignored the puzzled looks and continued, his voice calm and businesslike. "Charge portside guns and blank the starboard." Cook walked slowly from the navigator's desk to the weapons station on the port side of the bridge.

"Helm, pivot twelve points to starboard. Miss Palmer, lock target and prepare the portside guns; and...fire."

Nothing happened; the enemy ship's salvo missed the ship by a wide margin, but the *d'Artagnan*'s guns did not fire at all.

"Portside guns amain," Cook said in a weary tone of voice, and snapped his fingers; instantly, a red light flashed on the weapons console, showing that the main portside batteries were now ready to fire. He sighed, then walked to the captain's chair and placed his cup on the armrest before turning to face the crew.

"Really, Mr. Ashton," he said, his voice heavy with disappointment. "I thought these people were ready. But, obviously not."

The bridge was silent as a lifeless moon. It was apparent that things had not gone well, but nobody knew what had gone wrong—not even Janet, who had been too busy minding the helm to pay attention to anything else.

"Well, as long as I'm here," he smiled, sounding very much like an Academy instructor. Turning to every station in turn, his voice lacked harshness or rancor, but carried undertones of judgment that made clear the extent to which each had fallen short of what was expected. The effect on the crew was devastating.

"Miss Palmer, if you check the computer record you will find that you forgot to blank the starboard guns as I'd ordered. This meant a delay in charging the portside guns and caused us to muff our shot.

"Mr. Talbert, your course swung us too wide by nearly ten astrometers. Even worse, when corrected you made no attempt to amend your course plot on the navigation screen so that the helmsman could anticipate and adjust her settings. I expect you to plot us as closely as possible to the optimum; Miss Mendelson will ease us off whenever the laws of physics demand it."

Talbert was about to protest, but was cut short.

"Mr. Ashton," Cook smiled a bland smile; Jeremy thought he saw a momentary flash of amusement in the captain's eyes.

"Mr. Ashton—I will ascribe your failure to take a second reading of the enemy shields as we approached to the fact that you've been drilling in my chair, and have ignored your own station in the process. But mark this—I overlook mistakes like that exactly once.

"And Miss Mendelson," Cook began. He brought his index finger to his lips, as if choosing his words with the utmost care.

After a long pause, he said simply: "You almost have it."

Cook's eyes passed leisurely around the bridge, lingering briefly as his gaze crossed the rookie bridge officers.

"It looks to me like you people still have some work to do," he said at last. "Mr. Ashton, when you've mastered Level Three, you know how to reach me." He started toward the portside exit, sipping at his coffee.

"Excuse me, Captain." It was Talbert; everyone else on the bridge winced. Cook merely turned in place, fixing a curious gaze on his navigator.

"Yes, Mr. Talbert; what is it?"

Under the captain's merciless glare, Talbert felt his voice die in his throat, but it was too late for him to back down. "Excuse me, sir, but what do you mean by 'mastered?' "

"Mastered, Mr. Talbert," Cook said coldly, "means that the computer routinely gives you a perfect score of one hundred." He smiled grimly, as if he could read the shock on the faces of his bridge crew. "However," he continued, shifting his gaze to his first officer, "you may call me when your collective Level Three score hits ninety for the third time in a row."

"Ninety?" The words had spurted out before Jeremy had a chance to think; at the Academy, even his best scores barely reached the nineties.

"Oh, that shouldn't be too difficult, Mr. Ashton," Cook smiled humorlessly. "You can always use Mendelson's score to boost the average. Already I'd give her about a ninety-two, though the computer's probably a little more generous."

He nodded toward the rookies. "And I'll be satisfied with a Level Two score of ninety from the others.

"Actually," he smirked, "it should prove a rather close race. Carry on." And he left the bridge, the hatch door closing behind him with a soft whoosh.

"That arrogant son of a bitch," snapped Talbert, as soon as Cook was out of earshot. But nobody responded; not one of them even heard him. For the time being, each was lost in his own private world.

Jeremy swivelled his chair to face the system's station. He pushed a green button to the left of his center screen, activating the simulation computer to call up the helmsman's score from the last simulation. His heart sank when it appeared on the screen.

It read: "Helm: 93."

His heart pounding like a kettle drum, Jeremy called up the score for the command chair. The image from the screen burned indelibly into his memory.

"Command Station," read the screen. "Simulation Score: Timing—100; Strategic Design—100; Tactics—100."

* * *

The classroom fell silent as the instructor, a full commander, glared at the troublemaker. A plebe did not belong in the same classroom as upperclassmen, thought the commander—much less in an advanced class like Intra-solar Tactics. He snatched the paper from the student's desk and examined the marks the young man had jotted down. Sure enough, it was exactly correct, just like the last time. Just like every time. But this time, the teacher smiled; this time he was ready. He'd always known that this student was cheating. Finally, he'd be able to prove it.

"Stand up."

Slowly, the young plebe rose to his feet.

"How did you know the correct navigation plot before I even explained the problem?" the commander snarled.

"I just did," the plebe answered uneasily.

"Explain it."

"I'm sorry, Professor. I don't know how to explain it. I've always been able to tell."

"How?"

"I don't really know how. I just do."

"All this from someone who isn't even taking Navigation."

"I passed out of Navigation," replied the student, a slight edge to his voice.

Scowling, the commander returned to his desk and put another problem on the holographic screen. One that wasn't in any of the textbooks they were using. One of his own devising. And one that had an unexpected twist that would prove once and for all that the student wasn't as brilliant as all the other professors kept saying. Soon, the image of an imaginary star system appeared, with the mass and velocity of each planet marked on the screen, just as on a real ship of the line. Glowering as he returned to the young man's side, the commander he barked his command.

"All right, Midshipman Cook—set your course for Planet Two."

"Heading 810 by five degrees north," the plebe answered quietly, without hesitation; as he did, the instructor laughed mockingly.

"Hard when you haven't already gotten the answer, is it?"

"Sir?"

"Here is the correct plot," said the commander. Pushing a button on his controller, the computer displayed a navigation on the map, arcing in the opposite direction from the student's chosen course, and using the gravitational pull of the system's primary planet to accelerate toward the target planet.

"Heading 250 is the correct answer, Plebe. Swinging past the giant Planet Seven—which gives us our best trajectory toward *our destination. Now, do you care to explain why you're so far off, this time—when the problem isn't in one of our textbooks, and you couldn't have stolen the answer from the library's computers?"*

"With due respect, sir—that course is not optimal."

"I plotted in myself, Plebe."

"And if the computer was programmed along the same parameters," the young man continued quietly, "it would probably make the same mistake when you checked it."

"What mistake?"

"If you'll reset the controls and include the mass of the system's sun in the problem...."

His eyes widening, the commander pressed the button to recalculate the parameters. A sinking feeling in the pit of his stomach told him that he'd been so intent on using the giant planet that he completely forgot to enter the region's dominant gravity well into the governing equations. His heart sank when the navigation plot revealed the corrected optimal heading.

Heading 810, by five degrees north.

"Your heading would be best in open space, with no nearby star," offered the plebe.

His face softening, the commander nodded.

"It's almost like a melody I can hear," the young man whispered, squinting as he tried to explain. "All the vectors and gravity wells are kind of like notes and swells that pop into my head whenever I look at the stars. I just follow the melody...and that's the course to take."

"Thank you, Midshipman. Please take your seat."

* * *

"I STILL don't understand him."

"Welcome to the club, Jeremy."

Jeremy sipped his cold drink and placed it back on the coaster, then looked at Janet. The Officers' Lounge was almost empty; a junior engineer in the small study beyond the bend was their only company. Jeremy looked up at the observation screen looming over their booth. It showed eastward, toward Looking Glass and alien skies. There was a pensive, reflective gloss to his eyes that Janet had never seen before.

"He expects us to perform with machine tool precision, but he's never around. Never even lets us know what he wants from us. How are we supposed to live up to his standards if he doesn't care enough to show us how to do things his way?"

Janet laughed; she had a merry laugh, Jeremy thought, like a young lady swept up in the excitement of her first dance. "The Weapons Officer on the *Constantine* asked him that. Right in front of everyone on the bridge, sort of like Talbert did today...before Cook assigned him to laundry detail for a week. You know what he said?"

Jeremy shook his head.

"Skipper told him that he was a concert pianist and we were his keys, and that he refused to practice on an instrument that wasn't properly tuned."

They both laughed, and Jeremy noticed Janet's eyes brighten whenever she mentioned the captain. He felt something more than curiosity eating away his insides, but he was too much of a gentleman to ask any personal questions.

"You know, Jeremy—well, you were there before Cook's time, so there's no way you could know. But my first year at the Academy was just after he graduated. He was still a tangible presence on the campus, and I don't mean merely that his name was carved on all the award plaques. He was reflected everywhere that year: in the lectures of the professors, in the hallways and classrooms. Even in the eyes of the upperclassmen, and the way they approached their drills and studies. Nothing that he touched was unaffected. And I don't mean that he was universally admired or respected. He left as much bitterness in his wake as anything else. But he affected everyone there quite deeply. They either loved him or they hated him, and both with equal passion.

"Yet, by the time I left, he'd all but faded from memory. You still see his name plastered all over the grounds, if you know where to look. But the plebes who were there when I was a senior only vaguely recall the name. Today they know him only as the midshipman who still holds all the records. They don't have the slightest idea how he'd come to leave his mark, or how he changed the whole tenor of instruction there. Not the slightest idea. The cold record doesn't give any sense of what he was—what he is. You don't get that until you meet him in the flesh."

Jeremy smiled glumly.

"For instance," continued Janet, "you remember the Morgan Simulator—the standard aptitude test they give to all the plebes. You know, the test for multi-dimensional tactical conception?"

Jeremy nodded. "It's a humbling experience. The best score in my class was seventy-five out of two hundred. As I recall, the record was eighty-four, set by Commodore Jones when he was a plebe, a few years earlier."

"I came within five points of old Jefferson McKinley Jones—and the old record," said Janet, "and was the star of my class."

The corners of Jeremy's mouth turned up weakly. "I came in twelfth." He didn't mention his score; though well above the average score of fifty, it was not very impressive.

"Do you know what the current record is—set by none other than Roscoe Andrew Cook?"

"I don't think I want to know."

Janet leaned forward, as if sharing a dark secret. "His score was one hundred seventy-three." She laughed as Jeremy's eyebrows shot toward the ceiling.

"His instructor didn't believe it, either. She was so sure Cook was cheating that they retested him, with the rest of the class invited to watch, to help detect any sign of fraud. The second time around, his score was one-ninety-one. And you know what he said to the instructor then, while he was still strapped into the simulator and the rest of the class was busy checking for a glitch on the computer?"

Jeremy shook his head.

"He said, in that delicious accent of his: 'Shall I try it again? I think I'm starting to get the hang of this thing.'" Janet laughed brightly, her eyes shining like emeralds. "And you know why he's so tough on navigators—why, despite ourselves, we'll probably come to feel sorrier for Talbert than we will for ourselves?"

Janet didn't wait for an answer.

"It's because every ship that he commands will have at least two navigators. And one of them will be the greatest navigator in the history of the Cosmic Guard."

Janet mistook the look in Jeremy's eyes for disbelief.

"You think I'm exaggerating? Well, remember his order to me, to shave six points off Talbert's navigation arc as we approached the enemy ship? He wasn't guessing, Jeremy. Check the computer record and you'll find that we exceeded the optimum approach by exactly six degrees."

Now quite subdued, Jeremy shook his head. "Talbert's mighty fast with the figures, and Cook was wandering around the bridge like a gypsy. There was no way he could— "

"Don't you understand, Jeremy?" Janet interrupted, a distant sparkle lighting her eyes. "He doesn't need the computer. He knows exactly the right navigation plot before it could ever show on a screen. He sees it all in his head. And he does it without even thinking about it."

Slowly, Janet circled the edge of her glass with her finger. "And sometimes, he forgets that we can't."

Jeremy was silent. He sipped his drink and his eyes drifted once more to the viewer, letting his soul wander among the stars. Life in the heavens was often cruel, and often lonely. Friendships bonded men and women together, in the sky as on the ground, helping the days pass as pleasantly as the surroundings allowed, and it was a CosGuard tradition to make the best of things. But wherever fate led them, and whatever came in its wake, it would be hard having a genius in the family.

Chapter 14

"THE PRESIDENT WILL SEE YOU now, Miss Yang."

An overstuffed briefcase in one arm, and a thick file folder in the other, Suzie Yang eased past the receptionist, a matronly woman too busy being important to open the large oak door leading into the East Office for a mere staff aide. Hitting the door latch with her elbow, Suzie edged the door open and guided it the rest of the way with her forearm. Inside, she closed the door with her foot.

"Miss Yang!" Tossing some papers into a large pile on his work stand, Mikos Sarkisian, president of the Terran League sprang from behind his desk. "Here, let me help you."

He took the briefcase and escorted his petite director of communications to the oversized visitor's chair in front of the president's desk. The young woman plopped down, amazed that she had dropped the folder on her way from the North Wing only twice. The president put the briefcase on the edge of his desk. Outside, the sun shined gloriously in the cloudless sky. Through the window, Suzie could see the green leaves swaying in the breeze, and the sights and smells of the Presidential Gardens still haunted her senses. It was not the kind of day she wanted to spend inside, but she didn't have a choice in the matter.

"You wanted to see me, Mr. President?"

"Mrs. Dalrymple," said the president, pressing the button on the intercom. "Could you please bring us some tea?" Sarkisian sat on the front of his desk. He wore a ragged old coat, with patches on the sleeves. Suzie thought the president looked more like a professor than like a politician, and often wondered whether it was an image he tried to cultivate. His desk, after all, was immaculate—every item was in its place, and his in-basket was empty.

"Did you bring your family scrapbook, Miss Yang?" the president smiled.

"You said to bring the whole file."

"So I did."

Sarkisian walked slowly past the window, then resumed his seat behind the desk.

"Last year's trip to Mountain Villa was a logistical disaster," Suzie began. "You told Records to keep every brochure and paper scrap that we could piece together, so that things would go more smoothly next time."

Sarkisian looked inside the briefcase. It was the most disjointed collection of tourist memorabilia he had ever seen.

"Unfortunately," Suzie smiled wanly, "Records never did get around to organizing what they'd collected. The result is.... "

"I see the result," the president chuckled. "I guess we can forget about learning from past experience."

"As for the itinerary," Suzie continued, "the only definite commitment we have is the rally for Senator Hanlon. Everything else is flexible. The Villa Theatre even said they'd hold a box open at the opera for your entire stay, so you can have your choice of performances.

"But the big problem will be— "

"Sunday night's speech at the Lake Armstrong press banquet," Sarkisian finished. "I know, everyone expects a major address on some topic or other. And it seems that no matter what I say, they're always disappointed. The simple truth is that with the peace talks and Senate both about to recess, there's very little to say. Why can't these people accept the fact that they can't orchestrate history to fit a timetable? Besides, I've said about all I care to say on almost any topic you care to mention."

"The Tories will complain if you don't say something."

"The Tories will complain if I *do* say something, Miss Yang. The Tories are always complaining," Sarkisian snapped. He was sorry almost at once, and quickly apologized. There was no reason to vent his frustrations on everyone who worked for him; besides, Mikoyan already had that job.

"That's all right, Mr. President," Suzie said. "We're all feeling the pressure these days."

"And I want you to write the speech yourself, Miss Yang," the president smiled. "The rest of the staff hardly matches your grace of expression. I'll leave the topic to you."

"Is there anything I should know, Mr. President? The rumor mill is rife with speculation. A cabinet shuffle, perhaps? If there's anything you want me to avoid.... "

"No," the president said distantly. "There are a few projects in the works but it's best you know nothing about them. Military security and all, you understand."

Yang nodded, though CosGuard maneuvers were fairly routine, and the next scheduled exercise was a month or two away. It seemed odd that the president would worry about something like that, but she let it pass.

"Write something about the recess in the peace talks, I guess. How reconvening on an alien world is a great advance, how lucky we are to be alive at a time when Man is finally reaching across the heavens to clasp an alien hand in friendship, that sort of thing."

"You should write your own speeches more often, Mr. President. You have quite an ear for rhetoric."

The president chuckled amiably. "Part of the job, Miss Yang. Ah, here comes our tea."

* * *

"AS YOU WERE, men. You fellows need anything?"

"No, Skipper. Nothing here we can't handle. We've been over the relay switches once already. We're double-checking, that's all. These ancillary guns can be tricky."

"You are— "

"Patterson, sir. Crewman Technician Patterson. And that's Bartee, and Baughman, and Ramirez."

"You know, you'll get better readings from your circuitry block if you staunch the input valves on either side—like this—then ease the inserts into place so that they brush against the back of the galvo-meter...like...there. See?"

"Thanks, Skipper. Academy teach you tricks like that?"

"Hardly. It was a grizzled old yeoman, too impatient to stand by while some tyro blueshirt fumbled around, eating into everyone's down time. Got my head chewed off that time, but I never forgot the technique."

"How's the rest of the ship coming along?"

"Coming slow, but coming. Never a dull moment, you know. Carry on, gentlemen—and keep up the good work."

"Aye aye, Skipper."

"Wait. He's out of range now."

"I hear he's really reaming the blueshirts. They're sweating twice the bullets we are. And are even pulling triple shifts."

"Hey, enough of that. We've got work to do."

"Oh, come on, Paddy."

"You heard the Skipper, back to work. And with a will, this time. We're already behind schedule, and we'll never get things trim by New Year if we don't pull our weight."

"Oh, all right."

"Yeah, look who's bucking for yeoman."

"With a will, gentlemen, or you'll have a real greenshirt on your butt before you know it."

* * *

THE PORTRAITS and wall-hangings were stored in packing crates for the trip home. For diplomats and aides alike, the Terran wasteland was one lodging none were sad to leave. In friendlier surroundings, empty walls were symbols of passing; on this strange world, emptiness fitted the planet nicely. But the *glashenzhi* blossoms growing in a pot near the door gave the room a lilting fragrance, awakening the mood of renewal and warmth, and the promise that their long trip would bring them back to less rigorous surroundings. They were finally departing from the cold wasteland that the Terrans called *Sh'tar*, and they were leaving with hope. The talks would resume soon on the Crutchtan planet *Gr'Shuna*, the capital of the Shunite Region. And the Terran ambassador had promised to bring a response to their newest proposal for a two-generation moratorium on settlements.

Zatar sat alone in the small, windowless room that had served as the central meeting place for the delegation of the Grand Alliance. The floor was hard—Terran floors were not made for sitting—and most of the cushions were already packed for the trip. From the start, misgivings had haunted his thoughts, misgivings about the length of the trip and the harsh alien climate, but mostly about the Terrans themselves. When he arrived they had seemed so brusque and aggressive, like buduri guarding their harems. Even after the Veshnans arrived to take charge of the talks, Terran and Crutchtan negotiators could barely keep from shouting across the table. It had taken all of Zatar's skill as a diplomat to enforce minimal standards of civility at their early sessions, as the participants insisted on acting like uncivilized children. For the longest time, they seemed destined to measure their progress by eons. Zatar had even begun to entertain thoughts that the radical anthrobiologists might be right after all, and that the mutual aversion felt by Terran and Crutchtan alike might stem from passions deeper than simple rivalry. Scientific ridicule had long since buried the notion that organic chemistry had anything to do with racial antipathy, but there was something sinister in the visceral hatreds that he saw rising around him, something ancient and unsettling.

The wind gusted noisily outside and Zatar could feel the barrenness around him. Despite their mistrust, he thought with satisfaction, both sides had made substantial progress. The Crutchtans no longer insisted on foreclosing contact between the races, now and forever; the Terrans seemed willing to limit and delay their eastward expansion for the sake of peace. It confirmed what Zatar had long believed, that the essence of humanity was the capacity to transcend animal passions and soar to heaven on the wings of dreams. And with the arrival of *Gr'Raun-te*, the latest Terran ambassador, they had started viewing one another as they should have from the start—not as monsters, but as different species of human being. They still had far to go to achieve a real peace, but the first tentative steps had been taken. They now discussed their differences, rather than talking across their fears.

"Zatar?"

Zatar turned to see his favorite translator walking slowly toward him through the emptiness of the deserted room.

"Yes, Munshi. What is it?"

"Our belongings are packed and ready to take to the transfer point. Do you require anything else?"

Zatar smiled. "No, you and the others may leave when you like. I will follow shortly."

"You will actually miss this place, won't you?"

Zatar stood to look out the thin window. The narrow slit showed little of the outside, but he could see dust whipping through the air, like a pelting rainstorm on the warm worlds of home. Desolation was everywhere, even in the city. The Terran delegates themselves were often heard to grumble about holding such important talks on such a world, and Zatar could not imagine a less hospitable planet to host emissaries from other civilizations. At the same time, he had grown used to the heavy clothing the planet forced upon its inhabitants. There was a rough elegance to the landscape, like the pictures of the lifeless moons and asteroids he had first seen as a child. He had always found it difficult to imagine a place without rain or soft grass, in which sun and cold beat the senses with equal ferocity. Most of all, his soul burned with a hunger he had never known—for a place where men were looked upon as equals to be respected, not as distractions to be indulged, and where there was no need to prove that success was not a fluke, but was earned by the sweat of a back or the power of a brain. It amused and saddened him to know that among the Terrans, his status—the lone male in a house of Veshnan women—was the object of envy.

He turned to Munshi and smiled; she was so pretty, and her mouth danced playfully, a teasing promise of pleasures lurking just out of reach. On the Terran starbase, before the final leg of their journey to *Sh'tar*, she went into heat quite unexpectedly, causing a week-long delay in the talks before her cycle ran its course; even then, he wasn't the same for another week. Munshi was different from the rest; hers was the pleasure of soft summer nights, shared with a favored companion. Now, his nose told him that she was starting again; it would be a pleasant trip home.

"I miss people, not places," he said at last, quoting the old proverb. His smile was the tranquility of one at peace with his soul. "We've been here long enough. I'm ready to go home."

She eased close beside him and purred like a breeze. "The others have gone ahead. I told them we'd join them after checking our house one last time."

Gently as sleep, he stroked her face; she took his hand and led him up the stairs.

* * *

"FIRE!"

"Guns are still recharging, Mr. Ashton."

"Crap! Helm, hard about."

"Guns amain, sir."

"Crap!"

"Jeremy— "

"As you were, Mister. And put the damn plot on the screen. No, belay that, Mr. Dexter. Put a new simulation on the board, instead. Let's start over again."

"Do you want to know our sc— "

"No, Dexter— just put a new simulation on the fricking board!"

"We actually got an eighty-four that time, sir. Can you believe it? And that was despite— "

"Ensign—put a new simulation on the board!"

"Aye aye, sir— (*gee whiz, that's no reason to—*)"

"Ensign Dexter, did you say something you would care to repeat so that we all may hear it?"

"No sir ."

"Then put a new— "

"—a new simulation on the board. Yes, sir."

* * *

SILENCE FILLED Andersen's cabin, and Chief Connors found it a welcome relief. For as long as he could remember, he'd been chasing about the ship like a madman, trying to pull the pieces together, and it was proving too much for him. His feet ached. His eyes hurt. Every muscle in his body hurt, and his brain cried for sleep. Slightly dizzy from the beer they'd swiped from the galley, Connors sprawled on the couch staring at the ceiling, his boots on the floor and his feet propped on an armrest. Smiling like a cheshire cat, Andersen sat on the side chair, his own feet on the lounge table.

"I tell ye, Andersen, it's like to be drivin me mad."

"I know what you mean, Chief."

"I mean it's bad enough to be racing sideways to center when ye have an end in sight. That comes with the territory, an' no spacer worth his weight will carp over an isolated cruncher here and there. But this bloody thing goes on an' on, No tellin when it's going to bloody end."

"Well, you know there's an end coming eventually, Chief."

"Yeah, I suppose I do. But in my bones, I can't feel it comin. An' I sure as bloody hell can't be convincin many redshirts it's a-comin if I can't bloody well convince myself."

"I think they already know, Chief. At least some of them. The ones who really count."

"Ah, rot. Not the ones complainin to me, that's for bloody sure. On top of everything else, the Skipper won't even—ah, rot. Pour me another, Andersen. I've got more brain-numbin to do."

Andersen filled Connors' mug to half-full, emptying the pilfered beer canister of its contents. A knock sounded on the closed cabin door and instantly, as if he'd been expecting another visitor, Andersen sprang to his feet.

"I wonder who that could be?" he asked as he disappeared beyond the foyer panel. Connors was too lost in thought to pay much attention, until a familiar voice sounded from out of his sight.

"Is he here?"

"This way."

"Ah, rot," muttered Connors. He heard the door close, and the privacy bolt swing into place. Andersen stepped from behind the foyer. Behind him, and heading to pull an unoccupied chair next to the couch, was the captain.

"Don't get up, Chief," Cook smiled, his eyes twinkling devilishly. "Looks like you don't need the exertion." Connors grunted in return, and glowered fiercely at his fellow greenshirt. The Yeoman's unspoken code had few words for traitors, none of them kind.

"I understand you have some things on your mind," said Cook. "And they won't get said until we sit down to talk."

Slowly, and still scowling, Connors sat upright on the couch.

"Here," said Cook, handing Connors a package. It was wrapped in plain white tissue paper, with a broken shoelace for a ribbon.

"Call it a peace offering. Go ahead, open it."

Sullenly, Connors undid the bow, and let the wrapping fall on the floor by the couch. It was a bottle of brandy: Isitian brandy, one-hundred proof.

Andersen returned from the next room with three fresh glasses. He insisted they were clean, despite what his guests' eyes might tell them. "It's just the way the light hits them," he explained.

Shaking his head skeptically, Cook opened the bottle and filled the three grimy glasses half-way to the rim. "If that won't loosen your tongue," he told Connors, "there's more in the bottle. Now, drink up."

"But— "

"And that's a direct order, Chief."

A gruff smile crossed his lips. Connors lifted his glass and took a sip. Though it kicked like a stallion, the brandy was smooth as satin and burned joyously as it trickled down his throat. Moments later, he was feeling its effects. Grudgingly, he began to wonder if he hadn't misjudged this blueshirted young quirker after all.

"RIGLEY CLAMP RELEASED."

"Check.

"Musser Valve open."

"Check."

"Transmitter gauge normal."

"Check."

"IshCom reception pods cleared."

"Check."

"All right, Crewman, engage the Molecular Transmitter."

"Aye aye, Mr. Van Horn. Engaging."

Zzzzt.

"Oh, for crying out loud."

"Mr. Van Horn!"

"Damage Control Repair Crew, report to Molly Trans, on the double.

"Do you— "

"For the love of— "

"Mr. Van Horn!"

"Yes, I see it...."

"*Whew....*"

"Damage Control, please bring pod scrapers to Miss Molly."

"Wow."

"You may disengage the Molecular Transmitter, Crewman."

"What a mess."

"So it is, Mr. Agacinski; so it is."

* * *

"HA-HA-HA-HA-HA— "

"And then what, what happened then?"

"Well, funny you should ask," Cook slurred, and all three men burst out laughing. Even through a glassy haze, Cook's eyes twinkled brightly. He and Andersen sat on the floor; it was safer that way. Connors was still on the couch and getting wobblier with each passing second.

"No, really."

"Well, back then LaRue was a trifle pudgy in the first place. And the uniform curved in all the wrong places anyway, for all the obvious reasons. But mad as he was, he sashayed from his cabin, down Corridor A, fully halfway across the ship, and burst into my office. Suddenly, I find myself face to face with a homicidal, six-foot-tall executive officer— "

Tears were pouring down Andersen's cheeks; and Connors was laughing so hard his sides were aching.

"—with his belly sticking out where the top didn't quite reach to the bottom, and chest folds that looked like someone had taken a pin to deflate everything that should have bulged while a friend pumped up what was better left alone."

"And then?"

"And then, he stormed over to my desk and said—in his haughtiest French accent: '*Monsieur Commandre*—you see what zey have done to me. All my uniforms are like zis... someone at ze laundry pulled a switch. And now, I am left to dress like—like some *fille de joie*. I demand to know what you are going to do about it—how you are plan to help me out of zis—zis predicament'."

"And so you—" Andersen wiped his eyes with his sleeve.

"Well, what could I do? I told him: 'I'm sorry François, but I really don't have any lipstick. Perhaps if you asked Ensign Mendelson—"

Connors fell back onto the floor, barely managing to avoid cracking his head.

"—we could arrange something to tide you over till we reach port."

Cook joined in the laughter himself, spraying brandy over his companions as he tried to take another sip from his glass. "No, actually I promised to handle the investigation myself. And I assured him that I would bring the fiends to justice, no matter how long it took. Funny thing, though. I still haven't found any evidence. At least none that didn't get lost. I'm still on the lookout for fiends, though."

As the others gasped for breath, Cook gulped the rest of his brandy and poured everyone another refill. The bottle was down to its last quarter. Already, Cook was having trouble focusing his eyes, and he had the distinct feeling that he was pouring more brandy on the floor than in their glasses.

Connors struggled until he was sitting upright on the floor. "So ye—so ye do apperciate—*appreciate*—a good prank after all, don't ye, Skipper?"

"Of course I do, Chief. If it's clever enough."

"Then why in the name of St. George," thundered Connors, surprised at the anger in his voice, "don't ye let us have some fun with the tyros?"

"Chief?"

"No, Andersen—ye bloody well stay out of this. I want the Skipper to answer for himself."

Cook leaned back against the couch, to steady himself; his head spun like a pulsar. As slowly as he could, he turned his head so that he faced Connors. The Chief's face curled into a scowl, almost hidden by his beard.

"That's what all this is about?" The captain started to giggle, and brought Andersen along in his wake. Connors stared ahead, dumbly; the giddy spirits of his companions had suddenly left him behind.

"You mean—you mean to tell me— "

"Now, that's quite enough of that. I mean, beggin your pardon, sir. But that's quite enough of that."

"You mean to tell me, that all this—all this grief is over a few days of hazing? Not the seques—not the sequestration, not the double shifting. Not the lock on the beer vault—but the hazing? The skinned-knee, schoolboy 'eat-worms-or-you-can't-come-into-the-clubhouse' hazing?"

Despite himself, Connors joined in the renewed chorus of laughter, which seemed to their brandy-soaked minds to last a quarter-watch at least.

"Well, Chief—I'm sorry to have to say it, but that's not the way we do things on Isis," Cook said at last, when he had finally calmed himself down.

"Sir?"

"Hazing isn't rounders, Chief."

"It isn't what?"

"It isn't—well, it's just not very Isitian. Besides," he added, his mood turned serious. "I won't allow anyone under my command go through what I did my first week in the service. Or at the Academy."

"That's all what's behind it?"

"That's all," Cook nodded solemnly. "Of course, I did have my own way of dealing with Hell Week. I mean, I don't take things like that lying down. Even if I did have the meanest old yeoman on two legs—or was it three?"

The two yeomen perked up, suddenly curious. "What did you do?" Andersen asked, his giggling barely under control.

"Well now," Cook slurred, his lips inching toward a sly smile. "I considered the problem from all angles...all the various and sundry aspects and prospects, as it were...and planned—planned, mind you—the appropriate stragedy...*strategy*! The exaggly right stragedy."

"But what did you do?"

"And then I went and put it all—just put it into operation. 'Cause when Roscoe Cook sees what need to be done, he just goes ahead and— "

"What did you do?" the two yeomen bellowed in chorus.

"Well...I pulled rank on him," Cook shrugged, and took a deep swallow of brandy.

"You—you what?"

"Well now, it occurred to me that I still outranked the son of a bitch. At least when we were on duty. So the first duty shift we pulled, I just tracked him right down and gave him two direct orders.... "

"Direct orders?" Connors and Andersen both started laughing.

"Written orders! Direct written orders. And I made him sign a receipt so I could court martial the bugger if he disobeyed me... which I wouldn't have put past the slimy bastard, which is why I got it in writing."

"Direct—direct orders from—from a tyro blueshirt during Hell Week?"

"First order—don't bother me anymore when I'm off duty. Except when absolutely necessary to avoid loss of face with the rest of the greenshirts. I didn't want to humiliate the bastard, after all."

"Don't—don't bother you— "

"Second order—don't ever tell anybody about the first order. I don't know why the same thing never occurred to the other ensigns. But blueshirts never have struck me as a practical lot, you know? They don't teach it in officers' school so I guess some of 'em feel it's vaguely non-regulation. Here, have some more brandy."

The convulsing yeomen were too busy struggling to stay upright to protest. Cook drained the contents of the bottle until it overflowed the three glasses and started spilling onto the floor, then started to sing:

> Prime engines and set sail,
> Chop off a comet's tail.
> We'll walk no more Demeter's shore
> So bid your love good day-ay-ay.

Connors and Andersen joined the chorus; the Chief's heart throbbed dully in his head, spurred by the brandy and the pulse of the song. As much in wonder as to clear the fog from his brain, Connors slowly shook his head. He might have known: the Skipper was one of those maddening sorts who excelled at anything he tried. It stood to reason that he'd have one of the best singing voices on his own ship. Their singing spun circles in his mind, like the merry-go-rounds he loved to ride as a little boy, but the memory would bring little comfort when he awoke the next day:

> Ring 'round, the buckoes sing,
> We'll drink what fate may bring,
> While Rigel flares and Deneb glares
> Five hundred years away.

* * *

"Item ten— "

"And hopefully the last."

"Now, now—we're paid well enough. We can postpone our naps for a few minutes longer."

As Admiral Clay and the others chuckled amiably from his respective conference rooms, Weatherlee glanced down at his briefing papers. The last item on the agenda was the same as it had been for the past month. And it never failed to make him sick to his stomach.

"Updates on the new starships," said Clay, looking up from his papers.

"McKinnon reports that the shields and weapons systems are still inoperable on the *Buena Vista*. Something in the wiring isn't quite right and they haven't been able to figure it out yet. And Ebling reports that the computers on the *Covington* are still crashing," reported Miriam Wright, on Clay's left at the Command Center on Looking Glass. "Every time they load more than two bridge simulations before rebooting, the entire system freezes up, and it takes the better part of an hour to get things running."

"Wouldn't they be better off simply replacing the whole system?" asked the Admiral commanding the Hodges Outpost.

"They'd have to rebid the project," explained Commodore Wright. "And it would probably take the better part of a year before we could authorize a replacement."

"That's insane!"

"Those are the regulations," Wright smiled. "Unless we can prove a defect...."

"A crashing computer isn't a defect?"

"I just apply the rules," she replied. "I don't try to defend them."

"And Cook?" asked Admiral Clay.

"Actually, the *d'Artagnan* is the only one of the bunch that is anywhere close to being ready. Their computers are fully debugged, their systems are all minimally functional, and Cook's last report suggested that they were almost done with an overhaul of every engine coil on the ship."

"Still not starworthy, though?"

"No...but it's just short of miraculous that they've come as far as they have."

"I swear," Clay said, "I was rooting for him to pull it off."

"But the rules are quite specific...," Weatherlee began.

"Yes, Winthrop," Clay answered wearily. "As we've already decided, without their certificates, none of them will make Maneuvers."

"Exceptions would be— "

"No—we've been over that before."

Leaning back in his chair, Weatherlee took small solace in winning his point. These days, it seemed he won very few of them. And he seemed to win fewer with every passing year.

Weatherlee leaned forward, his eyes narrowing as he moved in for the kill. The Hawkins Massacre was still grabbing headlines across the whole of Terra. Panic over the alien menace had gripped Covington, and everyone was looking to the Cosmic Guard to set things right. But this Board of Inquiry had been cobbled together on the fly and he hadn't expected the proceedings to go quite so smoothly. In fact, he'd expected the arrogant officer in front of him to try lying and squirming his way around the facts. But the young officer's answers were exactly what the admiral had been trying to prove. Now, he could nail the little bastard's hide to the wall.

"Let me make sure I understand you, Lt. Commander Cook. Are you suggesting to this Board of Inquiry that you—an officer of the Cosmic Guard, sworn to uphold the law and protect civilians from whatever dangers space might present— maneuvered your squadron in such a way as to make it possible for the aliens to make good their escape."

"Actually, I'm not suggesting anything at all, Admiral Weatherlee," replied the young officer. "I am telling this Board of Inquiry that I deliberately interposed my ships between the aliens and their pursuers, to prevent any further bloodshed. The fact that the aliens escaped without anyone else getting killed means that I accomplished exactly what I was trying to do."

"For what purpose?" asked the presiding officer, leaning forward to hear the answer. Concern creased his brown, and his kindly brown eyes seemed genuinely puzzled.

"Our standing orders provide no guidance in dealing with aliens, Admiral Clay. Simply put, the aliens are beyond our jurisdiction. Our laws regard space as a common frontier that belongs to no one, and since they were not Terran nationals, it seemed to me that we had no legal basis to stop them. But beyond this—it was our first contact with an alien race."

"They attacked a mining camp and killed Terran civilians!" snapped Admiral Weatherlee. *"And you let them all get away."*

"As I understand, it was a rather bloody affair on both sides," the young officer replied calmly. *"At the time, the spacers were claiming several of their own had been killed and that the aliens they hadn't managed to finish off were getting away. I suspect that the terror and surprise was mutual—and either side could well have started the bloodbath. If we hadn't let them leave, then the aliens first taste of Terran hospitality would have been a massacre, followed by a pursuit, followed by a second massacre—which, given the reception they received at Hawkins Star, they'd probably have regarded as our standard welcome."*

"They killed Terran civilians!"

"We didn't know who or what they are. And, quite frankly, we still don't know. But it seemed to me that intervening in a way that separated the combatants—all of the combatants—and allowed the aliens to leave in peace gave us a better chance of sorting out the whole mess than we'd have right now if we'd just blasted away at them. Simply destroying them—which was the likely result of any attempt to stop them—may well have resulted in an interstellar war with an alien race of undetermined capabilities and intentions."

Admiral Clay nodded. *"So you decided, entirely on your own...."*

"I had no time to radio for instructions, Admiral Clay," the young man said. *"My squadron was there only by chance, and we arrived just in time to see the spacers closing in for the kill. My choice was to intervene, or to stand aside and let the spacers take their revenge. I suppose, in hindsight, staying out of it might have been the safer course as far as the High Command is concerned, since asking for instructions would have let me avoid taking any responsibility in the matter. But letting our first contact with an alien race end in the annihilation of their scouting party struck me as foolish in the extreme—and the kind of foolishness that History would not treat kindly. Even today, taking the safe way out would strike me as the act of a coward. And if I had the same choice to make, I suspect I'd act exactly the same way—though I'd probably deploy my squadron a bit differently, now that I think of it."*

Sitting back in his chair, Weatherlee felt a surge of satisfaction in proving his point. Later, when the Board retired to deliberate, he found himself smoldering with rage at what he was hearing. He'd done exactly what he set out to do. He'd actually proven that the arrogant prick was a traitor. But now everyone else seemed to regard it as a feather in the little snot's cap.

"I'll tell you what," laughed Porter Clay, the presiding officer on the Board of Inquiry as he rocked back and forth in his chair, "I've had my eyes on that kid ever since—actually, Winthrop, ever since that day in Covington when he topped off your tactics seminar at the Academy."

Clay slapped Weatherlee roughly across the back, and the rest of the board burst into laughter. They'd all been there. Every last one of them.

"I'll never forget it," roared Admiral Pendleton, and the rest of his colleagues started reliving the entire episode. "But hell, Winnie—we passed you anyway. It wasn't your plan that was the problem, you know. You just ran it into a goddamn buzz saw. The god-damndest one I've ever seen. And from a student, yet!"

Weatherlee closed his eyes and tried his best to push the experience out of his memory. "Even with all this evidence...," he began.

"That kid is the most brilliant young commander I've ever seen," said Clay, looking around the table. "And that decision of his took more balls than any of us have shown in our entire careers—and God as my witness, I think he made exactly the right call. DAMN!—but his instincts are remarkable. Hell, if it had been up to us we'd have spent two weeks debating it—and we'd still have fucked the whole thing up.

"No," Clay sighed, taking a deep breath. "We don't punish initiative in the Cosmic Guard, no matter what the press or politicians have to say. I move that this Board of Inquiry issue a statement calling on Covington to open immediate talks with our neighbors before another similar misunderstanding leads us to war. Then, we give that young man a medal—promote him to full Commander—and give him a cruiser to hone his skills. And you just watch: some day, he's going to be the best starship skipper in the whole damn fleet."

"*The vote will not be unanimous, Admiral Clay,*" Weatherlee whispered intently.

"*No, Winthrop,*" Clay replied coldly, "*I didn't think it would be.*"

Chapter 15

DAYS RACED BY IN A seamless blur, until one day a week or so later found Cook alone in his office. The writing on his viewscreen cast a soft glow on his face. Aside from the screen, and the clock on his bedstand, a small lamp on a corner table was the room's only light. When things around him seemed too hectic, Cook found it easier to concentrate that way. The time pulse on the chronometer read 470 Hours; little more than five cosmic hours remained in the current cosmic year. Time was racing by and there was still much to do.

He leaned back and re-read his message to Fleet Headquarters:

```
CGS 2001 <<D'ARTAGNAN>>
POSITION: SB 114, 43-110901/a2/15.6e
COMM REQ CODE III  cc:142-9994.7:
    TO:        EastFleetHQ/IshCom/FtAdmPMClay/
    FROM:      CaptRCook/
    SECURITY:  Standard/
    PREFIX:    Admiral Clay-Special Request/
    FLAGS:     yellow1;yellow2;green3/
    RE:        Maneuvers Eligibility
```
Preliminary repairs are nearing completion, but final adjustments will extend into cc:143; I estimate readiness for final inspection at 143-0150, and anticipate departure for shakedown cruise approximately ten days later, at 143-0250.

   With regular maneuvers scheduled for 143-1250, d'Artagnan will have a full cosmic month after departure to make all adjustments necessary to ready herself for maneuvers. Since the next scheduled exercises are set for 143-6250, the inspection deadline of 143-0000 will result in our ineligibility for maneuvers through the near future, unless the time requirement is waived.

   Therefore, I request that you extend the eligibility deadline for my ship, allowing us to qualify for the first-half exercises. Other

rookie ships, including all of the Challengers, may fall into the
same category, and would likely appreciate similar consideration.
   Capt R Cook//

Cook pressed the transmit button, sending his request to
Admiral Clay. He stretched his limbs as far as he could, and after a
few false starts he reached for the vidphone. He was already starting
to relax; he was sure he had made the right decision. As he entered
the number, he chided himself for leaving everything until the last
moment.

* * *

THE BRIDGE hatch opened with an airy whoosh, though none could
spare the time or attention to see who it was. Asteroids dotted the
viewer, and twin enemy cruisers a-flank the ship were firing almost
at will. Even the tyros, most of whom had not touched the controls
all day, were on the edge of their seats.
   "Incoming fire!"
   "Helm, slow to sublight, quarter-power and hard about."
   "Direct hit amidships, Mr. Ashton. Shields are holding but
weakened, at 60 percent power."
   "Divert power to midship shields, prepare to blank the aft guns.
Helm, prepare to increase speed."
   Jeremy stole a glance toward the entrance. It was the captain. For
the first time that Jeremy could recall, Cook was wearing standard
blues instead of his ratty fatigues. Jeremy felt blood rushing to his
head, but couldn't afford the luxury of worry.
   "Starboard shield amain."
   "Enemy cruiser coming tight about; number two is looping wide."
   "Increase speed to C-2; prepare to fire remaining guns."
   "Enemy slowing to C-1; range, ten klicks."
   "Incoming fire!"
   "Fire starboard guns!"
   "Shields are buckling. Heavy damage to enemy shields; second
cruiser approaching to port, now passing athwart to starboard."
   "Incoming fire!"
   "Fire all remaining guns!"
   "Missed him, Mr. Ashton."

"Starboard shield is gone, Mr. Ashton."

"Damn!" Jeremy hit his armrest with a balled fist and turned to face Cook. He wanted to say something, mumble some inane words that he didn't really believe about how much better things were going and how quickly they were improving. To his surprise, Cook motioned for him to step from the chair.

Wordlessly, a smiling Cook assumed the vacant captain's chair, swiveling from side to side as the simulator continued unabated. Jeremy quietly turned to assume the systems station from Dexter. Suddenly the bridge looked and felt different, crackling with anticipation, yet relaxed as a still night before a summer storm. The screen still showed the enemy cruisers closing for the kill, but the frenetic tension that gripped the bridge during the simulation had vanished, replaced by curiosity about what the captain had in store for them.

"Mr. Ashton," the captain, his voice quiet, but firm. "Replay the last simulation from two minutes before your last 'Hard About.'"

"We've never scored a ninety, Captain," Jeremy said. "I doubt we even—"

"Close enough, Mr. Ashton," Cook smiled patiently. "You're close enough. Now, replay the simulation, please." Soon, the screen showed incoming fire, and a graphic on the board registered the enemy score against the ship's shields.

"Slow the replay to quarter-speed, Mr. Ashton. Go on—quarter-speed." Winking at Mendelson and ignoring the quizzical looks of the others, Cook leaned back in his chair. "Everyone look at the screen, and remember what you see. This is your last simulation, slowed to more manageable levels. Look at it and imagine yourselves floating freely through time. The universe around you moves at this speed, but your own clock can beat to any time you find comfortable.

"This is how things should look to you during a battle. This is how they *will* look to you, once you've mastered your station. The flow of time has slowed, from a mad torrent to a placid lake of crystal clarity, and time itself has become your friend, one you can use and trust, whatever the dangers, whatever the enemy.

"Watch the screen," said Cook, a hardened edge creeping into his soothing voice. "Mr. Ashton deserves our thanks, for conducting these drills to help you to this point of proficiency, where you are at last capable and competent. It was a thankless task, and one that I find quite impossible, but it's among the most crucial for any new ship. His job is over now. He can only bring you part of the way. My job starts where he has left off, and I will bring you the rest of the way—to where your no longer have to struggle to do your job, and your actions will seem as natural as breathing—to where you and your comrades on the bridge are one with the ship."

The enemy cruisers completed their circling maneuvers, and were bearing down on the *d'Artagnan*, fully armed.

"Mr. Ashton, turn off the grader. The computer can give a rough measure of progress and you should all use it for your off-hours practice, but it's outlived its usefulness here. I prefer to evaluate you all myself. Now, release the simulator to manual control and let's keep things at this speed for a while, shall we? I think we'll find it more relaxing.

"One more thing," he added, smiling mischievously at his first officer. "We'll do it my way, this time." He leaned back in the chair, resting his elbows on the armrests and lightly touching his fingertips together as he gazed at the screen. Outwardly, he seemed the quintessence of calm repose, like a tenured professor sitting in his den for an evening of study and quiet reflection. But his eyes blazed in fierce concentration, sending chills down the spines of those on the bridge perceptive enough to notice.

"Miss Palmer—blank all guns, all power to shields, and stand by to recharge the keel guns. Helm—constant heading, prepare to drop us dead south, two hundred fifty degrees."

* * *

LIKE GIANT SNAKES, buried in layer upon layer of black insulation, the engine coils stretched in both directions before disappearing beyond the opposite bends in the ship. The dark corridor walls, wide enough to let two men pass comfortably abreast on either side, did nothing to relieve the gloom. The air dripped like jungle heat, dank and oppressive, but without even the prospect of rain to bring relief.

Crewman Technician Tom Sullivan's coil crew was still laying replacement cables in 277-port-12, as they had for the last week. Whoever installed the original coils had not gone overboard on quality control, he thought. There was scarcely a length of coil that didn't needed adjusting, or outright replacement. It was almost criminal, what these contractors got away with, and this was not the only pocket of trouble on the ship. If all the *Challengers* were like this, they'd be best off sending the lot back to the factory and demanding their money back. But that wasn't the way of any world in the Universe, these days. The procurement industry had too many well-placed friends, and there was no guarantee that anyone else would do a better job, anyhow.

"All right," he shouted. "Take ten. And Esshaki, try not to trip over the torch wires this time." He eased down to the floor and leaned back against the coil.

Sweat coursed from his pores. At his age, he thought, he should be thinking about his pension, not working like a jungle shoate on Demeter. Panting, he removed his shirt and tried to wipe his face and chest, but soon gave it up. The shirt was already soaked, and going bare-chested in this humidity didn't help at all. Soon, the rest of the crew gathered near the water jug, some rinsing themselves, others grateful for the chance to gulp a few mouthfuls of tepid water.

"Needing some comp'ny there, Sully?" Denny Barrett, his face dripping wet, came and sat next to Sullivan. Like Sully, Barrett was a Valhallan and full technician; together, the two of them supervised an eight-man crew. With too few yeomen to go around they'd been conscripted for nanny duty, and were beginning to understand why greenshirts were such crusty, cantankerous sorts. They had two apprentices and six raw recruits in the bunch, and had their hands full, explaining to the tyros what they should be doing.

"Can't say I like this any better'n I ever did," said Sully. "Leastways before, whatever else I did I got to see some progress. Now, seems like we butt our heads sideways against the wall just to stay even."

Barrett laughed. "Always a fountain of joy, eh Sully? Seems I remember a cute birdie on the old *B R McLintock*."

"Now, don't start up on me, Denny."

"Pert as a song, she was. And singing all day long the praises of one Thomas McGiver Sullivan."

"Denny, I'm telling you— "

"But there was always something, wasn't there, Sully? She was late for this or that, or too tired when you were in the mood to romp. Seems once I remember you arguing over a shade of lipstick you didn't much fancy. Then, one day—lo and behold—she's off with another and you're left complaining about that turn, too."

Sully sighed and rested his head against the insulation on the coil behind him. She'd been pretty, with lips like wine and a smile like a breeze, a ray of sunshine in a life of rain. He'd often wondered what his life would have been like, if only…but he banished such mawkish thoughts from his mind as soon as they arose. Cozzies had little room for nostalgia, and space was no place to dwell in the past.

"A-course," nudged Denny, "she did give old man Dugan a touch of Demetrian Flu—and Demmy Rot's a fitting climax to his career, wouldn't you say?"

The two old friends laughed. They'd been through a lot together. Seen all of Terra between them and knew all the redshirts on all the ships along the frontier. They'd laughed and cried, and hugged within an inch of breaking their backs when they found they'd drawn the same duty. For the first time in ages, and even in the midst of the newest ship of the line in the whole Fleet, the old-timers felt at home.

"Sully?" called a voice from the water jug; it was Martindale, the tyro from Ceres. He was holding up a cup, spilling water over its sides. Sully motioned for him to bring it; it was nice that some of the recruits showed their elders some respect, he thought.

"Here you go, Sully," he smiled. He was a tall lad, with tightly curled hair and olive skin. Hidden beneath his boyish looks and slender physique were muscles like strands of steel, and on top of everything else, he came from a family of spacers. It was little wonder that, almost alone among the redshirt tyros, Martindale won quick acceptance from the veterans, and respect for his knowledge of a ship's insides.

"If I didn't know better, I'd say your mother gave you birth in the engine room of a schooner. Thanks, lad."

"Must be hard on you old-timers," said Martindale, towering over his two supervisors, "stringing cable like this, day after day."

"Aye to that," called a voice from behind them. It was Bartee, another of the tyros. He'd finished his cup of water and was coming to join the group; the rest of the crew was close behind.

"I swear," he continued, "this crap goes on and on. No let up, no break, not even for New Year. And not so much as a word of thanks for all our hard work. That's something they never tell you about, when you sign the enlistment papers. The endless hours in a sweatshop, the fact that there's no end to it all."

"Now that's enough out of you," Sully snapped, startled by the fury in his own voice. Denny and Larsen, another new recruit, helped him to his feet. "No matter what I may think of you, you're a Cozzie now. A tyro, to be sure about it, but you're a full fledged Cosmic Guardsman. And if you think this is rough, you wait for the real work to start. You ain't done full watch in the midst of an ion storm, or battle with a pirate squadron whose only thought is spreading your atoms from here to kingdom come. I've had about all I'll stand of your belly-aching, and I'll not stand for it any longer."

"But if that tyrant of a bridge-rat had any sense— "

"And I'll not stand your bad-mouthing the Skipper, neither. Not unless you want me to tan your groundtoad butt myself. Skipper drives us tough—tough as any I've seen, maybe tougher. That, I'll grant you. But he's no shirker. He works as hard as any of us himself, maybe twice as hard. He won't have us doing anything he'll shy from himself. And he won't lean on us at all, without there be a reason for it. If he says sweat, then we sweat. And we'll do it from now until he says to quit, even if he takes us through every holiday from here to Rigel and back again.

"Am I understood?"

Bartee barely kept a sullen silence.

"Am I understood, Mr. Bartee?"

"That's no reason— " the tyro began, but his reply was cut short by the clearing whistle of the ship-wide intercom, muffled as it sounded through the engine coils.

"Attention," came a voice over the speakers. "May I have your attention, please. This is the Captain."   It was the third time Cook had used the intercom to address the entire crew. The first time, he announced that the galley would not serve beer until further notice; the next time it was to inform the crew that they were sequestered, and none of them could leave the ship without his written permission until the ship was starworthy. His voice on the speaker knotted every stomach on the ship.

"That's no reason...," Bartee began again, his voice dripping indignation; this time he was silenced by his superiors.

"Quiet," stormed Sullivan. "The Skipper's talking. Now be still, all of you."

> "This is the one hundred sixth-fifth day since I assumed command of the *d'Artagnan*. Many of you have been here almost since the beginning. In that time, we have found our ship needing constant care and attention to compensate for shoddy work in the factory. But we are professionals, dedicated to making our ship the finest in the fleet, even if it means endless hours of sacrifice and hard work. When the attention we lavish today turns into habit, we'll find that we cannot accept less than the best from one another, or from ourselves, simply because that's the way we've always done things...."

"DOES THAT mean we're all doomed to spend eternity checking engine blocks, Mr. Van Horn? Engineering duty's rough enough, without us— "

"Hold your tongue, Ensign Stewart, or I'll come over there and pull it out myself. And that goes for the rest of you, as well."

> "I demand a lot from my crew: loyalty; devotion to duty; devotion to each other; above all else, the highest devotion to excellence. For all of us, it should be a constant irritation to find the *d'Artagnan* in less than finest trim, for this hits at what should be our first and final objective—pride in our work, ourselves, and in our ship. That is why I've pushed us all as hard as I could, because we cannot and should not tolerate anything less than perfection...."

"ALL RIGHT, if you can't listen quietly, stand at attention, the lot of you. And Huntsman, get out from under that Scout. You can finish the overhaul later, when the Skipper's done talking."

"But Mr. Patterson— "

"You heard me, Crewman. Out of there and over here! On the double!"

> "But I will not bear down, or call for sacrifice, without an overriding purpose. By the same token, when it serves no

purpose, I will not exact an unthinking discipline, merely for its own sake. That does nothing but dull the sense of order aboard ship, diminishing respect due the captain from his crew—and the crew from the captain...."

CONNORS WAS leaning against the doorframe at the entrance to the molecular transmitter when he heard a voice call from down the corridor.

"What do you think it all means, Chief?"

Connors turned to see Andersen coming around the bend, on his way from the computer room, a quizzical look on his face. Connors leaned his head back and chuckled deeply. Slowly, he was coming to realize what the captain had in mind, and that the Skipper probably had it in mind since the beginning.

"I said— "

"I heard ye...now listen to him." The two men stood silently, listening to the captain's voice ring through the hallways.

"We have many reasons to be proud. Our ship is a fine one, and our hard work over the past weeks has brought her to the brink of starworthiness at a pace that is nothing short of miraculous. A new ship carries burdens as well as promises, and ship-shaping any vessel of the Cosmic Guard is a heavy responsibility. I have demanded a lot from everybody on board. My only regret is that we could not ready the ship for inspection by the end of the Cosmic Year, because it makes us ineligible to participate in maneuvers next quarter.

"I wanted us to be the first rookie ship in the history of the Cosmic Guard to win the gold medal, and I hate the thought of falling short of our first goal together as a crew. But any failure or disappointment we have suffered is not for want of trying. I am proud of the way each and every one of you has closed ranks, despite the hardships and self-denials I have made you endure. You've all tried your best. And while I will often demand even more than your best in the days to come, I will never call you to task for failing to do the impossible."

Andersen's eyes bulged wildly. "Is he saying— "
"Shhh."

"A captain has few opportunities to show his gratitude, and limited ways of showing his thanks. Therefore, effective at 800 Hours, I am suspending my sequestration order and granting liberty— "

No one heard the rest of Cook's sentence. In every corner of the ship, it was drowned out by a loud cheer that filled every deck and every station. Soon, half the crew had spilled into the corridors and hallways, all voices raised to give three cheers and more for the Skipper.

"You believe it, Chief?" Andersen shouted to be heard over the noise.

Connors shook his head and laughed, as much in gratitude and relief as in admiration. "That sneaky, duplicitous plotmeister. He had the bloody thing planned all along! Ever since the first day, I'll wager. The young bastard could out-diddle the flintiest Ceresian who ever— "

"What do you mean?"

"Look at those bellowing clowns." He pointed down the corridors, as everyone cheered their unexpected good fortune. "Two minutes ago they were grumblin over the color of their eyes and blamin it all on Cook. Now he's a bloody hero. Ye won't find a man or woman on this ship who won't follow him to Andromeda in a push cart. And they'll never think to complain again, no matter how hard he pushes'em."

"And you think— "

Connors shot back the wickedest grin this side of Pirate's Alley. "That man knows exactly what he's doing, Andersen. Exactly what he's doing. And ye can bloody well forget anything you've learned about dealing with blueshirts before. As a Skipper, he's one of a kind, Andersen. One of a kind. Ye can be thankin the stars that he's ours, for ye'll never see the likes of him again."

Connors stepped into the corridor to join the cheering. Soon, he and the other yeomen started calming the redshirts, making sure that they returned to secure their posts before liberty took effect. Whatever lingering doubts he had about the captain had vanished. Connors had already heard about his wizardry on the bridge, but with this bit of psychological sleight of hand, Cook had proven himself a master of all aspects of command. More important than anything else, the captain now commanded the Chief's respect as well as his admiration.

* * *

"HURRY ROSCOE, or we'll be late."

"I'll be right there."

"That's what you said ten minutes ago."

"I was set to go twenty minutes ago. This is your fault, you know...."

Vera could hear Cook busily rummaging through his closets, looking for something suitable. She knew that it really was her fault, at least in part. With shined boots and a fresh uniform, he had looked fine when she arrived. But fine wasn't stunning, and so she made him dig around for his dress blues. After all, she'd spent three hundred credits buying her own outfit, a low-cut, powder blue dress that flowed with her every move, and was not about to let her escort make her feel overdressed. Now, of course, she was paying the price, but how was she to know that he'd have to go through his entire wardrobe to find the one dress uniform he owned? She shuddered to think what it might look like; the stars only knew how long it had been stashed away in his clothes closet. Or whether he might not find it stuffed in his duffle bag.

She walked out the door connecting his cabin to his office. The chronometer read 950 Hours; they still had a half hour to get to McMorrow's party before Zero Hour. The office was a mess. Not as bad as his room, perhaps, but hardly likely to impress a visitor with its owner's organizational abilities. Vera started to tidy the desk, but stopped almost at once, as she realized that there was no place to put anything. Like a Grand Canyon of clutter, everything was in layers, perhaps revealing much to the trained eye about the problems of a starship captain readying his ship to sail, but buried under tons of sediment.

"Well?"

Vera's head snapped around, and a dazzling smile lit her face. Cook stood proudly in the doorway, a half-dozen of his smaller medals accenting the silken cloth of his dress blues. Slowly, he turned around to model his new attire.

"You look very handsome, Roscoe Cook," Vera beamed, "though I doubt anyone at the party will realize that neatness is not your natural state."

"Now wait a minute," Cook protested, but he knew that debating the matter was a lost cause. Vera took his arm and led him down the corridor toward the main elevators.

"How many are staying behind?" she asked as they waited for the lift cage.

"About twenty. All volunteers. I promised an extra three days' liberty to anyone who drew security detail."

The elevator door opened, and Vera stepped inside. But Cook paused at the entrance, a curious look on his face. Something had caught his attention, and he wandered out into the hall.

Vera left the elevator to stand beside him. She was about to ask what was wrong when she heard it—soft and distant, yet floating through the sterile corridor like a fresh summer breeze.

It was coming from down the hall, from the crew's common galley.

It was the sound of singing.

"THAT WAS good, Larsen, let's have another."

Andrew Larsen strummed his guitar and laughed. "Nah—not if I'm the only one singing. I hate playing to myself. I do that often enough in my cabin." His brown eyes danced merrily, flirting with the prettier part of his audience—a young ensign named Mathison, whose shy smile hinted that she shared at least some of his interests, and that missing Cosmic New Year on the base wouldn't be much of a disappointment for either one of them.

"We'll be joinin in this time—won't we, lads an' lassies?" Crewman Martindale grinned, mimicking Chief Connor's Demetrian brogue. "Else, ye'll be fodder for the brig, and salt for the mines."

"What'll it be?"

"Something slow."

"Something fast."

"Something sad," Mathison said softly. Larsen was too happy to oblige, singing a soft spacer's ballad that the local beer halls never did justice. They always turned it into another bawdy house drinking song.

Now the life of a spacer keeps changing,
As over the heavens he's ranging;
Past timeless horizons and yonder,
His spirit is destined to wander.

None of them noticed that two more had slipped into the galley; and not until chords began sounding on the refrain—and in the proper key—did they look to see that the captain had activated the keyboard.

For it's Springtime on Ishtar, m'darling,
It's payday, come lager and car'ling;
And my dusty dry glass needs a-filling,
By a lusty young lass who's a-willing.

"Do you mind," whispered Cook, as his hands helped the simple tune pulse smoothly in six-eight time, "if we're a little late for the party? I'd like to ring in the New Year with my crew."

Vera nodded her head but choked back a tear, determined not to show how hurt she was. Slowly, the startled remnants of the crew made their way to where Cook and Vera were seated, and soon the party was in full gear. Viewers linked the galley to each station manned for the duration of the holidays, and crewman and captain played every song known to Cozzie lore—including all but a few of the verses the men sang when they gathered alone, without their shapelier companions. Cook even helped break into Supply, to liberate some beer from the bowels of the food vault.

Though too good a sport not to join the others as the songs rolled from sad to merry and back again, Vera knew that she'd been fooling herself these past few weeks. Cook's life was his ship and his crew, and nothing would ever change him.

Chapter 16

REFRESHED AND RECHARGED FROM A few days away from the ship, *d'Artagnan*'s crew returned from liberty rested and ready to storm the heavens. Morale was high, and progress was brisk. For the first time everything seemed to break the right way, and tasks that seemed so hard a few days earlier now fell easily into place. As the ship neared readiness, all hands could sense that the ordeals and hardships of the past weeks were finally showing results.

The first successful test of the engine coils came at cc:143-0090. In all corners of the ship, the crew could feel the vibrating pulse that stirred beneath their feet, as the engines finally sent power coursing through her inner reaches. Loud cheers filled the corridors, and the captain ordered the entire crew to stand down for two full shifts in celebration. Two days later, Cook announced a temporary switch to single shifts for the redshirts, assigning all but the officers to one watch per day and promising to make it permanent if they could handle the work load and still make the ship starworthy by '0250. In response, the crew redoubled their efforts, each hand pulling as hard as possible, trying to justify the Skipper's confidence. Meanwhile, Cook drove his officers harder than ever, conducting two full bridge drills daily and accepting no excuses for sloppy work on or off the bridge. He expected all the officers to set examples for the rest of the crew; and as for his bridge team, he demanded that they set an example for the rest of the officers, requiring them to pull full ship-shaping duty in addition to their other responsibilities.

As the finishing touches neared completion, anticipation swept over the entire ship. At last, they began to see the final result of the efforts and a shared sense of adventure began to take root. They no longer thought of the hardships they'd endured, nor of the countless future tasks involved in keeping the ship in proper trim. All was forgotten in the glory of the moment. They began to dream of what might lie ahead of them in the dark reaches of space, and threw themselves at their work, filled with mounting pride at all they'd accomplished and determined not to disappoint their Skipper.

Finally, Cook pronounced the ship starworthy; and on May 22, 2551—on cc:143-0235 in the official records of the Cosmic Guard—Admiral Clay signed the order authorizing the first of the *Challengers* to sail. All that remained for the crew was to say their goodbyes to friends and loved ones on the base, and begin readying the ship for departure.

* * *

NEW BABYLON hung in the porthole window, a blue and white ball floating on a black, eternal sea. Now and then, spots of brown or green broke through the clouds, dappling the pristine beauty of the water below with splashes of life. The starliner's speakers filled the air with mindless music, but few seemed to notice.

Emerson Hollenbach sat in a cushioned chair in the first-class section, looking out the porthole, a glass of sherry in one hand, a smoldering cigar in the other. He'd requested a private booth, so he sat alone.

He was lucky to have salvaged as much as he did, he thought to himself. Once the Tories figured out how tenuous their hold on power would be, they'd threatened to back out and take their chances with the new elections. But that wasn't Schiller's doing: he might be a terror in the industrial world, but Schiller was an amateur as a king-maker and could have been bluffed. No, thought Hollenbach, that play came from someone else, and he chided himself for underestimating the Tory leadership all these years. There actually was a brain under all that fluff, after all.

But he could live with the changes. A triumvirate controlling CosGuard procurement might be imperfect, but at least he'd have a veto. More importantly, he did get to keep his committee, which was the source of his power. Besides, with the Tories in charge, his biggest worries would be a thing of the past, and he could even help do something about the lizards. The election he'd face in a few months scarcely crossed his mind; with the Tories neutralized, and no likely opposition in his own party, it barely touched his consciousness. But then, he always left such matters to his aides.

The music stopped, and the silence caught Hollenbach's attention. "Please be seated, and fasten your seat belts," a woman's pleasant voice called over the speaker. It was hard for him to remember that it was the voice of a computer. "The ship is preparing to sail.

"Please be seated...."

The ship shuddered, as her captain engaged the engines and a tractor beam eased the ship away from the spaceport. Soon, Hollenbach's bulky frame pressed lightly into the side of his chair, as the ship accelerated toward breaking orbit. Outside the porthole, the black terminator line began consuming the planet, and two bright moons came into view. Minutes later, New Babylon was nothing more than a blue point of light, quickly receding from view as the ship began its leisurely, six-day trip to Earth. Outside, in all directions, the stars glowed silently. Rainbow-colored and timeless, they danced across the icy blackness like an endless field of wildflowers.

"How long ye be gone this time, Macey?"

"Not long. Two or three months at most, I imagine."

"Ye be careful out here."

"I will."

Janey gave Mason a warm hug and handed him a bag filled with some bread and sausage. "It'll last ye for the first few days," she said. Her eyes moped along the floor of the hangar as she spoke.

"There's plenty of air, and there's more in the spare schooner. Ye can radio Nelson or Cifaldi if ye be startin to run low, or get to feelin lonely."

"C'mon, Mason!" Cyrus barked. He leaned over the gangway, impatience clouding his face. "The stars can wait forever, but I'll be damned if I will." Mason said goodbye and then ran down the gangplank. He turned at the hatch to wave to his woman and then disappeared inside the ship.

"Ye'll be spoiling her yet, Mason," Cyrus said, disapproval creasing his brow. Mason shrugged and slumped into his seat at the controls.

"Where we be goin this time?"

Cyrus chuckled as he engaged the engines. "East an' anticenter. We ain't been there yet. Not in a while, anyways."

Mason laughed out loud. "Ain't many been that way in a while, Cyrus. Leastways, none without a price on his head. But if the rumors about Wilkes be right ones, I supposed it does us good. If he's back to Pirate's Alley, I don't want to be around when the Cozzies get wind of it."

"An ye tell me ye've no head for spacin, Macey," laughed Cyrus. "To think ye've been holdin out on me the whole time!"

"What I got is no head for gettin shot."

Cyrus mussed his brother's black hair, then turned his attention to the helm. Soon, the ship eased away from its moorings, and disappeared into the emptiness of space.

"ANY MOMENT now," the pilot said in his native tongue.

Smiling, Zatar peered over the railing of the observation platform. He could see the speaker standing at the control panel with his back to the platform and his body partly obscured by the molded lounger beside his station. As was typical for his race, the young Crutchtan pilot had scarcely said a word for the entire trip, tending silently to his duties while keeping his emotions locked deep within. Now, as they neared familiar skies, he had started giving voice to his reports, and Zatar even thought that he heard the smallest hint of excitement in the very terseness of the pilot's commentary.

Of course, Crutchtan reserve found no echo in his own kind. The entire Veshnan delegation had come to the platform, to view the passage through the dome overhead. As the Crutchtans seated themselves comfortably and waited in silence, his own delegation fairly squealed with delight. It was as if they had taken it into their heads to let their Crutchtan hosts see the truth of the common stereotype, the excitable, gaggling Veshnan, too rapt in the thrill of the living moment to enjoy it in peace and quiet.

Zatar turned to look behind him, at the skies they were leaving. He could not see the star that had given them light until so recently; its brightness had disappeared from view many days earlier. The memories of the frozen, dusty land that had lent them its shelter would take longer to fade. Everywhere, heaven's blackness was the same; the calm tranquility was eternal and unvarying, and yet he was looking at Terran skies. It touched him with profound wonder to know that as he was seeing the alien stars of a strange race, the Terrans found comfort in the same heavens.

"The Great Divide is passed," called the pilot into the speaker, his voice echoing throughout the ship. "We are home."

Cheers rang over the observing platform. The Veshnan women hugged each other and sang songs of celebration; Zatar cried out in joy. The Crutchtans rose and clasped their friends by the shoulders, mildly protesting when the Veshnans came to embrace them more warmly than their ways allowed for *Lsh'Gelunsch*—or "Ones who are Not Mates."

Zatar looked overhead, from one side of the Observation Dome to the other. He could not explain the difference: the black sky held the same stars, and looked no different than before, but he felt the difference in his soul. No longer were they living amid strangers; now, they were among friends.

Glancing down from the platform toward the ship's controls, Zatar saw the pilot's face raised toward the arching dome. Like all of his kind, the Crutchtan's countenance looked featureless and inexpressive. And yet quietly glistening on his cheeks, tears flowed from the young man's eyes.

* * *

"COMMANDER ASHTON?"

"Engines are fully primed, Captain. Mr. Van Horn reports all clear."

"Mr. Underwood?"

"Ishtar Command gives us clearance for departure, sir. At our pleasure."

"Amid-deck hatches are secure, Captain."

"Thank you, Mr. Ashton. You may deactivate the grapplers whenever you are ready."

"Yes, sir."

"Mr. Underwood, sound the clearing horn."

"Aye, aye, Captain."

The alarm sounded throughout the ship, and soon loud cheers rose on all decks as the crew felt *d'Artagnan* begin to move beneath their feet. Slowly, as the charging engines sent shudders through the entire ship, the tractor beam eased them away from the base and into the nothingness of space.

THE DOCK Twenty-three Observation Deck was swollen with well-wishers and onlookers but the crowd was quiet, almost lifeless. Occasional laughter split the soft murmurs of conversation, and a few children played merrily in the playpit at the base of the deck. Most sat and watched in silence.

Silence greeted the ship's first appearance in the window plate; and silence followed her slow movement across their field of view. Like a gray ghost looming in the starlight, the great ship banked gracefully to starboard before gliding off into the Big Black. Stillness lingered on the deck until the ship was too faint to see any longer, and the well-wishing throng departed.

But a few stayed behind. Some tearful, some dry-eyed and stoic, they gazed into the distance, wistfully savoring the last flickers of *d'Artagnan*'s running lights. Most swore that they'd never again catch themselves aching after a fading point of light. Few remembered that they'd said the same thing before.

AHEAD, THE MONITORS showed the glowing red storms of the Ishtari Belt. Behind them, the starbase hung large in the blackness, its solar panels reflecting the yellow rays of Ishtar's sun, the spokes of the docks reaching into the heavens.

"Nearing the end of controlled space," Jeremy reported. "We should be clear in another two minutes."

"Thank you, Mr. Ashton," said the captain. "Please let me know when we're twenty seconds out. Helm?"

"Engines purring merrily at one-eighth capacity. Efficiency readings are smack in the middle of the dial."

Leaning back in the command chair, Cook closed his eyes and sighed. For the first time in ages, he was totally relaxed, totally at ease. Not that he was under any illusions about the future. Space always had a way of making things go wrong, he smiled. Whatever problems they had in store for them would probably arise at the worst possible time. And he suspected that his headaches were far from over. In fact, they were probably just beginning.

But not right now. It seemed forever since he'd felt so free of pressures and constraints. Today not even the croakers and worry-warts in the control tower were going to stand in his way.

"Helm, increase thrusters to one-half."

"Sir?" Janet worried. She'd seen him this way before, and it usually meant trouble.

Not chills-down-the-spine-and-pray-we-get-through-this kind of trouble, she knew. But still trouble.

"Thrusters to one-half," she replied. Despite herself, she couldn't help but laugh.

"Let's give ourselves a proper send-off, shall we?" the captain said briskly. "Helm—stand by for Academy victory sequence. Wing over wing, port over starboard."

"*Skipper!*" Jeremy exclaimed. "We're still inside the Red Zone!"

"Relax, Jeremy. We're almost clear. And I need to test my timing to see just how rusty I've gotten. It's been a few months since I've taken a ship into open skies."

Janet turned in her chair to face the command seat. "You know, we haven't practiced this maneuver."

"Sure we have. At least, I have."

"Not on this ship, we haven't."

"Well...just pretend it's the *Constantine*. The helm isn't all that different. At least, it wasn't on the simulator. Same omni-directional controls and all. Guess we'll just have to sort it out as we go."

"Some things never change," Janet muttered, shaking her head and returning to her controls.

"All right, people...sound the alarm, all hands to Condition Yellow."

As the bells sounded across the ship, summoning a thoroughly puzzled crew to alert, Cook leaned back in his chair and took a deep breath.

"Helm, stand by full throttle."

"Standing by."

"Red Zone terminus approaching," Jeremy said, nervously feeling the ship's power building all around them. "Clear in twenty seconds... mark!"

"Helm—full throttle. Power up and stand by to engage subspace engines."

"Engines amain."

"Helm—prepare for victory roll...and snap us out smartly at C-2, Missy. Heading 070 by 15 degrees north."

"Aye, sir."

"Stand...by...annnnd...*now!*"

As the ship wheeled on its axis, Cook could feel her main engines roaring to life, powering them out of their turn and racing toward the clear skies east and anticenter. He chuckled to hear groans filling the deck, as cross-currents of gravity yanked the bellies of his bridge crew in a dozen different directions. A moment later the ship came out of her roll, settling them onto their course. Ishtar Command became an insignificant dot in the blackness astern, and for the first time in a long while the captain felt he was home.

"JEESHUS!" CRIED a startled voice in the control tower. "Did you...did they...were they...?"

"They were clear of the zone by twenty-two feet."

"What a hot dog."

"Well, they were in port a long time."

"Did they file a flight plan?"

"I forgot to ask."

The story continues in
Book II of **The Guardians of Peace:**

The Star Dancers

ABOUT THE AUTHOR

JEFFREY CAMINSKY, a lifelong resident of Planet Earth, lives in Livonia, Michigan with his wife and family. His books include a book about soccer officiating, *The Referee's Survival Guide*, and *The Sonnets of William Shakespeare*, a guide to Elizabethan poetry. In an alternate reality, he is a public prosecutor in Detroit. His book *The Sirens of Space* is the first volume in the *Guardians of Peace* adventure series.

www.ingramcontent.com/pod-product-compliance
Lightning Source LLC
Chambersburg PA
CBHW020604250626
47154CB00004B/1357